# ELAINE COFFMAN

## BY FIRE AND BY SWORD

MIRA

ISBN 0-7783-2288-2

BY FIRE AND BY SWORD

www.MIRABooks.com

Printed in U.S.A.

For my readers

# *Prologue*

Any port in a storm.

—Anonymous

*Edinburgh, Scotland, 1746*

Revered and ancient, the brooding black crags of Castle Rock came into view. An extinct volcano, its ridges carved by glaciers, it seemed proud of its past—Bronze Age fort, thriving Roman settlement, royal residence, military garrison, prison and place of refuge.

It was all of these and more.

Sitting atop the great rock, Edinburgh Castle loomed over the city—besieged, bombarded, blockaded and captured, it had looked down upon Edinburgh since the twelfth century. One had only to look at its history to see both the strength and weakness of mankind.

Battles, massacres, treasons and murder: All have

left their stained mark upon the familiar stones of the castle, but how foreign they seemed to her now, wrapped in a mantle of ice and snow; sins of the past frozen in time.

Like Rome, Edinburgh was built on seven hills; like Rome, it had been attacked and rebuilt numerous times. And like Kenna Lennox, it had a turbulent past that it seemed destined to repeat.

These were the thoughts that occupied Kenna's mind as she waited for the yawl to dock at Leith harbor. Moments later, she walked down the plank and onto the pier. She was relieved to be in Edinburgh at last.

She dusted snow from her cape and continued on her way, beneath the ominous threat of dark clouds overhead. It had begun to snow shortly after she boarded the yawl at Alloa, but by the time they sailed down the River Forth into Edinburgh harbor, it looked as if it had been snowing there much longer.

She paused, and felt the easing of her troubled mind, for she saw there were a dozen ships or more riding anchor in the harbor. She was confident now that she would be able to find one to transport her to Calais.

A gusty wind blew swirls of snow, and drove them into drifting mounds around her. They looked as soft as milk. She walked on, her skirt skimming the snow and sending it spiraling around her like ethereal spirits, displaced and looking for a home. Perhaps they would find it at the castle—for it was said to be the most haunted place in Scotland.

She passed stone houses, where rows of chimneys

blew wraithlike smoke into the frigid air. Occasionally, sprays of glittering snow driven by currents of wind slid from the pitched roofs and fell onto the walkway. The afternoon would soon begin to fade, already the number of people she saw was diminishing. The world around her was cold and white and terribly silent, as if she were the only person left on earth.

Tomorrow was Christmas Eve.

She pushed the thought away, for it reminded her of home and family, neither of which she would see for a long time. The sting of separation was too new and raw, like a burn that would not heal. It was painful to think of the past, times both happy and sad, or the threat to her life by the evil Lord Walter Ramsay that drove her to leave. She quickened her step, not slackening her pace until she came to where she hoped she would find someone to row her out to a ship.

All she had to do now was to decide which one.

Her thoughts turned to her reason for being here, and she prayed she could find a captain who would be charitable toward her when she asked for passage to France. A thin ray of hope was born when she saw the snow starting to ease, then stop. She hoped that would last.

The change in the weather and the thin slices of sunlight piercing the clouds left Kenna filled with optimism. Soon, she would be on one of those ships and on her way to France.

She began to search the harbor for a ship flying foreign colors, for it would be more difficult to trace her passage on a foreign ship. Her teeth were beginning to chatter, and she pulled her cape more tightly about her, and then she saw it.

*Dancing Water...*

Even Kenna could see that the ship was a beauty and well cared for, and the best part was, she flew a pennant below the British flag that identified her as American. Probably a privateer, she thought, which suited her even better.

She could almost picture the ship sailing the West Indies, the sun shining, and waves made by the bow cutting through the water with splashes that sparkled like the glitter of an exploding star. It seemed as if the ship truly did dance upon the water.

Because of the dreadful weather, the waterfront and pier area were practically deserted, and Kenna was about to give up finding someone to row her out to the ship so she could make an inquiry.

And then she saw a man loading a few supplies in a small boat. She paused a moment to breathe deeply with hopes it would calm her jittery feelings. Up to this point, she felt confident and secure, for she was on her native soil. However, it occurred to her that once she set foot on a boat to be rowed into the harbor, control over her life and her person were no longer completely hers.

She knew she faced another problem: for women, especially of her social class, did not travel alone, but when one is running for her life, it is difficult to hire a traveling companion. In her mind, necessity outranked propriety.

She did her best to cover her mounting discomfort

by dusting a bit of the snow from her cape, and checking the clasp at her neck, her gloved fingers feeling wooden and numb against the metal.

The man was bundled in a jacket of coarse navy wool, and he took no notice of her until she cleared her throat and spoke. "Would you be available for hire? I need someone to row me to the ship, *Dancing Water.*"

He turned to look at her and she saw his lips were blue from the cold, and he was younger than she. A cabin boy, perhaps, she thought. When they began to discuss the price, she discovered he had no more mother wit than a bowl of oatmeal, but after a bit of bartering, she quickly changed her mind, for he was as shrewd as any man twice his age, and she ended up paying him quite handsomely to row her to the ship.

The only words he uttered during the entire trip were, "It is perishing cold for a lady to be out in the elements. I doubt you will be sailing today, even though the wind is strong enough to serve you well out of the firth."

He spoke the words like a seaman, but there was something in his expression that made her think he was naught but a young boy doing a man's work that was, more than likely, not of his choosing. She was disturbed by the look, which lay somewhere between stoicism and tears, in spite of all his rough ways and his attempt to hide it.

The wind whipping across the water was much colder than it had been on land, and she had to hold on to her hood to keep it from being blown back. As they drew closer to the ship she took one last look behind her and thought, this is the last time I will be this close to my homeland for some time.

She came close to crying at the idea of being away, not only from Scotland, but her family, but she convinced herself that she was doing the right thing, just as she had that night a few years past, when she made a similar trip from Inchmurrin to Edinburgh.

But this time, instead of riding through the night to Edinburgh to save her sister's life, she was fleeing to France to save her own.

Only God knew if she would be as fortunate the second time.

By the time they reached the ship, she could see a thin covering of ice coated the rigging, and everything was white, like a ghost ship. She was quite relieved to see there were a few crewmen milling about.

Once they helped her on board, she said, "I would like to speak to your captain."

# *One*

Ah, you flavour everything;
you are the vanilla of society.
—Sydney Smith (1771–1845),
English clergyman, essayist and wit.
*Lady Holland's memoir.*

What she got was a hot-blooded Latin. "I am Alejandro Feliciano Enrique de Calderón, and I am entirely at your service," he said with a bow.

Fate had been extraordinarily generous to him when it came to the male beauty of long, black hair, queued back, smoldering eyes and smile whose sole purpose for existing was to persuade women. Charm clung to him like lichen to a tree trunk. Any woman attracted to him would have a difficult time saying no.

"You are Spanish," she said.

"*Sí*, born in España, the youngest son of a noble Castilian family and a father with a name and title longer than mine. I am completely at your service, my lady," he said.

She was thinking he was as charismatic as Amphion, who built a wall around Thebes by charming the stones into place with the music of his magical lyre. Only in his case, he could use his smile in place of the lyre.

"Are you a member of the crew?"

He bowed extravagantly. "I am the best navigator in the world, and the most excellent friend of long standing of Captain Montgomery. I am an outstanding horseman, also exceptional with a sword. I dance and play the guitar with passion, tell stories, and make great love to beautiful women. And now, my lovely, I do apologize, but I must ask why you have gone to so much trouble to board our ship in such weather…and please…make it short, for you look like you are fast turning into a cake of ice."

How could she not like this passionate Latin, with his playful, wicked wit, brimming self-confidence and that mischievous gleam in his eye? He had to be the most flagrantly outrageous and perfectly charming man she had ever met—and so unlike the Scots. With his savoir faire and good looks, he did not have to tell her—she knew instinctively that he possessed a flair for attracting the ladies.

She liked him immediately, and that made her relax about following her intuition by choosing this particular ship. And since he was a good friend of the captain, then it stood to reason she would like Captain Montgomery and find him as charming as his navigator.

She gave him a weak smile—weak being all she could muster, due to the cold weather that was beginning to chill more than just her skin. She introduced herself, then said, "If you would be so kind, Señor de Calderón, I would like to see your captain."

He looked her over with all the attention to detail he would use when scanning the horizon for an enemy ship. "Aah, but not half as much as he would like to see you, I think."

Kenna struggled against a flare of displeasure and did her best to temper her words. "Do you always look a lady over in that manner?" she asked.

"Of course. Is it not better to be looked over than to be overlooked?"

She could get dizzy talking to this man who seemed to flavor a conversation the way a dash of vanilla does a cake. "Are you going to take me to see the captain, or make me stand on deck until I freeze to death?"

"I will take you, of course," he said. "Please, come with me."

She fell into step with him, just as he said, "I am puzzled why the captain did not tell me he had a woman coming."

She stopped suddenly.

He paused. "Is there something wrong?"

"I think we need to clarify something here. I do not know your captain, and I can assure you I am *not* here for the captain's *pleasure*," she said, emphasizing the word. "I have a business matter to discuss with him, and that is the sole reason I am here."

"What kind of business?"

"I have a request to make of him, and if you please, might I go someplace warm? I have never been so cold. My blood thickens."

"Pardon my lack of manners," he said. "You do look very cold. We will get you warmed up, but slowly. Have you been out in this weather long?"

"Too long," she said. "And the more we stand here, it grows longer."

He laughed. "Allow me to take these," he said, and reached to take her traveling bags, which she had dropped to the deck beside her with a thud.

"Please, if you will come with me, I will take you to see the captain."

As they made their way down the passageway, he told her the ship's owner was also the ship's captain— an American privateer by the name of Colin Montgomery.

"A privateer?"

"Yes...of sorts."

"Of sorts? I don't understand. What do you mean, of sorts?"

"It is quite simple. He is a privateer when it suits him, and a merchant the rest of the time. However, it is not something you should worry about. We are on friendly terms with Scotland."

"I would hope, considering you are anchored in the middle of the firth. And your captain does have a Scottish surname."

"I had nothing to do with it, *señorita*. His grandfather is responsible for that."

"His grandfather," she repeated.

"Sir Hugh Montgomery, twelfth Baron of Fairlie."

"The ship is flying an American pennant. I had no idea the captain was a Scot."

"Don't let Colin hear you say that. He is American by birth. His father was a Scot who found himself besotted by an American, so he married her and chose to live in America."

"If Colin's father was the son of a baron and chose to leave Scotland, he must have loved her very much, or else there was an older brother in line to inherit."

"No, his father was the only son, but he and his father did not look through the same spyglass. As for Colin, you couldn't entice him to live here with a ship made of solid gold. He is too much like his father when it comes to the grandfather, and Colin hates your Scottish weather. Unbelievable though it is, Baron Fairlie lives in a place colder than this. I went there once, and a more remote and foreboding place I have never been. It took only five minutes for me to understand why Colin's father left. One would need to have pure Viking blood to live there. They should have let the Norsemen keep it."

She smiled. "Caithness or Sutherland?"

"Sutherland," he said. "It would appear you have been there."

"Hmm," she said, and fell silent, for the thought of northern Scotland brought back memories of her own grandfather, and the happy times she had spent at Durness Castle as a child. They were all dead now…her grandparents and her mother, too, and now Durness belonged to her, but Kenna had not been there since she was a child.

When they came to the end of the corridor, Alejandro knocked on the cabin door. "Captain…"

While she waited beside him, she was thinking herself quite fortunate to have met Alejandro instead of some waterfront ruffian, for it was apparent that he was from a more privileged class.

It stood to reason that she would find Captain Montgomery as likable and charming as his navigator, not to mention that she and the captain had something in common—they both had grandfathers from northern Scotland.

# Two

The charms of the passing woman
are generally in direct proportion to
the swiftness of her passing.
—Marcel Proust (1871–1922), French novelist.
*Remembrance of Things Past*, vol. 4.

What he needed was a woman.

He was, by anyone's standards, drunk. He had been uproariously, outrageously and gloriously drunk for two days, and if the freezing wind and snow did not let up soon, he would stay that way.

His ship had been dogged by bad luck and bad weather since he left the port of La Spezia, and it left him believing he was long overdue for a change of fortune. To his way of thinking, he'd had more than his share of discomfiture from the elements. And even worse, neither he nor his crew had set foot off the ship for the past four days, all due to bad weather and the need to keep unceasing vigilance to lessen the risk of damage to the ship.

After each watch, the men hurried below with blue nails and aching wrists, results of the furious wind and the battering of an unrelenting snowstorm. Under such circumstances, everyone on board searched for ways to pass the time. Some whittled. Others wrote letters or played card games. A few even managed to catch up on their sleep.

Colin thought about beautiful women—both those he had known, and those he had yet to meet.

He sat behind his desk with his feet propped on the top of it. A bottle of Spanish wine and a half-filled glass sat a few inches from where his hand rested. He leaned back in his chair and took another drink of blood-warming wine. He had to hand it to the Spaniards—they knew what it took to warm a man's blood.

His mind went back to other ways of warming a man's blood, and if he was going to spend Christmas aboard ship, then being with a woman was the best way to spend it. There wasn't much that could go wrong in life that a little female companionship would not help.

A woman… That was exactly what he needed to take his mind off the abominable Scottish weather raging beyond the fogged portholes. A woman would be a good diversion, and a way for him to pass the time doing something besides drinking himself into a stupor.

In the absence of a real woman, he conjured one up…a true beauty, dark and sultry, with skin dusky as twilight. While he imagined what he would do once he had this phantom of delight beneath him, his body was ravaged with godforsaken longing that was fast becoming stone-hard desire.

Not the best time for someone to puncture his dreams with a knock at the door.

"Damn!" He stared moodily at the door; the urge to choke whoever was on the other side growing with each breath he drew.

Another knock, this one louder. Alejandro's voice called out, "You have a visitor, Captain. A *female* visitor."

Colin gave a snort. A female visitor indeed. "Pity that I know you for a carefree Spaniard of infinite jests," he called back. "Now, go away and leave me to my wine."

As far as jokes went, this was a pretty pathetic one—a female visitor in this weather? Was that the best he could do? Colin had never thought Alejandro capable of such stupidity—thinking he would believe something as far-fetched as that. His laugh was hardy enough to stir a gale into being. "Go away and leave me to the humors of wine and spare me yours."

Alejandro swore he was not joking. "Truly, Captain, there is a woman here to see you."

"Of course there is. I can see her now, this woman who simply appeared on my ship, in the midst of a snowstorm. How would she look, this daughter of father winter? She would be blond, the pale and pasty English-looking sort, all dressed in white, too shy to speak and frigid as a lover."

Colin could swear he heard a feminine gasp, and knew it had to be the wine.

After a few more exchanges, with Alejandro trying to convince him there truly was a woman on the other side of the door and Colin steadfastly refusing to believe such drivel, the musical tones of a feminine voice reached his ears.

"Please, Captain."

Whoever the wench was, she had a slow, husky voice that sent a shiver over him, and set him to thinking what sport he could have with the languid tart on the other side of the door.

Alejandro asked him again to open the door, speaking quite loudly this time.

Colin grinned. He had waited a lifetime for an opportunity like this. "It is open."

Colin had already decided that it was probably the crew's idea of a joke, born of extreme boredom. "And where is this insipid, whey-faced Englishwoman with no bosom and no behind? I have yet to see proof."

He heard a second gasp about the same time the cabin door opened, and Alejandro ushered a snow-caked bundle into his presence.

The bundle had a voice. "I assumed I would meet an American gentleman. I pray God does not strike me dead for using those two words together."

His head snapped back and his jaw dropped at the sight of an angelic face framed with a few wisps of coppery curls escaping from beneath the hood of her green wool cape. Hers was the kind of beauty found on ancient Grecian urns. And she was in *his* cabin.

Immediately parts of his body were responding to

the image of the rest of her, which he surmised to be lush and feminine beneath that green cloak.

Alejandro turned to the woman. "I apologize for this clumsy, inarticulate American. He is not normally such a churlish lout. Snowstorms that keep him confined bring out the beast in him."

"Don't make excuses for me," Colin said.

"You are right, of course." Alejandro turned to Kenna. "What I meant to say is, Colin is a fine sea captain. His other talents are drinking, wenching and adventuresome exploits, but don't take that to mean he is not a man of moral excellence and righteousness, for he firmly believes in loving his neighbor, and his neighbor's wife."

Colin rose to his feet and ignored Alejandro's comment, while he directed his words to the woman. "I apologize for my lack of manners. I erroneously thought this was a jest and I played along."

"I accept your apology, but you might try to remember that 'he who endeavors to ridicule other people, especially in things of a serious nature, becomes himself a jest.'"

"The *Decameron*," he said, and saw surprise on her face. "You see, American gentlemen are taught not only to speak, but also to read."

She smiled and dipped her head in a way to acknowledge his excellent retort. "Your point, Captain."

Colin turned to Alejandro. "Where did you find her?" He was mesmerized by her eyes…the most unusual golden eyes that were as distracting as her exquisite face. She was a beauty, all right, with coppery, red-blond hair, skin that belonged on a babe, save for the sprinkling of freckles across her nose. She was graceful, well-put-together and tall for a woman, and he had a vision of unbelievably long legs.

Colin could not believe his good fortune to have not only a woman seek him out, but a damn fine-looking one at that. He might be inebriated, but not even excessive alcohol could dull the impact of having before him, the very thing he was in need of. And this one went far beyond even his highly selective taste. Now he knew how Caesar must have felt when Cleopatra rolled out of the carpet at his feet.

"I did not find her. She found me."

"Even better." Colin just managed to stay on his wobbly feet while he maneuvered himself around the desk. "She is half frozen and shivering like a wet rat. I don't know how you Scots do it. Your blood must be three-quarters whisky."

He pushed the woman's hood back and a brilliant mass of red hair tumbled down over her shoulders, hiding most of her face.

"So, you have come to see me," he said, and lifted a red curl, noting it was cold to the touch. She began to shiver uncontrollably. "No, never mind responding to that. For now, we need to get you warmed up a bit and out of this frozen cape, before it starts to melt and gets your clothes wet."

He helped her out of the cape. What he saw beneath the fine wool made him frown. "Too late to save the dress. It's already wet. Hopefully, we will have better luck with you."

He handed the cape to Alejandro. "Put it in a warm place to dry."

Alejandro draped the cape over a chair near the stove.

Colin observed her. "Your clothes need to come off. I will not be detained in Scotland trying to explain how a half-frozen lass fell ill and died on my ship."

"Colin, can't you see she is a woman of breeding? You can't expect her to remove her clothes."

"Give me credit for telling the difference between a waterfront doxy and a lady," Colin said.

"I will not disrobe," she said, without looking at either of them.

Colin wasted no time in saying, "Oh, I think you will, or I will have Alejandro do it for you. You are, by choice, on my ship, and that puts me in charge. You are starting to shiver and that means your body is chilled below normal. A person can lose only so much warmth, and if you pass that point, what happens is not pretty."

When she did not respond, he turned to Alejandro, "Damn stubborn Scots. How does anyone deal with them? Look through her traveling bag and see if there is anything dry inside for her to put on. If not, take a shirt out of my chest."

"I have another gown," she said.

Alejandro opened her bag and found a blue gown. He offered it to her, but she did not take it.

"What is it to be, then? We leave and you change, or I go and Alejandro does it for you?"

She turned those unforgettable golden eyes toward him and Colin knew she was sizing him up and trying to determine if he was merely making idle threats, or if he meant what he said.

He was quick to reply with a half-sarcastic smile that was both challenging and bold, and he took obstinate delight in daring her to call his bluff. "I deal harshly with revolt."

It was almost humorous, the look on her face—two warring alternatives in one small head, held in check by dogged determination. He almost felt sorry for her: so free she seemed, so fettered she was. He would bet his silver-backed brush that she was thinking at this very moment, *If only I were a man...*

The desire to laugh in his triumph was so strong; it took some restraint on his own to repress it, although he did deem it wise to let her know who held the upper hand. "He who dares, wins."

She yanked the dress away from Alejandro.

Colin saw indignation flare hotly in her eyes, and he wisely asked, quickly as lightning, before she could vent her pique: "Who are you, and what insanity brought you out in the midst of such a snowstorm?"

"My name is unimportant. I came here because I want to buy passage to France."

"And I want to find King Solomon's mine." A muscle worked in his jaw. "This is a cargo ship. I don't take passengers, and if I did, I would not take a female."

"For what reason?"

"A woman on deck would be distracting to my crew. They are not accustomed to having passengers, and certainly not a beautiful one—who doesn't have any business traveling alone. You should go back home before it's too late."

"It is already too late."

There was something about the way she said that…it made him wonder who she was and what sad story she had to tell. But this was not the time to make inquiry. "Where you go is none of my business. All I am interested in is seeing that you leave my ship. I will not take you to France."

"I see…"

"I don't think you do. It is nothing personal. I cannot take you because we are not going to France. If this godforsaken weather ever clears, we are going to Copenhagen. We should have been there two days ago. Unfortunately, France is not on the way to Copenhagen."

"What would it take to change your mind?"

"A beautiful woman in any situation is tempting.…"

"Perhaps you have not heard, but we Scots gave up bartering in favor of currency centuries ago. I was referring to monetary compensation."

She put her hand to her head and he was hoping like hell that she would not pass out. "I am not so heartless to send you out in your present condition. When you are warmed and have had something to eat, I will have someone take you back. In the meantime, we will step outside so you can change…unless you need help, of course."

Not giving her time to reply, he ripped the blanket from his bunk and handed it to her. "When you've put on dry clothes, wrap yourself in this. I am sure you know that more layers will help hold in the warmth."

Colin opened the door and waited for Alejandro to pass before he said to her, "You have five minutes to cover anything you don't want to be seen."

He closed the door behind him with a click.

From the other side of the door, he heard her say, "Barbarian American brute! Who does he think he is, William the Conqueror?"

"She is obstinate as a headache and difficult to convince," he said as he and Alejandro walked toward the deck. "I hope she doesn't have a Scots temper to go along with it."

"Either way, she will be nice until she realizes she can't convince you to take her to France."

They stepped out onto the deck, and Alejandro tilted his head back to look at the sky. "Have you noticed that it has stopped snowing?"

The sight of breaking clouds and the red streaks of setting sun working through them did much to improve Colin's mood and lift his spirits. He tilted his head back. "The ice is beginning to melt on the mast. If it will only stay like this until we can get out of the firth. God knows we have been riding at anchor long enough. Scottish weather—fickle as a woman."

Alejandro studied the men who were now gathering on deck. "It seems the crew is as anxious to go as we are."

Colin called out, "Mr. Carlisle, keep an eye on the weather, and weigh anchor the moment you think you can get us out of here and bound for Copenhagen."

"Aye, Captain."

"What about the woman?" Alejandro asked.

"Give her another five minutes to dress, and then take her back to shore, or to another ship…one that is going to France."

"Why do I have to be the one to tell her? Why don't you tell her?"

"Because I'm the captain."

Alejandro grinned. "I'm the navigator, and I have a course to plot. Besides, she is in your cabin, not mine."

"That can be rectified."

"Oh no, I want nothing to do with this," Alejandro said. "She asked to see the captain and I brought her to you. You tell her we aren't going to help her."

"I am going to help her. If she wants to try another ship, there is a Danish bark anchored here by the name of *Aethelred II.* Take her there. I know the captain, Trygve Fischer. If he is busy, speak to the junior officer, Steen Willemoes."

"I still think you should tell her."

"I thought you liked her."

Alejandro put his hands in his pockets. "I do like her, but not that way. She reminds me of my sisters— a pain in the neck. Besides, it's obvious someone on Mount Olympus is bored and has decided to have a little fun with the two of you. Now that you've been put in each other's path, I will sit back and wait for the collision and suffer none of the heartache."

"She isn't my kind of woman."

Alejandro laughed heartily. "A woman hasn't been born that isn't your kind, Montgomery. You love all of them—some more than others."

"Do you—"

Alejandro interrupted him. "There is no point in trying to convince me. It won't work. You gave yourself away when you told me to undress her. If you weren't interested in her, you would have done it yourself."

"Observant, aren't we?" Colin said. "I will tell her, but I want you to row her over to the *Aethelred.*"

"Yes, Captain." Alejandro whistled as he went below to lay out a course for Copenhagen, and left Colin to decide if he should stick to their original plans for Denmark, or take a little longer by going to France first.

Colin went below and knocked on his cabin door. "Are you decent?"

"Yes, Captain, I am."

He opened the door and closed it behind him. He took a couple of steps into the room. She was standing a few feet away, in a dark blue gown.

"Where is your navigator?" she asked.

"He is, at the moment, laying out a course to Copenhagen."

Shouts and the thumping of feet penetrated the cabin. "What is happening?" she asked.

"It has stopped snowing. We are preparing to lift anchor and navigate the firth so we can get out of here, just in case the snow decides to start up again."

"You still refuse to take me to Calais?"

"I have no choice. However, if you will come up on deck with me, I will have you taken to another ship."

"There is no way I can convince you to take me to France?"

"I've already had too many setbacks. I have a cargo that is overdue in Copenhagen. It would cost me too much time to go to France first. I'm sorry."

Her face registered disappointment, and he thought he saw a glimmer of hopelessness in her eyes, before she turned away and said, "Very well, I shall gather my things."

He watched her collect her meager belongings, and wondered not only why a woman of her caliber would be traveling alone to a foreign country, but also why she carried such a small amount of baggage. She did not have much, but what she had was of the finest quality, and her speech and manners indicated she was educated.

But, it was still none of his business, and he pushed the matter out of his mind.

She had her traveling bags in her hands when she turned back to him. "I think I am ready now. Thank you, Captain Montgomery, for your help."

"You owe me no thanks. I have given Alejandro the name of a Danish bark, *Aethelred II*. She is bound for France. Alejandro will take you there. I know the captain, Trygve Fischer. He is a very upright man. You will be safe, and treated with respect on his ship." He paused a moment, looking her over, as if he was searching for an answer. "Why are you going to France alone, without much…"

"Please do not ask me that. I must keep my reasons as private as my name."

"Are you in danger?"

She did not answer straightaway, as if she was

weighing the question, and then all she said was, "Grave."

"Grave, as in life-threatening?"

"Yes."

"Why? Does someone have a grievance against you?"

"A vengeful man has threatened my life."

"This is why you are going to France?"

"Yes."

"To do what?"

"To protect myself, and that is all I will tell you."

Colin poured a glass of wine as he thought about her reply.

She focused on the glass for a moment before she said, "Captain, you can't be thirsty."

"I am a man who likes to anticipate things in advance." She held his gaze until he was certain her chin was aching from the strain of it. In case he had forgotten Scots were stubborn, he now had his memory refreshed.

"I don't mean to sound unappreciative," she said. "I am grateful for your help in trying to secure other passage for me. It is extremely urgent that I leave Scotland as soon as possible."

Her voice was low, and damnably arousing, too, with the soft caressing of her Scots burr that went over him like the touch of a woman's soft hand. Colin gave her a warm, teasing smile. "Perhaps, if it starts to snow again, we will have time to find out just how grateful you are."

"I'm afraid we would both be in our dotage before that would happen."

He nodded and offered the glass of wine to her. "Here, I poured this for you. Drink it. It will warm your insides." He almost found himself wishing he had not decided to send her away. He was certain that before he reached Copenhagen, he would regret his decision to let her walk out of his life so easily. He saw it as a chivalrous move on his part. She was obviously in some kind of trouble and hoping to outrun it. She didn't need him trying to steal her innocence on top of it.

But, oh my, he was tempted.

Before she took the wine he offered, she put her traveling bags and cape down, and seated herself. He watched her hold the glass between her hands, as she moved it slowly back and forth. Then she began to sip it slowly, and the cabin was engulfed in a quiet stillness.

He noticed, when she finished the last sip, that a slight tinge of color had stolen to her cheeks. She rose to her feet and handed him the glass, then thanked him again.

He placed the glass on his desk, turned, and leaning back against it, he folded his arms across his chest and regarded her with a level gaze.

There was a haunting sadness that clung to her like a vapor, difficult to see, and even more difficult to understand. *Heartsore* would be the way he would describe it.

"Your turn on deck seems to have sobered you," she said.

"Having *you* in my cabin was much more sobering than any time on deck."

He saw sadness in her eyes again, as she reached for her meager belongings. "Wait a moment," he said.

She turned back to him, her eyes questioning. Before she could guess what he intended, he caught her face between his hands and guided it upward, until their lips touched. As he kissed her, his hands slipped around her and he pulled her firmly against him and held her there. She was leaning back, held upright only by the strength of his arms around her, holding her body tight and firm against his.

He knew the kiss was undeniably tender, as his lips moved across hers, gentle and soft, for that was what he sensed she needed. With firm pressure, he forced her lips apart and kissed her deeply and with more passion, intensity and emotion.

He felt the tenseness in her body ease, only to be replaced by a newer, stranger sort of urgency that made her moan faintly, and he almost lost his steel resolve when her arms slipped around him. He felt the exact moment when something in him seemed to connect with something in her, and she was suddenly kissing him back with all the fervor of a woman who had not been kissed for some time…or perhaps one that had never been kissed at all.

He felt as if he could not get enough of her—her body, her skin, her mouth. His hands wanted to touch her skin, smooth and cool as cream. He wanted to comb his fingers through the long, silken tresses of her hair. He wanted to kiss her and keep on kissing her until she melted into him, open and yearning.

He wanted to go further—much further, but he did

not kiss her to seduce her, but because of the sad uncon-
nectedness he sensed about her, as if she was cut off
from every place and every person that was important
to her.

Wickedly impassioned seconds passed, but they
took no notice for desire seemed to hold them captive
in an iridescent bubble of rainbow hues, captured by
the magic of the moment. It was with a terrible sense
of loss that he eased his hold on her and withdrew his
lips from hers. As soon as he did, he felt the same
sense of deprivation and disappointment he read in her
eyes.

With softness that surprised even him, and a smile
to reassure her, he traced the outline of her lower lip
with his fingers and said, "That is why a woman in possession of a face and body such as yours should never
travel alone. Some men find the combination irresistible."

He had expected her to look sad and wan, but a moment later, he realized she wasn't as helpless as he first
thought. She put her hands around his neck and pulled
his face down to hers. He expected her to kiss him
with all the gentleness he had used with her, and was
completely undone when the kiss was undeniably passionate, and administered with such intensity that it left
both of them breathless and wanting more. He was
about to take it to the next level, when she broke the
kiss.

"That is what happens to a man who kisses a woman
and thinks he can use it to teach her a lesson."

The cracking sound of his laughter was something

he could not hold back, yet at the same time, in the back of his mind, he could not help wondering, who in the hell taught her to kiss like that?

The clanking sounds of the crew making the ship ready for sea, and the call of birds overhead invaded their senses and they both knew this rainbow bubble they were in was about to burst, flinging the two of them back down to earth with the jarring impact of cold, hard reality.

She glanced upward, where the noise on deck grew louder. He knew she must feel a sense of loss, and terribly alone in her uncertainty. He knew she had never taken a journey like this, and if he did not have to be in Copenhagen and if he wasn't already several days late, he would have personally escorted her all the way to wherever it was that she was going. It was not easy for either one of them, and he knew she, like he, was probably wondering just how did one gracefully go about extracting one's person from circumstances such as this, and maintain some semblance of dignity.

"If you are ready, I will walk you on deck."

She gathered her belongings once again, and said, "Well, Captain, I believe I am ready. If you would be so kind as to take me to your navigator, I shall get my journey under way, and let you do the same with yours."

Colin escorted her topside, and found Alejandro.

It seemed so sudden. One moment she was standing beside him, and the next moment, she was gone, over the side and into the waiting boat.

He moved closer to look down to where she sat, her

flaming curls peeking from her green cape, and her lovely face turned toward him.

The impact hit him like a fist in the gut, and he could not shake the feeling that he'd made a mistake in letting her go...a big mistake.

He cupped his hands and called out, as the boat pulled away from the ship, "How do you plan to protect yourself?"

She flashed him a stunning smile, as bright as a sunny day. "Why, Captain, by the sword, of course."

Stunned, he watched as the rowboat disappeared slowly, beginning with the bow, and ending with the woman in the green cape, an image that remained in his mind for some time, after everything else was gone.

# *Three*

West of these out to seas
colder than the Hebrides I must go
Where the fleet of stars is anchored and
the young star-captains glow.
—James Elroy Flecker (1884-1915),
English poet, playwright and novelist.
"The Dying Patriot."

The Danish bark, *Aethelred II,* did not have the sleek craftsmanship of *Dancing Water,* but she was clean and well cared for.

A gentleman to the core, Alejandro boarded the ship with Kenna and stayed to introduce her to Captain Fischer, before bidding her farewell.

"I leave you in very capable hands and wish you Godspeed, and a pleasant voyage to France."

"Thank you for your help, and please convey to your captain my gratitude for helping me procure this passage, which has helped me avoid a...well, simply tell him I send my thanks and gratitude."

"I shall tell him forthwith, lovely lady."

She was sorry the dangerous situation she was in prevented her from revealing her name, or much of anything else about herself. He had been kind to her, and to withhold herself from such kindness was not her true nature. She gave this warmhearted man a smile that she hoped would convey her pleasure in making his acquaintance. "Goodbye, Alejandro Feliciano Enrique de Calderón, 'most excellent friend of Captain Montgomery.' I should have enjoyed very much, I think, becoming your friend."

He took her gloved hand and kissed it. "You are already my friend, señorita. And never say goodbye. Where is it written that our pathways will never converge again? The arrow of fate has already been shot. Who knows where it will land?" He turned and walked away.

She looked over the side of the ship and watched him being lowered down to the rowboat. He stepped into it and turned toward her. "The world is not as big as you think," he called out, and they rowed away.

She watched for a while, before she asked Captain Fischer if she might remain on deck, then added, "I can be trusted to stay out of the way, Captain."

"I do not have a problem with that. If you have never sailed before, I know you would find it all quite exciting. I do think, however, that once we are under way, you would be more comfortable in your cabin."

Captain Fischer guided her to a safe place that was

both out of the way of the crew, and protected from the wind. She would have to admit that Captain Montgomery, in spite of his well-oiled state, did, at least, do a good job describing Captain Fischer, for he did appear to be an upright man, with kind blue eyes.

She knew the moment she saw him that he was unmistakably a man who spent his life on or around the sea. He was dressed in dark blue, with a rather jaunty brown cap that withstood the wind. His face was strong, and covered with a red beard, neatly trimmed. He had been a seaman so long, he seemed to have assimilated its primary substances—sand, water and salt.

The *Aethelred* was still lying at anchor. As the crew made preparations to weigh anchor, Kenna caught sight of *Dancing Water,* no longer riding at anchor, but now under way, her tall masts nothing more than graceful black lines, stark against the white of her sails and the dark gray of a gloaming sky.

She watched as the ship came closer, and she heard someone call out, "Cheerily, men… Cheerily."

She drew even with them, and Kenna could see a great deal of movement, men scurrying about the decks and others scrambling up the masts, or swinging from the rigging. Just as *Dancing Water* began to sail past, Kenna caught sight of Captain Montgomery, standing at the helm. As if sensing someone was watching, he turned his head and their gazes met.

She raised her hand in greeting, as if to show him she was not in the least piqued, or suffering from wounded pride because he had refused to offer her passage to France.

He brought his hand up to touch the brim of his hat, and as the sloop sailed past, it struck her that little remained of the man she met earlier, for he looked every inch the sea captain now—a man of pride, dignity and determination. Nothing remained of the man with a wild, reckless humor, and for some strange reason that made her just a little bit sad.

She touched her fingers to her lips, recalling the warmth of his mouth upon hers, and then leaning against the rail, she stood on her toes and watched from her place on deck, until *Dancing Water* sailed out of sight, with Captain Montgomery at the helm, on his way to Copenhagen.

Someone called out, "All hands on deck!"

Captain Fischer followed that with, "Weigh anchor and make sail!"

The anchor chains of the *Aethelred* rattled. Her sails began to flap, then filled with a loud snap as the canvas fluttered from her masts, and like a giant bird spreading her wings, she headed south and away from the ship with the magical name, *Dancing Water.*

Kenna's mind seemed to be snagged on the memory of the two men she had met—Alejandro and Captain Montgomery—so different and each unique in their own way. What are the odds, she wondered, that I shall ever see either of them again—a time perhaps, when I did not expect it that we chanced upon each other?

*Not very good...*

The ship was gone from her sight, and she knew she should do the same with the memory, so she forced the images from her mind. It was better this way, for if Captain Montgomery had agreed to take her he might have been more to her than just an American sea captain by the time they reached Calais.

It was just as well. There was no time for romance in her life now.

There was no time for Christmas, either, for tomorrow was Christmas Eve and she would spend it on this ship, away from her home, away from her family, on a ship and bound for a foreign country. She was close to crying, when she gave herself a mental shake. She would not allow herself to wallow in her own sorrows. She thought of all the families who were torn asunder after the Battle of Culloden, and how fortunate that her family had suffered no losses there. She had so much to be thankful for. It would be a dishonor to her family, her country, and most of all to herself to feel self-pity.

By the grace of God, she had made it this far, and by that same grace, she would see this thing through to the end, and come out victorious. She would.

Kenna headed toward Captain Fischer. "And where are you going?" he asked.

"I wanted to thank you for allowing me to stay on deck to watch our departure, and now I am ready to go below, if someone could show me where to go. Your crew has been very kind and tolerant. I hope you will tell them that."

"It is always a pleasure to pass along good tidings, and they will take even greater delight in knowing it came from you."

The captain called out to a man standing near the wheel. "Steen, I have a pleasant task for you."

As the officer came toward them, Kenna was thinking she had never seen anyone so tall and thin, and she wondered if when he turned sideways, he disappeared altogether. But he had the kindest pale blue eyes that reminded her of the waters of Loch Lomond.

"This is Steen Willemoes, our junior officer. He will take you to your cabin, but don't expect him to be as talkative as I am. Steen is what you call a very good listener, and he doesn't speak anything but Danish."

Steen did not say a word, and neither did Kenna, until they reached the cabin, and she thanked him for bringing her there, even though he could not understand the words, but at least he would understand her smile.

He smiled back and touched the brim of his hat. His face turned a bright shade of red, and then he was gone.

She opened the door and stepped inside, very happy to see her traveling bags awaited her. She realized she was quite exhausted, and there was really no reason for her to remain awake. She wasn't hungry. No one spoke English, save Captain Fischer, and his was difficult to understand. She was still embarrassed that when he tried to tell her he was of Dutch Huguenot descent and did not allow drinking, dancing or card playing on his ship, she had to ask him to repeat himself twice.

Her cabin was quite small, crowded a bit with wooden boxes and a large, locked sea chest. Overhead an oil lamp swayed back and forth with the rolling motion of the ship, and filled the cabin with an oily scent. She heard the ship's bell strike twice and knew it was the first watch. She dressed for bed, doused the light and, using the light coming though the porthole, crawled wearily into the hammock, only to find herself on the floor a second later.

It wasn't as easy as it looked. She rose to her feet and gave it another try. Same thing. She was thinking there must be a more clever way to do this. She made two more attempts, and was at the point of sleeping on the floor when her fourth attempt ended successfully.

As it turned out, the hammock was a better choice than the floor, for it compensated for the roll of the ship. The only drawback was, when she awoke the next morning, her nose was bent and poking between the netting at an uncomfortable angle. It was after the noon meal before the imprint from the rope vanished completely from her face.

The next morning she awoke to a knock on the door.

It was the cabin boy holding a tray of hot food and a mug of coffee. She knew it would do no good to speak since he did not know a word of English, which was exactly the same amount of Danish that she spoke, so she smiled and stood to one side, and motioned for him to enter.

He was obviously uncomfortable around her, and as soon as he put the tray on the trunk, he departed with unbelievable haste, tripping as he went out the door.

She picked up the mug of coffee and lifted the napkin to investigate the breakfast offering—a round, flaky roll with seeds, cheese and jam, all of which she ate, down to the last little seed that dropped on the plate.

For the rest of the journey Kenna either slept or occupied her special place on deck, where she watched the men scamper up the rigging in a matter of seconds. She decided climbing aloft was something she would not like to try, for they climbed ladders that leaned backward to get past the platforms, then climbed to the end of the yardarms by walking a rope.

She was beginning to feel like part of the ship and its crew, especially at the times when she observed them do the more menial chores—sweep, scrub, clean all surfaces, and then stand for inspection. She decided that even on a nice, clean ship, with a firm, yet congenial captain, it was a hard life.

Only once were the seas so rough that she thought she might be sick. Captain Fischer apparently noticed the greenish cast of her skin, for he offered her an apology for the rough weather, then said there was a benefit to having such robust weather.

"I cannot imagine what that would be," she said, while she tried to judge the distance to the side of the ship, in case she had to make a dash for it.

"It's true. Rough seas are quite good for us."

"Now, Captain, is that really true, or are you saying that to get my mind away from the condition of my stomach?"

His eyes were bright as stars. "A little diversion now and then is a fine thing, and a good sea captain will do anything to accommodate a lady, but in truth, the waves and wind have helped the ship achieve her maximum speed of seven knots."

"Seven knots... So, we are making good time?"

"We are making excellent time, my dear," he said, "and far better than I anticipated. No one in a comparable ship could do better than we are doing right now. If this keeps up, the *Aethelred* will reach Calais sooner than I expected."

That was welcome news indeed on such a gray, drizzly day.

Finally, after two days of questionable weather, they sighted Calais early on the morning of the third day, but then Captain Fischer said they might face a delay.

"What sort of delay, Captain?"

"If the tide is out by the time we arrive, we will have to wait until tomorrow morning when it is in again, since ships can only sail up the narrow inlet and into the harbor during high tide."

Fortunately, the tide was in by the time they sailed into a cloak of fog. Thankfully, it cleared by the time they traveled up the inlet and into the harbor of Calais. Now the fog was only a light drizzle, which ended shortly after they dropped anchor.

Captain Fischer kindly invited her to go ashore with him, where he would help her arrange passage to Paris. Strange though it was, her last thought as she pulled her cape about her and left the ship was that Captain Montgomery and Alejandro were a lot colder in Copenhagen.

# *Four*

She is Venus when she smiles;
But she's Juno when she walks,
And Minerva when she talks.
  —Ben Jonson (1572–1637),
  English playwright and poet.
  *The Underwood* "A Celebration of Charis.
  His Discourse with Cupid" (1640).

The weather when they arrived in Calais was cold and raw, but not as cold as it had been in Scotland. The ride ashore was chilling, though, and by the time they were safely on land, she was tucking her cape tightly about her, to keep out the cold wind.

"For your safety, I will take you to Dessin's Inn," the captain said. "It is only a short distance from here. Monsieur Dessin is an acquaintance of mine. You will be safe and well cared for while you enjoy a cup of tea. I will return as soon as I have made arrangements for you to continue on to Paris."

"Captain Fischer, you have been most kind, and I do regret the extra trouble you are going to on my behalf, although I must confess that a cup of tea would be a lovely way to begin my day."

"It is no trouble, I assure you. Captain Montgomery sent word with Alejandro that he would appreciate any assistance I could give you in procuring transportation for you to Paris."

She was struck with the sudden wonder of his words, because to hear the mention of Captain Montgomery's name was something so unexpected. Once she got over the surprise of Montgomery's request to aid her travels, she said, "That was certainly kind of him, and terribly generous of you, Captain. While I will accept your kindness in making the arrangements, I do insist upon paying the expense of it."

"Captain Montgomery has taken care of that as well," he said.

"Is this an example of American generosity? I cannot imagine someone I met quite briefly would go to such effort and expense."

"If I were one to play with reasons, I might think it had something to do with a guilty conscience. Nice though he was, he did send you away. Have you considered that as a possibility?"

She repressed a smile. "No, I had not, but I will think upon it. What else did that flamboyant Spaniard tell you?"

"Only that you were a lovely lady, who must withhold her identity, along with the reason for your flight. He asked that I respect that, and I hope I have done so."

"You have shown me much consideration, Captain, which indicates to me your generous spirit."

"There was something else he said. It was to the effect that every human being, at one time or another, finds it necessary to have a secret that makes him a mystery to those around him."

A frown creased her brow as she thought. "I can see that I misjudged, or more correctly, prejudged Alejandro. He is not all carefree and teasing, for beneath that thin veneer lies a man of considerable depth."

She could see the captain had a comment about that, but suddenly she remembered what she had forgotten. "Hout! I have left without my traveling bags."

"Don't fret. I made arrangements to have them delivered to the inn. They should arrive shortly. And now, if you will come with me, we will be on our way to Dessin's Inn, and that hot cup of tea I promised you."

Kenna felt a sudden panic, although she did her best to hide it. Before she left Inchmurrin Island, she had hidden money for France in the false bottom of one of the traveling bags, and her gold coins in the other. How could she have been so foolish as to leave it on the ship? It was too late now to do anything more than to pray for its safety.

He offered her his arm, and she started up the cobbled street, walking alongside Captain Fischer, with his red beard, cocked hat and a saber swinging at his side.

Along the quays the people of Calais bustled and stirred, unaware that Kenna had only recently arrived, and unconcerned with why she had come. She saw dozens of foreign sailors in peculiar attire speaking in

guttural tones that were harsh and grating. Robust fish-
wives hurried by carrying baskets of lampreys, herring
and capelin on their heads, calling out in shrill voices
to advertise their wares as they passed crewmen in
woolen caps and knee-length, baggy trousers, peasants
in heavy coats of sheepskin, the heavy sound of their
wooden shoes clattering as they tripped across the cob-
blestone streets.

They passed well-dressed tradesmen dressed in
black, and wealthy merchants wrapped in long fur
coats, and were almost run down by one king of the
city's merchants, who sped along in his two-horse ca-
briolet, a whip snapping. They paused at a street corner, to watch a fine-featured lady carried past in her
sedan chair, a fur robe tucked around her and her hood
lined with velvet.

The streets were still wet as they passed several men
sitting upon crates and playing cards. They looked to
be from one of the ships in the harbor, judging from
their earrings, curly beards and tarred pigtails. When
one of the men began to eye her in a way that made her
uncomfortable, she pulled her cape a bit closer, thankful that she had the captain's arm, and his sword beside her, instead of being left to her own devices to
make her arrangements to go to Paris.

By the time she saw the sign swaying in the breeze
over the door of the inn, Kenna thought she had seen
every class and nationality of personhood that dotted the
earth.

As soon as they stepped inside the inn, they learned
that Monsieur Dessin and his wife had gone to a wed-

ding in Amiens, but their daughter, Celeste, would take excellent care of the mademoiselle.

Captain Fischer waited until Kenna was settled cozily at a table near the fireplace in the embrasure of a window overlooking the garden. Although few flowers were in bloom at this time of year, it was a lovely spot nonetheless.

"I shall be very comfortable here, Captain, so you may take your leave with an easy conscience."

Once Captain Fischer was gone, Celeste brought Kenna a cup of tea and a basket of pastries.

"Would you care for anything more, *mademoiselle?*"

"No, thank you, Celeste. You seem to have thought of everything."

She could see that the sun had broken through the clouds, and now shed its pale, wintry light over the garden. While Kenna relaxed and let the warmth of the fire seep down to her chilled bones, she studied several paintings depicting scenes of Paris that were hanging on three of the walls, and one intricately woven Aubusson tapestry that decorated the other. With its exposed beams and old stonework, Dessin's Inn was charming and quaint, right down to the beautiful, hand-painted furniture.

Her reverie was interrupted quite unexpectedly, when she noticed passing by the window a tall, well-dressed gentleman, with a foil strapped to his side. The sight of it caused her heart to leap in her throat, and she wondered, am I truly going to France to train, to improve my skill with the foil, so I will be good enough to defend myself?

At the thought of fulfilling her lifelong dream, a wild heartbeat of excitement seemed to claim her and hold her within a magic bubble.

It was all true. What Kenna planned was to ask the best fencing master in France to take her as a pupil, so she could reach the highest level of skill, and thus feel confident in her abilities, talent and aptitude. Then she could defend herself, with confidence, poise and a clear-thinking devotion to the task at hand. Then, and only then would she be ready when Lord Walter found her…and he would find her. She was certain of that.

Few people knew that Kenna was skilled in the use of the foil, and even fewer had seen her talent firsthand. It was not something young women engaged in, but the Lennox women had always been a bit different and more daring than most. Some attributed this to their isolation on Inchmurrin Island, where they had more freedom and liberties than other women.

Kenna and her three sisters could often be seen riding around the island astride, rather than sidesaddle. They learned to swim at an early age, and all were skilled at hunting with a bow.

To his credit, their father also saw to it that they learned the things other young women their age knew, and that they were ladies in every regard as was fitting for the daughters of one of the most powerful earls in Scotland. Therefore, they were musically trained, and played several instruments. They painted, did needlework, knew how to dance and sing, spoke French and were well versed in the classics.

But Kenna did have one outstanding skill that her

sisters lacked, and that was the ability to fence. She had been captivated by the art at an early age, and from the time she was a small child, she would sit quietly, observing her brothers with their fencing master, absorbing each word he spoke.

Eventually, she managed to convince her brothers to let her be their fencing partner, and later, when her father found out, and threatened to confine all of them to their rooms forever, she managed to convince him to allow her to continue to practice with her brothers.

But it wasn't until the fencing master happened upon them one afternoon, and saw her send the foil flying out of the hand of her brother Kendrew, that things changed.

The fencing master asked her father if he might instruct Kenna, and quite naturally, her father refused. Adamantly.

"Surely you jest, sir," the earl said. "Instruct a woman in the use of the foil? Preposterous! Impossible! Unheard of! And, completely asinine," he said. "Just look at her hands...those lovely long fingers that bring out the magic of a piano, or a harp. And her needlework...exceptional! I have, since the death of my wife, tried to see that my daughters were schooled not only from books, but in artistic endeavors as well. But fencing? Name me one woman who claims to excel in the art. Just one name."

"I cannot in the present time, although there have been many women who took up the sword in the past, your lordship, but that should not influence your decision concerning your daughter. You know yourself that

Kenna is not like other girls. So why would you try to compare her?"

"Go on."

"Your daughter is an exception, and I ask this, Lord Errick, because she is a natural. I have observed her, with her slender height, her grace, agility, her ability to think quickly, her focus. She is aggressive and excels at anticipating what move her opponent will make next. She is even-tempered, capable of tremendous concentration, and has a drive to succeed that equals that of the finest swordsmen. She has a natural skill that I have rarely seen in any man. It isn't her fault she was born a girl, and graced with a man's gift for sport. Why deny her?"

"Since I cannot come up with an adequate response to that question," the earl said, "I suppose I must concede, so I say, very well, but do not go putting big ideas into her head. I do not want my daughter to think she can saddle up with the clan members when they ride out to confront an enemy. And she will wear a dress at all times. Is that understood?"

"Perfectly, my lord. I will see to it that your wishes are respected. And I shall, if I may, take the liberty to say I know your lordship will never regret this decision."

"I am holding you personally responsible to see that I do not," the earl said. "And by the by, respected is not what I asked for. I want my wishes obeyed."

"Obeyed… Yes, your lordship, I understand, and I will see to it."

Kenna sipped the steaming tea, flavored with honey

and cream, as her gaze traveled around the room once more. It was such a lovely spot after the emotionally charged and exhausting past few days, which made her feel a little regret that she would be leaving it so soon, for she saw Captain Fischer coming up the street, with the rolling gait that seemed particular to men of the sea.

"When I saw you enter the room, Captain, I thought, now there is a man who looks as if he has accomplished something, and is glad in the doing of it. I know you will be pleased to have me settled in a conveyance of some sort and on my way to Paris, snug in my green wool cape, and my traveling bags tucked close to my side. However, it may surprise you to know that I actually enjoyed my time on the *Aethelred,* and I am richer for the experience. I feel my words are inadequate in expressing my appreciation for your help."

"It has been a true pleasure to make your acquaintance, and to offer my assistance," he said, and for the first time since she had met him, Captain Fischer seemed to be struggling to find the right words. He mumbled a bit, and tinkered with the butter knife, and then cleared his throat and said, "I must tell you that I met with great success in regard to your transportation. I have hired a *berline* and four horses to take you to Paris, for a very good rate of twelve livres. Two of the livres the *voiturier* is obliged to pay to farmers for permission to cross their land, and if you hire a carriage, you must pay twelve livres, or half a guinea, for every person who travels in the coach."

"How many will be traveling with me?" Kenna asked.

"None. I must say that this was requested by Captain Montgomery, although I would have insisted on the same. Consequently, I arranged for you to travel alone. You will find that more comfortable, and of course, more in line with what you are accustomed to. There is another reason as well. The common coach between Calais and Paris is such a conveyance as you have never seen. No sane man would dare use it, and certainly no lady, if she has any regard to her own comfort and convenience. Undoubtedly no one of sound mind would pay a single coin for passage on anything but a private coach."

"I am truly in your debt, Captain, and rendered quite speechless."

"Truly, madam, it has been the greatest of pleasures for a crusty old seaman like myself to be of assistance to such a lovely lady." He looked as if he was about to say more, but his attention was snagged by something he glimpsed through the window.

She turned to look, and saw a *berline* pull to a stop. The coach was still rocking to and fro, when one of the two postilions jumped down and came into the inn.

"It looks as though your coach is here," he said. "I will accompany you to the coach, in hopes it meets with your approval. And once you are settled, your journey can begin."

Once again, he offered his arm, and taking it, she left the inn in much the same manner as she had entered little more than two hours ago.

The driver nodded at her as she passed, then buttoned his heavy caped coat and gathered the reins in his rough hands. The door of the coach was closed with a bang. Captain Fischer handed her inside, and without anything further to be said, he closed the door with a loud snap, while the horses stamped restlessly as the postilions scrambled onto their backs. At that moment, the sudden clang of church bells began to ring throughout the city. She waited until they stopped, then leaned forward so her face was framed in the window and said, "Goodbye, Captain Fischer."

Before he could reply, she heard the driver crack his whip, and they were off with a sudden lurch that had Kenna grabbing for a handhold. She looked out the window and saw Captain Fischer was smiling, and then he gave her a salute.

The sun was beginning to warm things a bit by the time she was completely settled in the coach. She had placed her traveling bags on the opposite seat, after she verified that her money and jewelry were still there.

She was now ready to face the second part of her journey. With a sigh, she leaned against the well-padded cushions and considered herself off to a new beginning, and a new life. She thought of the purpose that had taken her away from her family, and brought her to France, but such thoughts were painful, and she forced her attention, instead, to what she would be doing once she arrived in Paris.

She relaxed, serenaded by the rattle and clank of chains, the crunching of wheels skimming over rocks, the snorts of straining horses as they worked to gain momentum and settle into their collars.

In spite of her anticipation of the future she was racing to meet, her thoughts fell back to the most recent past. A whispering of a name flitting through her consciousness...

Colin Montgomery.

She imagined him lingering in the shadows, sphinx-like. Colin Montgomery, an enigma sifting through her mind like dust through a locked window—an ingenious assembly of handsome features that both attracted and frightened her. And then it vanished like the flash of a falling star, gone before she could gauge its brightness.

He stood alone now, enclosed in the purple shadows of her attraction, his appeal strong and magnetic, drawing her deeper into her fascination with him. She knew it was the unknown quality that was seductive, for what woman would not be drawn toward a man surrounded by mystery as thick as a Highland mist?

She recalled the way he looked, his body long-shanked, hard and aggressively male, the image sending a shivering quiver of awe and fear spiraling down her spine. Her body coiled tightly at the memory of his dark, glossy hair, tied back, the lean hardness of muscle, the perfect symmetry of elongated bone, the startling contrast between broadness of blade and slimness of flank.

She gave pause to the direction of her thoughts. Just why was she still conscious of him; why, after their brief meeting, was her mind still held captive? Was it because he was part rake, part rogue and all masculinity? The coiling thread of desire wrapped itself around her when she considered the truth: it was because he was a man who indulged without restraint in all the physical pleasures of life.

Even in his inebriated state, he stood out among the men she knew, and he had come out of nowhere, like lightning that strikes from very far away. Insistent, powerful and easily read, it was the soft seduction in his eyes that captured her.

*"That is why a woman in possession of a face and body such as yours should never travel alone. Some men find the combination irresistible."*

Even now, the sonorous sound of his voice enticed her. Puzzling, inexplicable, he was a challenging *riddle wrapped in a mystery inside an enigma.*

And she was simply enraptured.

She was smart enough to realize being besotted with a man she would never see again was a futile undertaking, so she forced her thoughts away from him to focus on the reason she was in France. It was just as well, she thought, for she did not need herself to be distracted by a devilish rogue when her life was at stake.

She could not hide the excitement she felt within at the thought of holding a foil in her hand once again. She was determined that she would work twelve hours a day, or if necessary, fourteen—whatever it took for her to become even more skilful than her fencing master, and then, when that hungry-faced villain, her murderous enemy, Lord Walter Ramsay, appeared on the scene, she would show him that she was no longer the young, inexperienced girl she had been when he murdered her father and three brothers, and became the guardian, and chief tormenter, to her and her sisters.

She had foiled the hollow-eyed bastard once, when Lord Walter had kidnapped her sister, Claire, and held her captive in a deserted castle, where he tried to starve her to death in a dirty dungeon. Claire's crime was to refuse to hand over their father's title and the family fortune to him, by way of marriage to the son of Lord Walter's accomplice. It was Kenna's daring ride through the night, from her home to Edinburgh, to get help that saved Claire's life. The Grahams, led by Jamie, the Earl of Monleigh, and his brother Fraser, hurried to rescue Claire, who was close to death by the time they found her.

At his trial, Lord Walter, brimming with hatred, lashed out at Kenna, his mouth foaming, as he spewed his venom-laced curse, where he vowed to make her pay for what she had done, no matter how long it took. "You spawn of the devil, you will know no peace, for you will look for me in every dark place, and jump at the sight of every shadow, never knowing the exact day, or the hour I will come. But mark my words, *I will come!*"

When he had entered their lives, Kenna and her sisters were too young to know about such evil, or to ask what could transform a man into such a monster.

She still did not know the answer to that, but she knew the young should learn about villains and monsters from fairy tales, not real life.

The coach made one stop between Calais and Amiens at a post house to change horses. Kenna dined on a lunch of herbed chicken and potatoes, before they continued on. It was almost dark when they reached

Amiens, and she watched the shadows against the trees and rows of houses, cast by the coach lanterns as they passed. She spent Christmas Eve at the Golden Leg Inn, a modest but reasonably clean accommodation.

After breakfast, she was in the coach again, and as they had done the day before, they stopped to change horses at another post house, where she had her Christmas lunch—a lovely little meat pie flavored with onions and potatoes. Just when she thought she was finished, the waiter took her plate and replaced it with a luscious plum tart.

He told her it was a special "Christmas tart" and hoped it would make "Christmas away from home a happier one."

She thanked him, so very touched that someone understood what it was like to spend Christmas away from family and country. To show her appreciation, she ate all of it, down to the tiny crumbs on the plate.

When the man returned he looked at the empty plate and said, *"C'est formidable, n'est-ce pas?"*

She responded with a confident air, *"Oui, c'est formidable, formidable!"*

Shortly thereafter, she was in the carriage again, and on the final segment of her journey to Paris. On they went, through sleepy little villages and dark, shaggy woods, across burns and bridges, until the rhythm of the coach overcame her and she was rocked to sleep.

# *Five*

Enter these enchanted woods,
You who dare.
—George Meredith (1828–1909),
English novelist and poet.
"The Woods of Westermain" (1883).

Kenna was uncertain how long she slept when she was suddenly awakened by the crack of a pistol that pierced the quiet. A shout—the sharp scraping of brakes—and the coach came to a sudden, jerky halt.

Seconds later, the horses began to snort and stamp about in confusion, their movements rocking the coach. She heard shouts, and parted the curtain to take a peek outside, but she could not see anyone. Suddenly, the opposite door of the carriage was yanked open, and a man leaped in and closed the door. She saw he was not much older than she, which made her bold.

The horses nickered. More shouts. "Have you murdered the coachman?"

"Murdered? Do I look like a murderer, *mademoiselle?*" he asked, and answered his own question. "Of course not. I have murdered no one."

"I am not an imbecile. I distinctly heard a shot."

"Only one shot, *mademoiselle,* fired to halt your coach."

"And why, pray tell, did you do that?"

"How else would I stop it? Do you think I would be so foolish as to dash in front of a speeding coach and wave my arms? As for your coachman and postilions, my friends are keeping them occupied at the moment. They will not be harmed."

"You have forced us to stop. I have reason to concern myself with that."

"I assure you that you have no reason to be alarmed." He had a soothing voice and honest eyes. That, and the fact that he did not look like a highwayman helped her relax somewhat—although she had to admit to herself that she had never actually seen a highwayman.

As for his face, he had a marvelous one, with high cheekbones and a refined, yet masculine nose. His eyes were a silver-blue, set in a tanned face framed with curly, dark blond hair. But it was his mouth that was so attractive, wide and sensitive, with the corners lifted slightly in a smile—and she could tell it was a mouth that did a lot of smiling.

"I mean you no harm, and I am not after your money or your jewelry." He was elegantly dressed, poised and obviously accustomed to a life of wealth.

"That is just as well, for I have little coin and no jewelry, but I cannot help but wonder, if you are not after money, then why have you stopped my coach, *monsieur?*"

"We were set upon and robbed by highwaymen, and our coach overturned. They took the horses, and left us with no transportation. One of my friends is hurt. We need to get him to a doctor."

"He is the only one that is wounded?"

"*Oui,* unless you count the wounded pride of Alexandre, who tripped and fell while stepping out of the carriage and into a ravine he could not see in the dark. Took quite a tumble, he did, but I think his pride is wounded more than anything else."

"And you wish to take my coach and driver and leave me here?"

"No, of course not. *Mademoiselle,* what do you take me for? A villain? We only wish to ride with you to Paris, so we can find a doctor for de Lorraine."

"In what way is he injured?"

"I believe he has broken his arm, for it looks more like the letter *L* than an arm at the moment. He is in a great deal of pain."

"Very well, bring him inside the coach, so we can make haste to Paris—and tell the driver I said it was all right to do so."

He left, and she heard the exchange of voices before the man returned to the coach a few minutes later. When the door opened, she could see he and his friend carried the wounded man, who was screaming from the pain in his left arm, which dangled, with the upper arm bone at an unnatural angle. She knew broken bones were painful, and that there was nothing they could do for him to ease his pain, for there was not so much as a dram of whisky in the coach.

"Place him on the seat next to me," she said, and they lifted him inside, with him howling anew with each movement.

She guided him, so his head was in her lap, to give him more room to stretch out. One of them told the driver to continue on, and the coach started up again.

She looked down into the face of de Lorraine, who was alternately cursing and praying with fervor, interjecting the name Macarius several times in his plea for the pain to be gone.

"Who is this Macarius?" she asked.

"It is *Macarius the Wonder Worker,* his patron saint," the one with the dark blond hair replied.

"It looks as though he is getting no reply," de Bignan said. "One should never mix prayers and oaths."

The blond said, "Do not ridicule poor de Lorraine, although I am not convinced his writhing like a dying fish is doing much for his pain."

Kenna, meanwhile, was doing her best to keep from laughing, and as a diversion, she looked down at de Lorraine, whose face was perspiring. She wiped his brow with her kerchief and pushed his hair away from his face.

De Lorraine mumbled, *"Merci, mon ange,"* then began to gasp with pain as he turned himself slightly, to look at his two friends. "When I am well, *mes amis,* I shall break both your arms and then tell jokes and wait for you to laugh."

It was a good and much-needed chuckle, and when it ended, they fell quiet. The coach rocked along in silence, while she observed the other two men, noting that the three of them were all blessed with striking male beauty. She noticed the scratches on de Bignan's face, and found herself wishing she could have seen him step proudly out of the coach and into the ravine. He was fortunate he received only a few scratches.

She noticed the blond was studying her in great detail. "You are not French, *mademoiselle*."

"Is my French that bad?"

He laughed. "No, *mademoiselle,* it is excellent, but you do not *act* French."

"That is as it should be, for French, I am not. I only arrived in France yesterday, and have hired this coach to take me from Calais to Paris."

"You are English?"

"I am insulted to be called so."

He laughed. "A Scot, then?"

"Proudly, I say that I am."

"Aah, a supporter of the Pretender," he stated, with a glance at his friend sitting beside him, as if he knew ahead of time that she was a Jacobite.

"I am a Presbyterian, and neither a Jacobite nor a supporter of the man whom you mention."

"And therefore, you cannot tolerate even the sound of your Scots name for him…Bonnie Prince Charlie, upon your lips?"

"That I cannot."

"May I ask why, *mademoiselle?*"

"For too many years his cause has brought chaos,

devastation and ruin to Scotland, and what happened at Culloden delivered us into the hands of the English. They are murdering clan chiefs and seizing their land. They are passing laws for the sole purpose of bringing the Highlanders to their knees by destroying the clan system. We have only begun to see the repercussions of it."

"Conquered, but not convinced," he said.

"Never conquered nor convinced," she replied. "There is a difference between being conquered and being ruled. They have seized the Highlands by force, they will make us obey their laws, but they will never conquer our determination or kill our spirit."

He laughed. "Well said, my little fire dragon. I thought I touched a nerve, but I see that I unleashed a lightning bolt."

"What is your name, *monsieur?* Since you have taken over my carriage, I would like to know the names of the gentlemen who accompany me."

"A slight oversight, *mademoiselle,* please forgive my discourtesy and allow me to correct it. The wounded man is Jules François Joseph de Lorraine, Comte de Lorraine. My friend who does not look before stepping out of coaches is Alexandre Antoine Auguste de Rohan-Chabot, Vicomte de Bignan, Baron de Kerguehéneuc."

And you, *monsieur?*"

"Philippe Henri Louis Marie de Courtenay, Duc de Bourbon, Marquis de Marigny, Comte de Rochefort, Vicomte de Rohan…"

"'De Bourbon'? Are you related to…" The moment

the words escaped her, Kenna realized she had committed a grave error and snapped her mouth shut.

"Related to whom, *mademoiselle?*" de Bourbon asked.

Her heart began to pound as she strived to think quickly, for this was a learned man she was trying to divert. She had made a terrible mistake asking that question. The duke was not an imbecile. Royalty cut their teeth on intrigue. He had Bourbon blood. That made him a relative of King Louis, which in turn, gave him some kinship to Sophie, who was Claire's sister-in-law, who was also a cousin to King Louis.

Kenna tried to think of a way she could gracefully extricate herself from the situation she had created. When no reasonable way out came to mind, she supposed it did not hurt to tell him about Sophie, who was now married to Jamie Graham, the Earl of Monleigh. It was not likely that this Frenchman would cross paths with Lord Walter.

No, she thought, no more than you would cross paths with someone related to Sophie. It was sober learning, and she prayed she would not commit such a faux pas again.

"Who were you thinking of, *mademoiselle?* Perhaps it is someone I know."

"Oh…I was distracted a moment, trying to remember the name. It was someone I met once, in Edinburgh…at a ball, I believe, although the name now escapes me. She was quite charming, as I recall." The moment she spoke the words, she realized she should not have revealed so much. Now he knew it was a woman. She noticed, at that moment, a gleam in his eye that said his quick mind had already made a connection, all because of her foolish mistake.

A large smile seemed to wrap itself across his face in a cleverly skillful way. "I am certain I know who it is," he said, with confidence so strong one could walk on it. "Sophie Victoire de Bourbon, the daughter of Louis-Alexandre de Bourbon, Comte de Toulouse, Duc de Danville, Duc de Penthièvre, Duc de Châteauvillain, Duc de Rambouillet—made an Admiral of France at the age of five, and later he became the Grand Admiral of France. Is that the person you met in Edinburgh?"

She wished she could step into a ravine herself—anything to get out of this predicament. Her heart beat triple time as she tried to maneuver out of and minimize the significance of her blunder, for well she knew, such mistakes had upon occasion served to change the course of history.

"I truly cannot say, Your Grace." She tried to discount it with a little humor. "With such a long title, I may have dozed off before they got to the end of it, and forgotten the name completely."

He did not seem to find that amusing, so she added, "It was a short introduction that took place a few years ago. Much suffering and sorrow has come to Scotland since those days."

"But the Bourbon name must have been familiar to you, no?"

Aah, flattery, she thought, and proceeded to use it. "Bourbon blood flows in the veins of the kings of many great countries. The illustrious House of Bourbon has been one of the most powerful ruling families in Europe for centuries. Its famous name is known to everyone the world over, and I am certainly no exception. As for the woman I was trying to remember, I have no way of knowing if she is the one you speak of, because our meeting was such a minor event. One does not always attach a great deal of significance to every introduction."

"Of course," he replied, but she could almost hear the wheels turning in his head, cranking out possibilities.

"Was there something particular that I said that made you think it was the woman you mentioned?" Kenna asked. "I only ask because I am certain there must be many women with Bourbon blood about."

"I thought of this particular woman for two reasons, *mademoiselle:* her Bourbon blood, of course, and the fact she lives in Scotland. I know of only one woman who fits both descriptions. She is a Bourbon, and she married a Scottish nobleman—a duke, or an earl, I believe. And yes, she is related to me. My uncle was the Duc du Maine, a natural son of Louis XIV. King Louis was also Sophie's grandfather."

"Aah, I understand now, how you would think of her. Unfortunately, I do not know anyone married to a Frenchwoman." Kenna had nothing more to add to that, so she remained silent. If the duke wanted to discuss it further, then it would be up to him to broach the subject again.

"And your name, *mademoiselle?* You have not introduced yourself, and I cannot help wondering if that was intentional or an oversight."

"I do apologize, Your Grace, but I am in a quandary, and I hope you will understand. I can tell you that I left Scotland for personal reasons, and cannot, therefore, divulge my name, or the reason I came here. I can give you a false name, if you like."

The *duc* laughed, and his silvery eyes held a spark of delight.

Alexandre was smiling, but it was the *duc* who said, "I do believe that is the first time anyone has asked my permission to tell a lie." He could not manage to say more, for at that moment he was overcome with laughter. "I would like to call you something other than *mademoiselle,* but I respect your decision to keep your identity secret. It is something I have been forced to do myself, from time to time."

"I appreciate your honesty and indulgent understanding, Monsieur le Duc."

Silence engulfed the coach; everyone was lost in their own thoughts, but there were no visible clues as to what direction those thoughts were taking.

After a short while, Kenna allowed her curiosity to get the better of her. "I am puzzled as to why the three of you are traveling on Christmas Day, instead of being home with your families."

"We had plans to be back in Paris four days ago, but our carriage overturned south of Dunkerque," the *duc* said. "We managed to set it upright, and made it to the next post stop. We sent for a blacksmith, who told us the good news, that we needed a new axle. We were forced to wait there until he could make a new one."

"A terrible inconvenience, it was," the *vicomte* said, but the worst part is spending Christmas in a coach."

"Yes, it does not seem like Christmas at all," she said.

"And yet, life goes on, does it not?" the *duc* said.

"I do believe de Lorraine has fallen asleep," the *vicomte* noted. "We haven't had a shriek from him for some time now."

The Comte de Lorraine was, indeed, asleep, and after a few more miles of nodding, the *vicomte* joined him.

"I am afraid that leaves only the two of us to carry on the conversation," Kenna said, but she noticed a short time later that the *duc* had joined his friends in slumber.

It was not much longer before the carriage clattered over the cobblestones of Paris, and everyone began to wake up, all, save the poor *vicomte,* who took a turn at pulling back the curtain to find familiar landmarks.

"We are near Rue de St. Denis," the *vicomte* said, and turned to ask de Bourbon, "Is this not the street where your physician lives?"

A few minutes later, Kenna bid her three traveling companions goodbye as the carriage set off down the street once more, taking her to the home of Madame Guion.

Kenna had acquired Madame Guion's name almost two years ago, from Sophie, the same Sophie Victoire de Bourbon that Philippe, Duc de Bourbon, had spoken of in the carriage earlier.

It happened after Lord Walter was sent to prison, and the Lennoxes returned to Lennox Castle. When Kenna went to bed that night and opened the shutters in her room, she glanced at the moon and saw a halo encircled it.

Kenna knew what that meant: a ring around the moon was a bad omen.

If the moon shows like a silver shield,
you need not be afraid to reap your field,
but if she rises haloed round,
where you stand is cursed ground.

It was confirmation that the curse Lord Walter had placed upon her was real. In his mind, Kenna was to blame for his misfortune. Instead of enjoying the Lennox wealth, he would spend his life in prison, thanks to her. He would take great pleasure in his revenge, and that twisted mind would demand nothing less than a horrible, painful and torturous death for her. A simple murder would not do. He would want bloodcurdling revenge.

Since that night, Lord Walter had become her nemesis, the man who would stop at nothing to bring her down. He had murdered before. He would not hesitate to do so again.

She had trouble sleeping after that day, and her family thought it would be good for her to take a trip to the Continent. It was Sophie who suggested that Kenna go to France, for Sophie had many friends and relatives there that she could rely on.

Everyone agreed that France would be the perfect place, especially since French was a language Kenna spoke with fluency. Sophie did her part by writing letters of introduction to several prominent friends, and supplied Kenna with a list of people she might find helpful. One of those was Madame Guion, and the other was the Comte Debouvine, who, according to Sophie, was the best fencing master not only in France, but all of Europe.

But Kenna never went to France. She changed her mind about going, and the trip was forgotten, along with the packet of introductions and lists Sophie had given her.

"Why, Kenna?" Claire had asked. "You were so looking forward to this trip."

"I know, but now I feel different. I think to go would be running away. I feel very strongly that I should stay here and face the devils that rob me of my peace. If I go to France, I think it highly likely that those same ghosts will still be waiting for me here, when I return."

No one questioned her change of heart, and the subject was never broached again.

Things were different now. Lord Walter was out of prison and looking for her, and that made her decide for the second time in her life to go to France.

Only this time she followed through.

This time things were different.

She was not running away from ghosts. She was going on a journey to perfect herself, to train and to learn, until such time she felt confident to face her enemy.

Fortunately, she had kept the letters Sophie had written for her, which had been lying in the bottom of her trunk. The night before she left home, she tossed back its lid and threw the contents in five different directions, looking for the letters at the bottom.

She removed the small metal box and unlocked it. Inside, she found Sophie's packet of notes and introductions. It was all here—the names of friends and relatives, places she should visit and the letters of introduction.

She tucked the package into her traveling case along with only essential clothes she would take to France—two extra gowns and a riding suit. She could not risk taking the trunk, for it would draw more attention to her and be cumbersome to travel with.

And now, she was here, in Paris, and on her way to the address Sophie had given her for Madame Guion.

# *Six*

But words are words; I never yet did hear
That the bruis'd heart was pierced
through the ear.
—William Shakespeare (1564–1616),
English poet and playwright.
*Othello* (1602-1604), Act I, Scene 3.

Madame Jeanne-Marie Guion was a most agreeable lady who insisted she would never charge the sister-in-law of Sophie de Bourbon more than three guineas a month.

She had opened her home to a select few since her husband died, and prided herself on both her home and the quality of the people who stayed there.

Her son and two maiden sisters shared the large house, which was well furnished, with four bedchambers on the first floor, a large parlor below, a kitchen and "should you ever have the need, you are welcome to use the cellar."

Madame Guion also took care to warn Sophie about

her son, Jean-Claude. "*La!* He is a handsome enough young man of five and twenty years. He is good-natured and quite obliging, although in possession of a goodly amount of vanity. However, his one downfall is women…especially beautiful ones, and therefore you are at risk. He is a bit of a libertine, *mademoiselle,* so be on your guard."

Sophie had already warned Kenna about Frenchmen, and how their vanity was the ruling passion of the most volatile of them. Kenna was actually looking forward to his returning home, so she could see just what Sophie meant by volatile men whose vanity was their ruling passion.

Jean-Claude arrived home, and entered the room as vain as a peacock, with his strutting walk, his sword tasseled and hanging to his side. Immediately, Kenna realized Sophie had described him perfectly, right down to the bright red tassel.

When Kenna saw his saber, she said, "*Monsieur,* I thought gentlemen in Paris were not allowed to wear swords about."

"*Oui, mademoiselle,* what you say is true, but due to my position of importance with the government, I am permitted to wear a sword."

Upon further questioning, she discovered, too, that he had never used it, nor would he be so obliged, as he put it. "It is the effect of the sword, *mademoiselle,* that attracts attention, not the using of it. It is much more fashionable to display ornamentation, rather than running around brandishing a sword at each and every person you meet."

Madame Guion added, "Jean-Claude is so trustworthy that he is the receiver of the tithes of the clergy in our district. It is an office that gives him command of a great deal of money."

After she had finished dinner, Jean-Claude devoted himself to boring Kenna to death in the parlor, with mind-numbing descriptions of his uncle's château in the country; intentionally dropped hints of the fortunes that should have been settled upon his maiden aunts; boasted of his connections at court; and assured her, "It is not for money that my mother lets their lodgings, but more for 'the pleasure of enjoying the companionship of such lovely and well-connected persons such as yourself.'"

Kenna smiled inwardly as she remembered what Sophie said: "He will tell you of his connections at court, but I must warn you that they are confined to a clerk in the secretary's office, with whom he corresponds by virtue of his employment."

Jean-Claude went on to tell her of his accomplishments with the fairer sex, and when his mother left the room for a moment, whispered that he did, indeed, keep a *fille de joie*. In his best, broken English, he also admitted, "Can you believe *mademoiselle,* that in the past year alone, I have fathered six bastards...and all boys."

Thankfully, Jean-Claude was human enough that he had to eat, and when he went to the kitchen, Kenna hurried up to her room and locked the door.

She was up early the next morning, and after her toilette, she dressed and sat down to write a note to the

Comte Debouvine, by way of a *petite poste*. She included the letter of introduction Sophie had written to him.

She received a reply two days later, hand delivered, with an invitation to dine with the *comte* four days hence. He would send a carriage for her.

Because she had brought only a small amount of clothing with her to France, Kenna did not have a large number of gowns to choose from. She decided to enjoy not having to waste a great deal of time making a decision about which dress to wear. The riding suit was out, so that left only three choices. She easily selected a silk gown of deep, burnished gold, trimmed with dark brown, braided cord. She was aware that she would become very tired of this dress and the others she brought with her, and reminded herself to find a seamstress.

Kenna believed clothes possessed a very powerful influence, and to know she was dressed well gave her a sense of peace and well-being. With her gaze focused on the standing oval mirror in the room, she turned from side to side, and gave herself a critical going-over. The gown was both elegant and simple, and the braided cord added a jaunty military air. Yet, it needed something, and she settled on her mother's pearls.

When she had finished paying great attention to the smallest detail, she gathered her cape and was about to go belowstairs to await the *comte*'s carriage, but before she had her hand on the door, she heard the clatter of carriage wheels.

A quick peek out the window and she caught sight of the *comte*'s carriage, its brightly polished brass lanterns all aglow and two postilions riding tall as it rolled through the arch and into the courtyard, stopping in front of Madame Guion's home.

Thankfully, no one was about when Kenna went swiftly down the stairs and was handed by one of the postilions into the carriage. With a crack of the whip, the carriage was off and through the courtyard arch, then down the streets of Paris, to leave Madame Guion's home behind.

To say the Comte Debouvine had a home was an understatement, for it turned out to be a very palatial château on the outskirts of Paris.

Immediately upon her arrival, she was invited into the vestibule, where she barely had time to notice the exotic fabrics and lacquered grandfather clock before she was greeted by a *majordome*.

"I am Gaston, the *majordome* of Monsieur le Comte. May I take your cloak and gloves?"

She handed him her gloves, and he helped her out of her cape, which he placed on a chair before he said, "If *mademoiselle* will come this way, the footman will show you to the Salon Rose, where you may await Monsieur le Comte Debouvine."

A white-stockinged footman magically appeared, liveried and powdered, to conduct her down the long hallway. On the way, they passed the grand salon filled with exquisite furniture, tapestries and priceless paintings. The *comte* had cultivated taste, and it was obvious that he was very discriminating; she only hoped he was not quite so discriminating when it came to accepting her as a pupil.

Suddenly, the footman stopped and, throwing wide the doors of the Salon Rose, said, "If you will be so kind to wait here, the *comte* will arrive shortly."

After he was gone, she walked around the salon, with its great fireplace beneath ancestral portraits. The room was octagonal shaped, done all in gold, white and blue. She walked to the open doors and looked out to see the magnificent gardens spreading out behind the château, highlighted by a spectacular fountain. Echoes from the past seemed to haunt the setting with balustrades, terraces, sweeping stone stairways and beautiful walkways through avenues of lime trees. Further over, she caught a glimpse of the greenhouse and stables.

A moment later, she heard footsteps, and she turned as the doors opened and a slender man of medium stature entered. He was an impressive and graceful figure clad in a white cambric shirt, a green-and-cream damask coat and dark green satin breeches, with his once-black hair, now streaked with silver, unpowdered and tied back with a black velvet riband. The gold buttons on his coat bore his family crest, as did the gold signet ring on his left hand. A sparkling diamond ring graced his right.

His dark blue eyes widened when he saw her, then grew suddenly warm as a smile appeared upon his lips.

She knew very little about him, other than his repute as a fencing master and as one of the greatest swordsmen in all of Europe, and that was enough to intimi-

date King Louis himself. There was much myth and romance associated with his name, and her first impression of him was of a man of enormous reputation. His
age, personal history and marital status, were nothing
more than a matter of conjecture, and her fertile mind
was fast at work filling in the gaps with her imaginings.

He could have easily passed for a prince, so regal
was his bearing. She found it difficult to believe this
wealthy man could be the *comte* who mentored those
who wanted to learn the secrets of the sword. She knew
she was looking at the real mortal man, and not the
demigod she imagined from the stories she had heard,
where she could not help picturing him as a dashing
swordsman, fighting for honor and his king, and ending up with the hand of the king's daughter in marriage.

But, she reminded herself that she was racing off on
a tangent, and she knew nothing about the *comte*. In
truth, she could not really tell by looking at him that
he had ever picked up a sword.

But, as she stepped closer, she saw the trace of a
faint scar that ran from his right ear across his throat
to disappear beneath his collar, close to the collarbone.
She also noticed a small scar near his left temple,
though it was hard to drag her attention away from his
unbelievable, crystalline blue eyes.

"Lady Kenna, I have been looking forward to our
dinner this evening." He bent over the hand that she offered and brushed it lightly with a kiss. His lips were
cool, yet the hand that held hers was warm and strong.

He lifted his head and looked her directly in the
eyes. He was a handsome man, and she felt certain that

in his day he was quite sought-after, not only for his obvious wealth, but also for the beauty of his face. She wondered how many women he had seduced with his charm; how many men he had dazzled with his swordplay.

"It is an honor to make your acquaintance. It is something I have anticipated since receiving your note and the introduction from Sophie de Bourbon...forgive me, I understand she is now Lady Graham."

He spoke in French, and Kenna answered him in the same language. "It is a pleasure to meet you as well, Comte Debouvine. I thank you for extending your courteous invitation to a complete stranger to dine with you this evening. I am most appreciative for Lady Graham's generous introduction. She speaks very highly of you, and also said the two of you were acquainted, but she did add that it did not mean you would necessarily remember her."

"Not remember a beautiful woman who raised the ire of her cousin the king, by leaving France rather than marry the man of his choosing? Such a woman is not forgettable, my dear. I remember a great deal about your friend, Lady Graham."

"I must be truthful with you, Monsieur le Comte. There is a family connection there as well, for Sophie is the sister-in-law of my sister Claire, in her own right Countess of Errick and Mains."

"Your sister is a countess?"

"Yes. She is married to Fraser Graham now and has one son, Alex. She has spoken of her intent to pass the title to Fraser, who would have to change his name to

Lennox. He would then be known as Fraser Lennox, Earl of Errick and Mains."

"She will do this for her son, I assume."

"Yes, so he will one day inherit the title and continue the line of Lennoxes who bore the title."

"By the way, I must compliment you on your honesty. It is good to know you are a woman of principle and truth."

She could feel the heat as it rose to her face and she cast her eyes down to the floor. "I am not as saintly as you paint me, Monsieur le Comte, and cannot accept your praise. I do my best to tell the truth in every situation, but I must confess that there are times when I have found it necessary to stretch it a wee bit."

When he recovered from his laughter, he said, "I will be honest with you as well. I already knew of your family connection with Lady Graham, and was most curious to see if you were going to tell me of it. Your French is excellent, by the way."

"Thank you. So is yours," she said, knowing her eyes were alight with humor.

His aristocratic brows went up, and a slow smile curved crookedly across his mouth. She noticed the sparkle in his eyes that told of his pleasure at her comment.

"You had an exceptional teacher," he said.

"Yes, my father. He was a student of languages, and insisted his daughters learn French and Latin. My brothers were taught Italian and Spanish as well."

"Aah, a learned father, which is why you are so proficient. There is nothing like having someone close to you give instruction. When you care about someone, you naturally want to please them. It makes both learning and teaching a joy."

"That would apply to you as well, Monsieur le Comte, for it is evident that you have enjoyed your time as a fencing master, and it is quite obvious that you did not do it for the money."

He laughed, and began speaking English. "You have a quick mind and a fine wit. I am going to enjoy dining with you very much."

"And I look forward to dining with you," she said.

He offered his arm, and she slipped hers gracefully through his as they walked from the Salon Rose, which she found a little sad, for it was such a lovely room.

She needn't have regretted leaving the Salon Rose, for the *salle à manger* far surpassed it, with a carved stone buffet, high ceilings, ornate chandeliers and splendid boiseries, ornate, gilded and intricately carved.

"A magnificent room…actually, the château is magnificent. Has it been in your family long?"

"My family has been on this land about a thousand years," he said, "and the house has been added on to many, many times, to get to the state you now see. On several occasions it was almost demolished." His words were measured in that self-assured way many of the nobility have of speaking.

"One would never know by looking at it now."

"Please, Lady Kenna," he said as he pulled out her chair, waiting for her to sit down before he seated himself.

They dined by the light of candles and the moon coming through the glass doors that led to the gardens. She could only imagine the setting in the springtime, when the doors were open, with the scent of flowers and the serenade of the muted notes of the fountain drifting inside. Still, there was a lovely, crackling fire that provided both warmth and a bit of melody, along with an occasional display of brilliant sparks.

"I must say I was surprised when you asked in your note to see me, and that you would be coming alone. Surely you have not traveled from Scotland to Paris unaccompanied, Lady Kenna."

"Yes, I did, although it was not my preference to do so. Certain events necessitated the decision, and I was forced to make a choice—come alone, or not at all. It was not circumstances of my choosing, or something I settled on easily."

"A courageous decision, then?"

"My father always said a wise man makes his own decisions. Only time will tell how wise or courageous mine was."

His aristocratic brows were knitted together in disapproval.

"I understand that you would not commend a woman for doing such a distasteful thing as traveling alone."

"It is a dangerous undertaking. You know what kind of things might happen."

"Yes, I do, but the things that would happen if I remained in Scotland were far more unpleasant. And I have been very fortunate in my travels thus far."

After some moments, he said, "So, you have emulated your friend Lady Graham?"

"In a way, I suppose our cases are very similar. I cannot deny that Sophie was inspiring to me. I felt if she was able to take control of her life, then I could do the same with mine. Of course, our motivations were nothing alike."

"You did not come here to escape marriage, then?" His voice was firm, and smooth, and his command of English, excellent.

"No, I am not betrothed. My flight from Scotland and my home were similar to Sophie's, but my reasons for coming are entirely different."

She wondered if he would press the issue and inquire as to the circumstances that forced her flight, but his breeding proved to override any curiosity—at least for the moment.

"I am a bit confused about a comment in your note, when you referred to a most important matter you wished to discuss with me. Now that we have finished our dinner, I feel I can politely broach the subject with you."

"I have come here to ask you to take me as a pupil and become my fencing master."

To describe his reaction as *surprised* would be to give the word more expressive power than was its due, for his face registered much more than wonder or amazement, or even something unanticipated. In fact, no one word would do it justice, for it was an expression that combined all the elements of *overwhelmed,* *stunned* and *astonished*...the kind of shock one would expect to show if they suddenly opened the door and saw Leonardo da Vinci standing there with Mona Lisa at his side.

It took him a moment to recover. "I beg your pardon, but I must have missed the meaning here. You did not mean to say what you said. Either that, or your words were meant in jest."

"No, I meant what I said and I jest not. I am very serious, Monsieur le Comte. I wish to become your pupil. I decided upon you because you were once the greatest swordsman in Europe, and then you became the best fencing master. I wish to hire you."

"This is most improper. Forgive me, Lady Kenna, but you are a female, and fencing has yet to become an acceptable pursuit for women. It simply is not done."

"Someone must be the first, although I know there have been female swordsmen before me."

"That is of no importance." He paused a moment to study her face, and finding no answers there, he asked, "What did you hope to accomplish by coming here like this?"

"I needed a fencing master and I chose you. It was worth the gamble, for I had naught to lose."

"A gamble? Go on."

"I knew if I came for wool, I might come home shorn myself, but a desperate man will grasp at water, and I had naught to give my unfed hopes. My only recourse was to try. I am not a gracious loser, Monsieur le Comte. It is a wide streak of stubbornness that plagues all Scots," she said. "We are like burrs, we stick."

"You are awfully young to speak as you do. You should be going to balls and taking rides in the park and be counting your suitors, not harboring visions of yourself with a sword in your hand. You are young. Enjoy it."

"I cannot afford the luxury of being young. It is more important that I survive."

"I see. I am sorry to have to refuse you, but I would never take a woman for a pupil."

She started to reply that her being a woman should not have anything to do with it, but he rose to his feet and offered to show her around his grand château, and she read his meaning correctly. The matter was closed.

"Of course I would love to see it," she said. "And I would enjoy it immensely if you would honor me with a peek at the place where you conducted your fencing classes."

She saw the muscle in his jaw flex, and the scar across his neck became red. "In spite of your persistence, you must understand that I have retired from all of that, but I will show you the Salle des Chevaliers if you will come with me."

Upon hearing the *comte* mention the French, Salle des Chevaliers, or Knights' Gallery, reminded her that the room dated back to the time of chivalry, and that helped prepare her for what she would see.

The *comte* unlocked the door and she stepped into a gallery vaulted in the Gothic style, with stone arches that towered high overhead. It was like stepping into a cathedral.

Splendid trefoiled windows, set high, lined two

walls. At the far end of the gallery, she could see the sculptured coat of arms, and along one wall armory from the château's early years—suits of armor, halberds, pikes and a stack of large stone balls for catapults. Then she saw the assortment of swords…sabers, rapiers, foils, épées.

"It is magnificent," she said. "I am almost speechless at the overwhelming sight of it. It is so much more than I expected." She turned to him and said with warmth in her voice, "It is like stepping back centuries, for I can imagine it looking exactly the same at the height of the Crusades."

"I am glad you appreciate fine architecture, for it is exactly as it was when it was first built, save for the additions of the more modern swords."

After their tour, she took a glass of port with him in the library, where the fire in an enormous hearth warmed the room and the hallway beyond.

She seated herself across from him. "I hope my request did not offend you."

"It isn't offensive, but that is far from the point. I hope I was not too blunt in my refusal, but you must understand my position. You are a very persuasive woman, Lady Kenna, and if you asked almost anything else of me, I would grant it. However, there are two very good reasons why I cannot honor your request. First, I would never instruct a woman. Second, I am retired. When I put down my foil and closed the door to any future students, it was permanent. Besides, I doubt I would live long enough to train a novice."

"But I am not a novice, Monsieur le Comte. I have been fencing for many years."

"You cannot be serious if you make such a statement."

"It is the truth. My father allowed me to be instructed by the same fencing master who taught my brothers."

He simply stared at her, and she saw the white knuckles around his glass and hoped he would not shatter it. "I cannot imagine the father who would allow his daughter to learn weaponry of any sort."

"My father was not a barbarian, I assure you. He was a powerful earl, and the laird of the Lennoxes, a very old and noble clan. His power reached beyond even Scotland."

"I have heard of the Lennoxes," he said, "and I apologize if I said something to cause you grief. Is your father still alive?"

"My father and three brothers were murdered."

"I am sorry to hear of your loss. Do their deaths have something to do with your coming here, and your wish to further your fencing skills?"

"I would be lying if I said it did not."

"I understand. Perhaps you should seek out another fencing master. I can give you the names…"

"It is imperative that I have only the best."

"Thank you for your flattery, and the honor you give to me by saying I am the best. That might have been true once, but times change."

"Yes, that is my point exactly. You said women did not take up the sword. Times are changing. I want to change along with them."

"I am not holding you back, Lady Kenna. I am only refusing to be the one who teaches you."

"And you would not consider taking one pupil…to be the first fencing master in France to instruct a woman?"

"You cannot bribe me with fame. I must ask you not to persist with this request. The answer is no, and the answer will remain no."

He seemed to be searching her face, or perhaps her eyes for something…truth? Shame? Humility? She had no real inkling.

He sighed, and said, "Come with me."

She went with him into the library, where after a moment of searching, he drew forth, with an exclamation of, "Aah… I have found it…a book by Petrarch. Give a listen, if you will."

He indicated a chair for her to sit in, and she obliged, with a nod of her head as she sat down.

"In 1343 the Italian poet Petrarch wrote of one woman warrior, an Italian named Maria. He called her 'a mighty woman of Pozzuoli, sturdy in body and soul…. Her body is military rather than maidenly, her strength is such as any hardened soldier might wish for, her skill and deftness unusual, her age at its prime, her appearance and endeavor that of a strong man. She cares not for charms but for arms; not for arts and crafts but for darts and shafts; her face bears no trace of kisses and lascivious caresses, but is ennobled by wounds and scars. Her first love is for weapons, her soul defies death and the sword. She helps wage an inherited local war, in which many have perished on both sides. Sometimes alone, often with a few companions, she has raided the enemy, always, up to the present, victoriously.... I saw her again a few years ago...and I barely recognized the wild, primitive face of the maiden under her helmet.'"

He closed the book and turned to her. "Now, tell me you would like to emulate this woman's life."

"Of course I do not wish to emulate Maria's life. I wish to remain myself, just as I am, but with the skill of a highly skilled swordsman."

"And I suppose you see no reason why you cannot have everything you ask for?"

"I see no reason why I cannot have everything I work hard to achieve."

"This is preposterous. A woman swordsman...I daresay I do not know the proper way to even address her. Swordsman does not seem fitting for she is not a man...and swordswoman, besides being difficult to say, sounds utterly absurd. Swordsperson identifies no gender. Swordette? It sounds like a dance. But never mind, I cannot perceive a female learning the art."

"Aren't you forgetting your own La Maupin?"

His face registered surprise. "La Maupin? How in the devil do you know about her?"

"I know a great many things, Monsieur le Comte. I was privileged to have a father who believed in enriching the minds of his daughters. In my studies, I learned there have been many such women, Monsieur le Comte. I would be happy to tell you of some of them if you like."

"You are the daughter of a Scottish earl. Why would a woman of your breeding and station want something like this?"

"Perhaps I want more out of life than polite conversation and serving tea. Perhaps I want to survive and live my life in peace. Perhaps a woman can want the same things as a man."

"And what is that?"

"Adventure, control of her own life, confidence in her ability to defend herself."

He did not say anything further. He stood and walked to the bookshelf and put the book back exactly where it had been. He crossed one arm across his middle and brought the fingers of his other hand up to his cheek and drummed his fingers several times. Then he stood there, with his face toward the books, as if in deep thought…or could it be that he was considering something?

When he made no move to turn back to her, she tried to understand what this meant. Perhaps it was his way, or the French way, of dismissing someone.

After a few more minutes, she decided he was waiting for her to go, as a way for both of them to save face. So, she rose to her feet and without saying a word, walked to the door of the library, then turned.

"Let me ask you something. If you were in my place, would you meekly surrender and give up, or would you keep trying?"

"You ask an unfair question, and one I cannot answer, simply because I am not a woman, and do not think like a woman."

"Do you have a wife and children?" she asked.

"I did once, but my wife and two sons were killed during a botched robbery."

"Forgive me for asking. It was inconsiderate of me to put my personal needs before your right to privacy. I am fortunate to have three living sisters. However, having lost my mother and all the male members of my family, I do understand your loss."

"I am sure you do," he said icily. He glanced at his watch. "The hour grows late and you have to traverse the distance back to Paris. I will escort you to your carriage."

Kenna suddenly felt bereft of even the power to charm, which had always served her so well. What could she say to him that would not make her motives seem self-serving and selfish? She bit her lip to hold back the tears. It cannot end like this, she thought.

It cannot…

Of all the things that could have happened to her, during the trip to Edinburgh, the travel by ship, the coach ride from Calais to Paris, she'd arrived in Paris and had her hopes thrust back in her face, and her dreams shattered.

If I do not learn to protect myself, I might as well send Lord Walter a letter telling him where he can find me, she thought as they walked in silence to the carriage.

So much planning and now everything was falling apart; her center could not hold. She needed something to hold on to, something to retain her equilibrium. No longer rich with hope, she was alone with nothing to do but weep and curse her fate.

It was raining when they stepped outside, and she was thankful for that, at least, for it would hide the tears that began to spill in spite of all she did to hold them back.

In defiance of her despair, she managed to compose herself long enough to give the *comte* her hand, even though she was sick at heart.

"Thank you, Monsieur le Comte, for a lovely evening and dinner. And please accept my apology for intruding on your privacy with my humble, albeit persistent request. I can only say in my defense, that I am an educated woman of good breeding and genteel manners, but there are things that can happen in life that push you from your center and leave a person with little hope of saving herself. You are most fortunate that you have never in your life been in such a desperate situation that you were forced to go beyond the bounds of etiquette and propriety to humble yourself in your desperation. It humiliates and damages one's pride and dignity to be forced to put more faith in begging than in prayer, begging, as a dog would do for scraps. You have no idea what it is like to be without hope. I compliment you on your steel reserve, and your iron will. I pray the dark shadow of fear never wraps itself around you, for you cannot imagine how the fear of one evil can lead you into an even worse one. I hope you never have to dread each hedge and tree you pass and wonder if the breath you now draw will be your last."

With her head held high, she stepped into the carriage, and pulled the door closed behind her.

"I am strong enough to bear this misfortune, and I

will overcome even this, and be stronger in the doing of it," she promised herself as the carriage sped into the darkness.

# *Seven*

There are two levers for moving men—
interest and fear.
—Napoléon Bonaparte (1769–1821),
French general, emperor. Quoted in:
Ralph Waldo Emerson, *Representative Men,*
"Napoleon; or The Man of the World" (1850).

Disheartened, she returned to Madame Guion's, and was disconcerted to see through the window that Jean-Claude was sitting in his favorite chair by the fire. She was certain he was waiting in the salon for her to return home.

Not now, please God, she thought, for I cannot speak of this evening to anyone, for the pain of it bleeds throughout my being, like the puncture of a foil, straight, deep and lethal.

She needed time alone, and quiet surroundings where she could nurse her wounds, still so raw and burning, and Jean-Claude was such a blot on the beauty of silence. She did not want to discuss anything with anyone, especially one of the Guions' household, for they would never understand the strongest minds are the ones heard least.

She stepped into the foyer and paused to close the door with a soft click, followed by the snap of the turned lock. Although she did not know why she bothered to close it carefully, for Jean-Claude would hear even the slightest whisper of her silk slippers upon the floor.

She stepped farther into the room, and thought it odd that Jean-Claude, with so much self-centered energy did not immediately leap from his chair upon hearing her enter.

She walked quickly to the doorway, which was a few feet from the stairway. After a quick glance into the salon, she went limp with relief. Jean-Claude, whom she prayed earlier would develop a sore throat, was actually asleep. It was the first scrap of good fortune she had experienced since coming to Paris.

The next day, she lived and relived the harrowing appeals she had made to the *comte,* feeling like a desperate beggar who flings all pride and self-respect to the wind.

By the second day, she knew she had to move beyond this disappointment and reorganize herself, so she could come up with a new plan. After all, there were other fencing masters in France. All she had to do was find the right one.

But saying is easier than doing, and by the passing of the second day, Kenna was still despondent over the results of her attempt to convince the Comte Debouvine to come out of retirement and take her as a pupil.

It was agonizing to leave the house on the third morning, but she had to do so in order to escape Madame Guion's prying. The only beneficial part of it was she found a good *sempstress,* and was fitted for a dozen gowns to be made from what the *sempstress* called "rich Renaissance fabrics and colors"—cut velvet, damask and silk in the colors of burgundy, teal, dark blue, deep gold, ruby, onyx, russet, carnation, maid's blush, silver, and a sumptuous gold-and-garnet silk. She also selected day dresses, several riding outfits and was fitted for undergarments, which went beyond torture. She did, however, refrain from telling the *sempstress* that the women in Scotland did not wear so many torturous devices.

The fourth day Kenna spent shopping for hats, gloves, fans, parasols, fichus, shoes, boots and shoe buckles. And then it was all done—everything purchased, gowns ordered, and nothing left to do but go back to Madame Guion's and decide how she would find a new fencing master.

She had borrowed writing paper from Madame Guion to write the Comte Debouvine, but now that she would be writing to other fencing masters, she needed to purchase her own paper, and that meant one last stop, to view *le stock d'un marchand—papetier de Paris, Louis Richard,* or in her own tongue, to view the stock of the paper merchant of Paris, Louis Richard.

It was half past four o'clock in the afternoon when she left the shop of Louis Richard and returned to Madame Guion's. She arrived almost on the hour for dinner, where she was beset with obstinate questions from both Madame Guion and Jean-Claude. Were there ever two more opinionated, stubborn and boorish people born into the world, than these two? she wondered. When she could take no more, she begged to be excused from dessert, in order to take a powder for her head as she felt as though "someone had taken an ax to her brain."

Kenna did not have a headache, but she was exhausted from her long day, and on edge from all the questions during dinner, so she removed her clothes and put on her dressing gown and lay down to take a nap.

She had no concept of how much time had passed, when she was awakened by someone knocking on the door.

A moment later, Madame Guion called out her name loudly, "Lady Kenna, you have a letter from the Comte Debouvine."

Kenna cracked her knee on the bedpost as she sprang from the bed. She was still rubbing it when she opened the door and stared at the white vellum in Madame Guion's hand.

She took the letter and looked it over, recognizing the *comte*'s loopy handwriting as she looked at first one side and then the other. "When did it arrive?"

"Only moments ago…delivered by the *comte*'s own groom, it was. I am sorry to wake you, but I thought it might be important. Were you expecting a letter from him?"

Kenna gave her a puzzled frown as she read her name on the envelope. "No, I was not expecting a letter from the *comte,* and have no idea what it could be about."

She started to close the door, but Madame Guion's ample being was in the way, and she did not look like she was budging anytime soon. Kenna said, "Thank you for bringing it up to me, madame. I will read it after my head feels better."

Madame Guion opened her mouth, then hesitated, as though she was contemplating saying something more but thought better of it. She closed her mouth and took a step back. "Do let me know what the *comte* has to say," and then, as if realizing just how prying her comment was, she tried to soften it somewhat by adding, "That is, I do hope you will share any news of general interest."

The woman's curiosity was insatiable, and Kenna felt Madame Guion was meddling in her private affairs, but she was too gracious to say such. "I will tell you of anything of general interest, rest assured…and thank you for bringing it to me."

She closed the door and turned back into her room, where she paused in front of the mirror. The woman staring back at her had a visage she did not know; a pale face that had taken on that quiet, delicate beauty of death, lifelike and yet so intensely still.

She seated herself on the bed and tore open the envelope, and was shocked to see it was another invitation to dine with the *comte* tomorrow night. After he signed his name with a flourish, the *comte* had penned an addendum:

*"I do hope you will decide to dine with me, Lady Kenna, in spite of the way our last evening ended, for I have something of the utmost importance to discuss with you."*

*The utmost importance*, she thought, and found it unlikely the *comte* would want to discuss anything with her, and certainly not something of the "utmost importance."

Try as she might, she could not think what they could discuss. And she knew full well he had not changed his mind, nor would she ever forget the way he had politely said, "*Je suis désolé.* I am sorry. I have had several requests from others like you, hoping to change my mind, but it is firmly made up."

Oh yes, the Comte Debouvine would most assuredly come out of his recent retirement now…just long enough to take up the foil and stab her with it.

As a last resort, she thought it might be that he had some names of possible fencing masters she could contact.

It wasn't much, but it was all she had to look forward to.

It was almost nightfall when Bastien Lievin, the Comte Debouvine, stood in the midst of the magnificence of the *salle à manger.* The ornate chandeliers were not lit, and only a single candelabra cast a dim shadowy light that fanned out across the floor, to where the table was set for two.

As he had been doing for the past few days, he was thinking about the Scottish lass he dined with a few evenings ago—an evening much the same as this, with pale light shining through the glass doors that led to the gardens, accompanied by the musical notes of the fountain.

The sound of those last few words brought a smile to his face, for he remembered how she had com-

mented on the lovely sound of the fountain that serenaded them. "Such lovely golden notes that capture me
with silver hooks," she said, and he found it quite odd
that he had never really taken any notice of the fountain when he had dined in here before.

What daring she had, not only to leave Scotland
and travel to Paris alone, but also to ask him to come
out of retirement and instruct her. Somehow, she had
managed to make it all sound so perfectly natural. As
though he was asked to instruct women on a daily
basis.

He still thought it absurd and a bit incongruous that
she not only had the nerve to *want* to be instructed, but
also to ask him to do it. And yet, how many times when
the absurd had been prevented the noble was also sti-
fled?

He was curious as to why such a beautiful woman
would make such an out-of-the-ordinary request. She
wanted to become skilled in the use of the foil...who-
ever heard of such?

Oh, he would grant that there had been a few women
warriors scattered throughout the pages of history, but
that did nothing to promote her request. He almost regretted not asking her why she wanted to learn to fence,
although she did give him some hint when she indicated she was in grave danger—but, from whom, and
why?

To ask such a question would have been out of line
for a man of his position.

He picked up his brandy and retraced the steps he
had taken that night when he showed her around the

château, then took her to the Fencing Gallery. He recalled her delight in being allowed to see it, and the way she walked along the display of swords and rapiers, with a rapt look upon a face so radiant he wondered if her destiny was akin to that of Joan of Arc, who was divinely summoned to take up the sword and lead the forces of the true French king into battle.

Like Lady Kenna, she had been audacious in her actions, for she had declared to the English, *"Allez-vous-en en Angleterre,"* go away to England, or she would *"bouter vous hors de France,"* drive you out of France.

And she had shocked many when she donned the suit of armor the king had made for her, and carried a sword and a banner. Although she never killed anyone, she did expel prostitutes from the camps at sword point, and on more than one occasion, she gave them whacks across the back with it.

But unlike Joan of Arc, he knew the cause Kenna had taken up was not a religious one, but one of her own survival.

And that one fact intrigued him, especially when he added the spice of her spirit and determination to fight her own battles. To do this, she had shown great courage and strength of character: admirable qualities, both.

He felt a sudden sense of emptiness and loss for his long-ago decision to never marry again, after the death of his wife and his sons. He counted the years, and realized Kenna could have been his daughter. He imagined how his life would be different with one such as her, so full of life and determination, filling the château with her vibrancy and joie de vivre.

Aah...to have such a daughter.

*And what would you do if she wanted to learn the use of the foil? Would you send her away in humiliation?*

He finished the brandy and chastised himself for such thoughts. Yet he did wonder, what would he do if Kenna was, in fact, his daughter?

A woman taking up the sword...did she really think this was a skill needed by a woman of her position? But, she did say she had taken lessons from her brother's fencing master for years, with her father's approval.

He considered that for a moment. She was tall and slender, and from what he could tell, she was limber and supple, and she was hungry....

"*Pardon moi*, Monsieur le Comte, but Lady Kenna Lennox has arrived," Gaston said. "Shall I show her in?"

"Yes, by all means," the *comte* said, anticipating her entrance into the *salle à manger*, for he knew she would be as despondent as she had been when he saw her last. Yet the moment she swept through the door, swathed in emerald-green silk, with magnificent pearls gleaming against alabaster skin, he knew she was a woman who recovered, or covered, her emotions easily.

She could almost read his mind, could hear him thinking as clearly as if he had spoken the words: this is a woman of strength and resilience, not a woman who had gambled and lost, and I am a man who admires strength and resilience, for the ability to spring back quickly after being wounded, humiliated or defeated should be utmost in the mind and character of anyone who picks up the foil.

*Excellent,* she thought, *for that is precisely what I wanted you to think.* "Good evening, Monsieur le Comte. It is an unexpected delight to be invited back to your lovely château, and I am honored once again with the pleasure of your company at dinner."

"The honor and pleasure is all mine, Lady Kenna."

"I must admit, Monsieur le Comte, that I am most confused as to why you invited me here tonight."

"Suffice to say, you have my attention, Lady Kenna. Now you must capture my interest."

"I am not sure how I should go about doing that," she said.

"Just be yourself. And may I say you look absolutely ravishing tonight? Were I thirty years younger, you would be in grave danger of being seduced."

She laughed. "I shall make a point to wear this dress more often then, if it draws such a reaction."

"Oh, it does. Believe me. When gauging a woman's beauty, the eye never fails, no matter the age." He came closer, and she offered her hand, which he kissed in that charming manner that only he was capable of executing with such flair, and after he had finished, he kept her hand in his and, pulling it through his arm, led her to a comfortable chair by the fire.

She barely had time to seat herself when Gaston entered with a bottle of champagne and two glasses. He must have handled the explosive liquid many times, for he quickly uncorked it and poured her a glass. "Is this supposed to help me drown my sorrows?" she asked.

"Do you have sorrows that need drowning, Lady Kenna?"

"No, but if I did, drinking champagne is better than being drowned in a barrel of malmsey, don't you think?"

It seemed to her that it took great effort for the *comte* to keep the corners of his mouth from lifting…far be it that he should smile and give some indication that he was enjoying himself.

"Has anyone ever accused you of being enchanting?" he asked.

She thought about that for a moment. "No, but I have oft been called exasperating."

The beautiful room reverberated with the sound of his laughter. "Your frank honesty is a bit unsettling for a Frenchman, for we are accustomed to the evasive techniques employed in the salons."

"I am sorry if I came across as unrefined, but asking if I had been called enchanting, well it made me sound quite antique, like some fairy, tripping half naked across the moors, with long, unkempt hair, or an ancient hag peppered with magic straight from the charmed forests of Celtic history, long before the sacking of Delphi."

This time, she was certain his boisterous laughter could be heard all the way to Paris.

"I would like to offer you more champagne, but I dare not spoil the sharpness of your wit that is so evident tonight. To what do I owe the pleasure of it?"

"You might say, it stems from pure relief, for I have no worries that I must say or behave in a certain way that would influence you to accept me as a pupil."

He saw immediately that she thought she had said the wrong thing, for his face took a sudden serious turn.

"And yet, your wit and your humor have managed to extract from me that which your serious persuasion could not."

"Well, Monsieur le Comte, it is your fault for plying me with champagne, so now you must…"

Suddenly, his words penetrated her consciousness like the abrupt blast of a north wind sweeping across Sutherland. "Monsieur le Comte, if this is your idea of a jest…"

"My lovely little Scot, I have never had a more serious moment in my entire life."

"Then you will…"

"Take you as a pupil, and may the good God above grant that I should not wake up in the morning with a headache and a heart full of regret for the words I uttered this night."

"Monsieur le Comte, I doubt that is possible, for you have yet to finish your first glass of wine."

"Lady Kenna, allow an old man the opportunity to blame something other than the weakness of his own fortitude."

"You are not old, Monsieur le Comte."

"I have recently passed my sixtieth year, Lady Kenna. And now, let us sit down, for I have seen Gaston pacing the hallway beyond our door, fretting that the lamb will not be eaten at the peak moment of its perfection."

Gaston must have been pleased for the lamb was, as the *comte* promised, at the "peak moment of its perfection," and once the meal was over, the *comte* invited her to share a glass of port in the Salon Rose.

As she entered the room, she paused beneath a wall of ancestral portraits. "I do not see your portrait, Monsieur le Comte. Will it hang here one day?"

"I am trying to resist the supernatural soliciting that I feel each time I pass by. I rather think it is bad enough to be condemned to tolerate the stares from faces of the past, without feeling compelled to perpetuate the images. Have you ever noticed there is always something wrong with the mouth? They are endlessly the same, either seriously grim, or a smirk."

"Except perhaps, for Mona Lisa." She studied one portrait in particular. "This must be your father, for I see a strong resemblance. There is much continuity in the Roman nose."

"Yes, I come from a long line of highly unattractive people."

She smiled at that comment, and proceeded to study the painting of the woman next to his father. Was it his mother? With an elegant dress, jewelry and a gold chatelaine, she was certainly a lady of quality. And the ring was obviously her wedding ring, considering it was on her right index finger. She decided it was his mother, for the clue was in the crystalline blue eyes. "Your mother was beautiful."

He stopped next to her and studied the portrait, almost as if it were the first time he had looked at it. She knew then that he had been very close to this woman. "My mother always hated that portrait. She told the artist it would never be considered a masterpiece, and the artist replied that to paint a masterpiece, the artist must first have a beautiful subject."

The smile became a laugh. "Monsieur le Comte, I would have never known you for a man of great wit and humor."

"It is nothing more than an opportunity to resist the nascent attempts of approaching age to stir the blood of kinship."

"Did you have a large family?" she asked.

"Two brothers and three sisters. All are dead now."

"I am sorry you have suffered so much loss, and sorry that you are all alone."

He raised his brows in surprise. "But, I am not alone. There is a young woman living here. Josette Revel is about your age. She is no blood relation, but she is like a daughter to me. I think the two of you will enjoy each other's company and companionship."

"When shall I meet her?"

"She should return tomorrow. Josette is Romany… a Gypsy by birth. Although she has spent most of her life here at my château, there are times when she will go back to the place where she was born. She feels it is important that she not forget who her people were."

"And she travels alone?"

It was the first time she had seen the *comte* throw his head back and truly laugh.

With charitable zeal, Kenna quickly said, "No one should lose their past and where they came from."

Humor still danced in the *comte*'s eyes. "She would agree with you, for she likes to remind me that I am noble by heritage, and human by choice."

"I look forward to our meeting, and hope we shall be good friends."

"I am confident you will. Josette is a woman who is passionate about many things, just as you seem to be. Of course, I could be wrong, and the two of you could dislike each other from the start, for I have arrived at the age where one oft expresses himself with a palsied heart and a jaundiced eye."

"What made you change your mind about me, Monsieur le Comte? Was it the fortuitous aligning of planets, or the mere whim of merciless fate who tossed me into the center of your retired life?"

"Fortuitous situations form the molds that shape the events in our lives, whether some are by accident or the decree of ordaining fate, one can only suppose. As to your particular situation, it's been several days since you were last here, and during that time, your parting words have not left my mind, primarily because I find them to be quite haunting. I decided I would know more of this woman, so lovely and so young, who knows a great deal about suffering. You mentioned things that can happen in life to push you from your center, leaving you with little hope of salvation. That comes not from reading but from experience. I would like you to tell me of it. Please," he said, moving to the sofa, "do sit down."

She seated herself and studied the hands in her lap for a few moments, as she wondered where to best start.

The *comte* took a chair close to her.

"It began with the murder of my father and my two eldest brothers by an aunt and her lover. Isobel Lennox was married to my father's brother. She had a son, Giles McLennan, by a previous marriage. She was a beautiful woman, but vain and greedy. She was always pushing my uncle to buy bigger castles, so she could live like a queen."

"A wife like that has been the ruination of many men," he said. "It usually causes the honeyed milk of romance to curdle."

"Apparently, it did in Isobel's case, for she had a lover for years—an Englishman, Lord Walter Ramsay. My uncle was barely in the ground when he moved into the castle with her. She had my uncle's wealth and his property, but before long, the money was gone and she began selling off his holdings, and when that was squandered, she turned her greedy eyes upon my father's money and holdings, and his title. About this time, my father and two eldest brothers were murdered while returning home from visiting the Grahams. One of my brothers was beheaded and his head hung on a pike."

She paused a moment to collect herself. "We never learned who did this or why, for it was not robbery. Almost immediately, we learned that Isobel and Lord Walter were appointed our guardians. They slowly poisoned my youngest brother, Kendrew, and after his death my sister Claire inherited our father's earldom, and became the Countess of Errick and Mains in her own right. It was their plan to force Claire, who was only fifteen at the time, to marry Isobel's son, Giles, which would put the control of the Lennox title and wealth in their hands. Only Claire was not as malleable as they thought. After treating all four of us cruelly for months, Lord Walter decided he needed to speed things up and took more severe measures with Claire. He locked her in the dungeon of an abandoned castle in a remote area on the coast of Caithness and starved her almost to the point of death."

"And she escaped?" he asked.

"No. I spied on him and learned where he was taking Claire, and then I put on the trews of my dead brother and rode to Edinburgh to the home of Fraser Graham, to get help. Fraser and his brother, the Earl of Monleigh, and several men rescued Claire."

"And what happened to Isobel and Lord Walter?"

"Isobel preferred death to prison, and drank poison. Lord Walter was imprisoned in England, which brings me to the reason I am here. After the Battle of Culloden, the King of England released Lord Walter. I was warned that while in prison, he vowed he would get even with me for ruining his plans and causing the death of Isobel."

"So you came here to improve your skill?"

"Yes."

"Why did you decide to handle this yourself, instead of allowing your family to protect you?" he asked.

"Lord Walter killed all of the men in my family. He

almost killed my sister. I could not bear the grief of losing another family member to this evil man. I made the decision to ride for help to save Claire. I am the one Lord Walter seeks his revenge upon. I will not allow someone else to settle my score with him. If I face him, there is a chance—if I am proficient enough—that I could prevail. If not, and I lose my life, that is preferable to a lifetime of grieving and guilt over the loss of a loved one."

"You have taken a great deal of responsibility upon your slender shoulders, while at the same time placing a tremendous burden upon mine. For now I must not only improve your skill, I must teach you how to save your life."

"I have no doubt that you and I can do this together. That is why I chose you as the man to entrust with my life. I did not come here for sympathy, or to court favors. I came to persuade you to teach me the art of survival. I have a quick mind, a strong heart and a willing spirit. When I care about something, I give it my all. I am not a quitter, and I will not give up easily."

"We will soon see what you are made of, for there will be ample opportunities for you to prove yourself worthy. But first, you will move your belongings to the château tomorrow, and you will reside here for as long as you are my pupil. I will control your life henceforth. I will order your meals, and tell you when to go to bed and when to rise. You will work the entire day, save for a break for lunch and dinner. You will dress as I ask, and obey me no matter how foolish my request appears."

Her eyes watered, and she dared them to spill. This man was no tyro, no beginner and no old man out of practice. He was the greatest fencing master in the history of the French school and he had agreed to instruct her.

"I will never be able to repay you for this," she said.

"You may not want to, once your work begins. It is a grueling routine even for a man. You will come to hate even the terms you have to memorize and execute...*parade de septime* replaces the slower *parade de prime*...always use the *parade de seconde* instead of the *parade d'octave,* which is weak...the *parade de tierce* is stronger and readier than the *parade de sixte.* You may wish you were anywhere else when you engage a man who could carve you like a goose before you had time to say *parry.* You will be expected to drill repeatedly to bring your body to the peak of perfection, for only then will you realize that flexibility of movement, quickness, steadiness and lightness of touch are preferable to endurance, determination or even brute strength."

"One day I will look back upon this as a day of good fortune," she said.

"The opposite is also possible.... In any case, you shall be a welcome addition to my household and, I hope, a close friend to Josette."

He stood. "It is time for me to retire. I have enjoyed our time together. My coach will come for you and your possessions at ten o'clock tomorrow. Once you set foot in that coach, your life is no longer your own."

# *Eight*

You told a lie, an odious, damned lie;
Upon my soul, a lie, a wicked lie.
—William Shakespeare (1564–1616),
English poet and playwright.
*Othello,* Act V, Scene 2.

It was not Gaston who opened the door of the château on Monday, when she arrived with her belongings.

Taken aback by her surprise at seeing a woman where Gaston should have been, Kenna seemed to have lost her voice. Before she could introduce herself, the woman greeted her.

"Welcome to your new home, Lady Kenna. The *comte* is expecting you."

Kenna stepped inside. "I apologize for staring so, but I was gorgonized from head to toe expecting to see Gaston open the door, not an exquisitely beautiful woman. And please forgive my manners for not introducing myself. I am—"

"I know who you are. The *comte* told me about you. I am Josette Revel. I live here. I am not an employee. I am not his daughter. I am not his paramour. Like you, I am someone the *comte* has opened his home and his heart to; unlike you, I have no interest in fencing, nor can I imagine why any woman would want to go to so much trouble and travel so far for fencing lessons."

Kenna began removing her cape. "I will not hold that against you, and to tell you the truth, leaving home and coming here was not something I dreamed up out of boredom, but rather I was forced into it."

"Why?"

"Mine is a long story, just as I am sure yours is, so I will save it to share with you when you have time to tell me yours."

Kenna knew she was looking at a woman who must have a paralyzing and stupefying effect upon men. With her exotic Mediterranean bone structure, olive complexion and voluptuous figure, she could put a goddess to shame. Kenna was especially taken by her big, almond-shaped eyes, which were a lusty velvet brown with a hint of sea green.

Sensuality seemed to drip from her, and left Kenna feeling her more classic beauty, pale skin and red hair had just taken a tumble in the dust.

Josette wore a colorful dress of gray wool, trimmed with Kenna's favorite Venetian raised-point lace, which the Italians aptly named *punto in aria*, and truly it was a stitch in the air, exquisitely fine and delicate—the richest, most sumptuous of needlepoint laces, and also the most expensive.

"Your gown is of beautiful design and workmanship. The delicacy of the lace is remarkable."

Josette gave her a flat, measuring look. "Were you expecting me to wear several long, flowing skirts with an abundance of flounces all in bright colors, gold hoop earrings and a dozen clanking bracelets?"

"Since I did not expect you to answer the door, I had not given any thought to what you would look like or what you would be wearing, and since I arrived in Paris with only three gowns plus the one I had on, I am not in a position to criticize how anyone chooses to dress. However, if flowing skirts, brightly colored flounces, gold hoop earrings and a dozen clanking bracelets are what you prefer, then I think, by all means, you should wear them."

Josette looked at Kenna sharply, as if she had not suspected her capable of sarcasm. "If you will come with me, I will show you to your room. It is on the second floor, next door to mine."

She did not say anything more until they reached the stairs and started up them. "The *comte* thought perhaps you might prefer to have someone nearby, so that is why I chose this room. If you would like more privacy…"

"I come from a large family, Josette. I have three sisters. I do not think I would feel at home if I did not have someone close by to talk to. I am glad you don't mind having me next door."

Again, Josette looked at her with a measuring, suspicious expression. "I did not say I did not mind having you here."

"When you finish being caustic, I hope we can settle into being friends."

"I will let you know when I feel the same."

"Please do," Kenna replied, "for even a moment of friendship lost is a terrible waste."

"I wouldn't know. Friendship has been something I have never experienced from anyone other than the *comte*. I am Romany…a Gypsy, which means I come from a long line of thieves and liars, so that may eliminate any desire for friendship on your part."

There was fierceness in her, and at the same time, vulnerability. Kenna could almost feel rage curling her fingers into fists at her side, for she was sorry someone so intelligent and lovely had, at some point in her life, suffered degradation by the mean, petty and suspicious.

"I am Pict, Celt and Scot, which means I come from stoic, distrustful and dour stock. I am strong willed, outspoken, determined and stubborn. That may cause you to keep your distance, or our two heritages may cancel each other out, in which case we are back to the beginning. Shall I go back and knock on the *comte*'s door again?"

Josette studied Kenna's face for some time, as if doing so would validate her words. She did not smile, but Kenna did see something in the depth of her eyes. It was neither warmth nor amusement, but lay somewhere in between.

Josette opened the door and stepped into the room, and Kenna followed her inside. The room was beautifully appointed, with everything done in the loveliest shades of yellow, green and cream, including the carpets.

Kenna was studying the bright shafts of yellow sunlight that spread lazily across the floor, warm and inviting, when Josette opened the glass doors to the balcony.

"I chose this room, not only because it is near mine, but because of the view," Josette said.

Kenna followed her and stepped outside to gaze out over the vastness of the *comte*'s estate. She lifted her face to the sun, ignoring the cold, to feel the kiss of warmth against her skin. "Such a lovely view this is," she said.

They stepped back inside and Josette closed the door. "Your baggage will be placed in your room. Would you like a maid to unpack for you?"

Kenna smiled. "No, I don't need help with unpacking three gowns, and I am sure the maid could use her time more effectively than coming all the way up here to tackle the trio."

"Very well. I will have a tray sent up for you with the noon meal. You can eat, rest and unpack at your leisure."

Kenna was thinking if that obstinacy could be exchanged for smooth dispose, what could this woman not accomplish? "I am most appreciative for your assistance, Josette."

"It is nothing, Lady Kenna. I will see you at dinner. We dine at eight. Do not be late. The count greatly admires punctuality."

"So do I."

Kenna watched Josette until she disappeared down the stairs, before she stepped farther into her bedchamber and the new life she was beginning.

At dinner that night, Kenna did more than simply eat and be entertained by charming company. She learned, upon considerable observation, that the *comte* was mentally equipped for the art of fencing, with steady nerves to augment the natural ability of his lean and vigorous body.

She only hoped that he would not see her as a bungling dilettante, or that she would prove to be one. It was never very far from her mind that here was the most famous, and best swordsman in Europe.

"How old were you when you were first introduced to the art of fencing?" the *comte* asked.

"I was quite small when I began observing my brothers practice...not more than seven, I think," Kenna replied.

The *comte*'s brows went up and an animated expression danced across his face. "I am surprised it was so young. And when you began working with the fencing master, how old were you then, Lady Kenna?"

"I began fencing with my brothers when I was ten. Two years later, I started with the fencing master."

The conversation had gone quite pleasantly along the same vein, that is, until Kenna was about to take her first spoonful of *Vichyssoise de champignons à l'angélique*, a cold soup of mushrooms and angelica.

The spoon was halfway to her mouth when the *comte* said, "Josette was a little older than that when she harassed me to the point I conceded to teach her a few basic fencing moves. She was a lot like you were, I imagine, for it soon became her master-passion."

The hand that carried the spoon fell back to the table as Kenna directed her gaze hotly upon Josette's face. "Pardon me, *mademoiselle,* but did you not tell me a few hours ago that you had no interest in fencing, and that you could not imagine why any woman would want to go to so much trouble to learn it? Was there a particular reason you chose to lie to me?"

Josette shrugged. "I did not lie. I simply chose not to tell you the truth."

"Then am I to understand that your master-passion is not only fencing, but denying the truth…lying, if you will?"

"I see myself more as a woman of two truths," Josette said. "At the time, I did not feel up to a lengthy discussion over two women accomplished with the sword. A little denial sometimes saves a great deal of explanation. Don't tell me you have never done such."

"We are not talking about me. I did not lie to you."

"You are upset by my admission. Perhaps the truth is too appalling for a moralist. Everyone lies. You tell lies yourself, unless you prefer to lie about it."

"Of course I have, but I differ from you in that I am more altruistic. If I do tell a lie, it is out of good manners, or a wish to spare someone the pain of the awful truth. I consider it to be a fabrication for politeness' sake."

"And I think you owe Kenna an apology, Josette."

"Very well, I apologize, Lady Kenna, and tonight I will pray for forgiveness for each lie I have ever told."

"I think it will take more than one night," Kenna replied.

The *comte* smiled. "If I were you, Josette, I would lie fallow for a while."

It was a good way to end an evening, with a round of laughter, a fine meal, and for dessert, *flamusse de potiron à la châtaigne,* a warm pumpkin-chestnut pudding, so comforting on a cold winter night.

The next morning, Josette bustled her out of bed before the sun came up.

Kenna was sleeping soundly when she was rudely awakened by the sound of someone coming into her room.

"Time to get up!"

Kenna lifted her sleepy head from the pillow as Josette came swiftly into the room.

"What time is it?"

"Six o'clock, and time to get up."

"*Sacre bleu!* Why so early?"

"We are going into Paris."

Kenna sat up with a yawn occupying her mouth for the moment. Then she stretched lazily and asked, "And the purpose?"

"You need proper attire for your classes, so we must leave early if we are going to have enough time to find suitable clothes and shoes for your lessons with the *maître.*"

Josette turned and went to the wardrobe, and proceeded to fling the doors wide. "Oh, my, this will never do. You certainly need clothes."

"I have been measured, poked, prodded and mercilessly pricked with pins for an abundance of clothing that will be ready in two weeks."

"That is all well and good, but in the meantime, you need something to wear during your time with the *maître*. You and I will go to Paris, where we will find you some suitable clothes to wear during your classes with the *comte*, to supplement all that you have ordered."

She pulled Kenna's green gown out of the wardrobe, held it up for inspection. She gave it a shake and tossed it on the bed. "Put this on and meet me downstairs in half an hour."

# *Nine*

When shall we three meet again
In thunder, lightning, or in rain?
—William Shakespeare (1564–1616),
English poet and playwright,
*Macbeth* (1606), Act I, Scene 1.

In the weeks that followed since he had met the red-headed lass, she was too often in his thoughts for, since the night of her departure, he had wondered if he was more despondent because he had let her go, or because he had done nothing to learn where she went.

About the same time Kenna was preparing for her shopping trip, Alejandro walked into Colin's cabin. "Oh dear, I come seeking a ministering angel and find in its stead a churlish priest. How long are you going to sail the sea of doldrums? If you've a fondness for the Scottish lass, why don't you try to find where she went?"

Colin gave him a sour look. "And sometimes you

come across as a learned man, and sometimes like a flippant, laughter-loving idiot, or is it a scatterbrain? Faith! Has the devil chosen my friends for me? If not, then why the criticism?" he wondered.

Alejandro put away his smile. "You are right. You need more than encouragement or criticism. You need your backside dusted with gunpowder. What will it take for you to go after her? Do you want me to do it for you?"

"By all means. Find her, if you can."

"I can damn well come closer to finding her than you can sitting here, daydreaming and draining wine bottles."

"It won't be easy to find her. We do not have her name."

"No, but I came in here to tell you the *Aethelred* has just sailed into Copenhagen and dropped anchor. I assume you know what to do with that bit of information, or shall I go inquire of Captain Fischer as to what he did with the golden-eyed beauty?"

"I can damn well take care of finding a woman."

"I am glad to hear it, because you have made a poor showing of it thus far. I assume you are going over to the *Aethelred,* so my next question is, do you want me to go with you?"

Colin stood and put on his coat. "If you can be *nice!*"

"Charming," Alejandro said. "When I have to, I can be perfectly charming."

"Come on. You can row us over to the *Aethelred.*"

An hour later, they walked into Captain Fischer's

cabin. "Well, bless me," the captain said when he looked up. "I did not expect to see the two of you." He put down his pipe and stood to shake hands with Colin and Alejandro.

"I was just thinking a moment ago that I would come over to see you, and you have saved me the trip. Do sit down."

As soon as they were settled, Captain Fischer asked, "Have you come to inquire about your Scottish lassie?"

"Yes," Colin said. "I want to know how she managed during the trip to Calais, and what you did with her after that."

Captain Fischer was a man of great detail, and he took at least an hour to fill Colin in on each bit of information stored in his brain. He started out with the usual about how she fared on the ship, and how the men took a liking to her, and then told how he had left her to have tea at Dessin's Inn, while he procured her passage to Calais. "I made good use of your money, Colin, for I found a new *berline* with four horses and two postilions, to transport her to Paris, all for twelve livres, and that was for her to have the coach to herself, as you requested. She insisted I let her pay for it, but I told her you had already done so. I will say again that it was a great pleasure to be of assistance to such a dear lady."

"Do you happen to remember where you hired this coach?"

"Why, at the posting station. The driver was the son of the proprietor."

"Do you remember his name?" Colin asked.

Captain Fischer's expression began as puzzled and

ended up enlightened. "Oh, I see now. You did not come here for a report on my wisdom in spending your money, or to inquire as to whether any was left, which there was, but you are interested in finding her."

"And if I am, would it be in line with your agreeable nature to tell me what I want to know? Or have you adopted a protective, fatherly nature concerning her, and find my roguish life not up to her standards?"

Captain Fischer laughed and opened his drawer to take out a pouch. He offered it to Colin. "Here is the rest of your money, by the way, and as for your lass, you have good taste, my friend. May I offer my felicitations to you?"

"I will accept your gracious felicitations, but only if you keep the money. I insist. You earned it."

"Very well, and thank you. And to answer your earlier question, I do remember the Frenchman's name. Marcel Favier, it was."

"What did Monsieur Favier look like?"

"I would say he was a man about forty, of smallish stature, and walked in a rather humped-over manner, for I never saw the man stand straight. I suppose he has leaned over the reins of a coach for too long. His hair was dark and his eyes blue…but that is true of most Frenchmen, is it not? I hope that helps you in your quest."

"So do I," Colin said.

"When do you sail for Calais?"

"As soon as we're back on the decks of *Dancing Water.*"

Captain Fischer's eyes seemed to brighten with satisfaction. "May I entice the two of you to stay long enough to have lunch with me?"

"That could be arranged," Colin, said, and true to his word, they returned to the ship after they had dined with Captain Fischer and set sail for the port of Calais.

Once they arrived in Calais, they went immediately to the posting house and learned Marcel Favier was due in from Amiens later that night.

Alejandro and Colin went to dinner, returned two hours later, and waited another hour before Marcel Favier's coach stopped at the station.

"The Scottish woman?" Marcel said, when Colin inquired about her. "Yes, I remember her quite well."

"Did you learn her name?"

"No, she preferred to remain anonymous, and not even the Duc de Bourbon could wrest a name from her."

"The Duc de Bourbon…I was under the impression she traveled alone," Colin said.

"Oh, she did travel alone, *monsieur,* but our coach was flagged down not far from Paris by the *duc* and two of his friends. One of them was wounded when their coach was robbed by highwaymen. We gave the three of them a ride into Paris and dropped them off at the doctor of the *duc.*"

"And the lady?" Alejandro asked. "Where did you leave her?"

"I do not remember the name of the street, *monsieur.*"

"Damn! It's the end of the road," Colin said.

"*Non, monsieur,* not the end, just a slight delay. I will be driving to Paris on the morrow, and if you and your friend would like to come along as passengers, I can show you where I left the *mademoiselle.* I never forget where I have been, *monsieur,* but I am not so good at remembering names."

The next day, Colin and Alejandro traveled to Paris with Marcel, and once he had dropped his passengers at the posting station, he drove them through an arch and stopped in front of a neatly kept home. "This is where I left the *mademoiselle, monsieur,* for I remember this arch very well."

Alejandro paid Marcel handsomely for his help while Colin knocked on the door. A moment later, they were gazing upon the rotund countenance of one Madame Guion, who eagerly invited them into her salon and insisted they take tea.

While Colin tried to balance the rattling cup on his knee and cursed Alejandro's amusement under his breath, Madame Guion proved herself to be as she called herself, *une trouvaille,* which Alejandro translated to be "a lucky find." Colin was quick to agree.

"Lady Kenna Lennox is who you are looking for, *monsieur.* She came very highly recommended to me, I must say. Her sister is a sister-in-law of Sophie de Bourbon, who is the granddaughter of King Louis, the Sun King. Sophie married a Scottish earl and now lives somewhere in Scotland. She gave Lady Kenna a very nice letter of introduction for me and also one for the Comte Debouvine, who invited her to dine with him almost immediately."

Alejandro and Colin exchanged looks.

"Who is this *comte?*" Colin asked. "What does he have to do with Lady Kenna?"

"Why the *comte* is known all over, *monsieur.* I am surprised you have not heard his name, for he was the greatest *maître d'armes* in Europe, or he was up until his retirement."

"Where is Lady Kenna now?" Colin asked.

"Why, she is living at the *comte's* château, and very grand it is, too. Rivals anything the royal family resides in, with the exception of Versailles, of course."

"Are you saying that a titled lady would move into the home of a man she just met? That sounds rather far-fetched to me," Alejandro said, "for the nobility of Europe does not behave in such a manner."

"*La!* I did not mean to imply she is the *comte's* paramour. On the contrary, she is his student, for she was able to do what no one else has done, and that was to persuade the *comte* to come out of retirement in order to be her *maître d'armes.*"

"Fencing master?" Colin said to Alejandro. "You know, I remember before she left the ship I asked her how she intended to protect herself and she said with a sword. I thought she was jesting, naturally."

"Oh, it is no jest, *monsieur.* She is most assuredly the *comte's* pupil."

"Can you tell us how we might find this *comte?*" Colin asked, and Madame Guion was near to bursting the seams of her snug gown to accommodate them.

"Where to now?" Alejandro asked.

"We will get a hotel room," Colin said.

"I think we need a hotel room *and* a tailor," Alejandro said, "if we are to present ourselves to a man as important as the Comte Debouvine. I know, being an American, you are not exactly enamored with titles, even though your grandfather has one. We would never get past the footman if we went sauntering up to the *comte*'s château and asked to be admitted dressed like this. These things need delicacy and finesse. You leave that to me."

"What difference will delicacy and finesse make? If we tell the *comte* we have come to see Lady Kenna Lennox in order to see how she fares in France, he will naturally ask her if she agrees to speak to us."

"We are completely at the mercy of this Comte Debouvine. If he considers us to be foreign riffraff, *canailles,* he will not even mention us to a lady of nobility."

"My point exactly, and in order to show that we are not the *canailles* he might imagine us to be, we will bring to his attention that we are of the upper class."

As it turned out, it was a week before the tailor could deliver their new clothes. When they arrived, Alejandro purchased the finest stationery Colin's money could buy, and set down to pen his masterpiece, which he began with a flourishing hand, *Monseigneur Comte Debouvine...*

It seemed to Colin, who had been quietly observing, that Alejandro's letter writing deserved a fanfare befitting a state occasion.

Colin did not understand all the fuss over the painted pomp of European codes of conduct any more than he did the rules of correct behavior regarding nobility, but he knew Alejandro had a long procession of names and fancy titles trailing from his family line, so he deferred to him in this matter, and busied himself trying on all the dashing finery Alejandro had persuaded him to purchase.

"I have clothes like this on the ship," Colin said.

Alejandro paused, mid-flourish, to answer, "And I as well, but that fact does neither of us any service now, does it?"

"I am beginning to wonder if all of this is worth doing for a fascination with a woman who may lay waste to all my imaginings. Had I known she came equipped with a title, and all its trappings…well you know my interests have never gone in that direction."

"There are two things to remember when you pray for something—to ask for what you want, and pray that you enjoy it. Sometimes, the second is more difficult to achieve than the first."

Colin felt a growing irritation at the delay. "Are you not finished with that novel you are writing?"

"Patience, my friend. Everything has a beginning… except the equator, of course," Alejandro replied, and signed the letter, Señor Alejandro Feliciano Enrique de Calderón, son of *Don Álvaro Enrique Luis de Calderón, Marqués de Málaga.*

# *Ten*

Our failings sometimes bind us to one
another as closely as could virtue itself.
                                    —Luc de Clapiers,
                        Marquis de Vauvenargues (1715–47),
                                            French moralist.
        "Réflexions et Maximes," no. 176 (1746).

On the morning of her first lesson, Kenna was up
early. She dashed her face with cold water, before
going to the wardrobe. When she threw back the doors,
she was greeted by the sight of a great many more
clothes than she had the day before.

It was a fine feeling to see more than her customary four choices, and that added to her euphoria as the
thought of her first day with the *comte* had already set
her heart to beating faster than normal.

She chose a riding skirt and a shirt, soft as thistle-
down, which was the latest Parisian fashion for young
boys, and far superior to anything to be found in Scot-

land. It fitted close to the body, yet allowed her freedom of movement.

A knock at the door, and the maid came in with her breakfast. "Good morning. Where would you like your tray?"

"Put it on the *secrétaire,* please."

Kenna looked at the tray after the maid left, and knew there would be no time for a leisurely breakfast this morning, so she poured a cup of tea and ate a roll, which she finished off hastily with several gulps of tea.

Afterward, she braided her hair and let it hang down her back in one long plait. She considered herself ready and was about to leave, when she remembered she was missing her shoes, or rather a soft pair of leather half boots, supple and light.

As she hurried down the stairs, she hoped she would arrive ahead of the *comte.* But, she did not have long to wait by the door to the gallery when the *comte* arrived, dressed all in black in the traditional manner of the fencing master, or as the *comte* preferred, *maître d'armes*, which she shortened to *maître.*

"Good morning, *Maître.*"

"Lady Kenna," he said with a nod. "I see you and Josette were successful in finding you suitable clothing. May I inquire as to how the two of you managed your close confinement in a coach to and from Paris?"

"We were able to refrain from scratching out each other's eyes, if that is what you mean. It might also interest you to know, she taught me how to play *tarocchi.* Do you know it?"

"Aah yes, the Italian card game. She is very good at it, you know."

"Yes, so I found out. I also discovered that she likes to win, and if she is not winning, she cheats. However, I have to give her credit, *Maître,* for she did warn me in advance."

She paused and, with eyes mischievously bright, considered him. "You are smiling, *Maître.*"

"I was thinking how much I think I shall enjoy having two daughters instead of one."

He opened the door and followed her inside. They were greeted by the sight of early morning sun streaming into the gallery through the trefoil windows, which threw warm, scalloped patterns across the cold stone floors. When she stood in the center of the pattern, she could feel the warmth seeping into her boots.

She walked farther into the gallery, passing rows of antique weaponry, and paused to study the display of swords. She moved for a closer look and said with surprise, "You even have a claymore."

"No collection would be complete without one."

When she turned around the *comte* was looking over her fencing garments, and she could tell by the gentle expression in his eyes that she was officially sanctioned as being appropriately garbed in the dark green riding skirt, white shirt and half boots.

Comte Debouvine was a man of commanding presence, loose-limbed and regally erect—a man who carried his still handsome head with an air of unconscious pride. She watched him walk toward the rack that held numerous and assorted swords, and was almost mes-

merized by the way he moved. He had a measured
grace that seemed to be inborn rather than histrionic.

From his vigorous body, she had guessed, upon first
meeting him, that he was no more than forty or forty-
five, not a man with enough years to total sixty. His
face, lightly tanned, was noble and strong, with a hawk-
ish nose, more Roman than French, with a high and
prominent bridge.

It was his eyes that captivated her, and what she
considered his best quality, for they were a deep, dark
cobalt-blue, and seemed to know her thoughts even before she did.

His mouth was well shaped and usually held firm,
but when he smiled, it totally changed his countenance,
replacing the harsher features with an air of gentle
charm. Red-tinted, brown hair was only beginning to
gray at the temple, and today it was queued back with
a riband.

Black clothes suited him, and the black velvet jacket
with its silver buttons was obviously made by an expert tailor. His black satin pants outlined the strong
muscles of his slender legs.

"From this day on, your life will change, Lady
Kenna. Fencing will occupy your days, your nights
and your mind. Over and over again, you will repeat
the five figures of the wrist…*prime, seconde, tierce,
quart* and *quinte*. You will wonder why you must remember all of them, when the first is of very little use,
and the last is of no use at all."

He paused, as if considering how she was taking
all of this, then he continued, "But you will remem-

ber them, nonetheless. You will find yourself practicing the movements of your wrist when you get into bed at night. And in the privacy of your room, you will practice the placement of your feet as you assume the stance. The terms will roll like the discharge of cannons, or a volley of oaths. *Attack...defend...in guard...a lunge in quart...parry in disengaging...parade of tierce...pushing seconde...the feint or half thrust...sword on the outside...the recovery in guard...*"

He was right, for already her head was swimming with the familiar words.

He walked over to the wall opposite the paneling and removed two foils. He returned to where she stood and handed one to her. "First, I must find out how much you know...or do not know, as the case may be. Take your place on the *piste*, if you please, Lady Kenna."

Kenna moved to the *piste* and took her position.

"Now comes the test. Let us see if you know how to use a sword, or if you simply beat the air with it."

"I have not held a sword for some time, *Maître*. I am sure to be impaired from lack of practice."

"This is the last time you will offer me an excuse." He approached the *piste* and took his position. "Try to score a hit. *Allez!*"

She moved quickly to attack with the foil.

He deflected her weapon with ease.

"The way you are going you would not be able to accomplish anything, even if you had centuries in which to do it. If that is your best, you cannot possibly have had a fencing master in the past. You move as if this is your first time."

She came at him again, determined to show him she was better than he thought, but he easily dodged or deflected each maneuver she made. To further humiliate her, he switched the blade to his left hand, and stared at the ceiling, and yet he countered her every attempt.

The blades slid and tinkled against each other. She was becoming frustrated, and he added to it by taunting her.

Cool and easy, the *comte* was on the defensive, not finding it necessary even to move, casually deflecting every thrust and lunge sent against him in swift succession. To make it harder, he played her close, with his elbow flexed and using only his forearm and the forte of his blade, defeating her time and again, with a minimum of exertion. She, on the other hand, was already greatly winded.

"*Ça alors!* Good grief! Come, come…where is your staying power? Would you have me brand you a liar? Have you ever even seen a sword, Lady Kenna? I wonder, for you use it as if it is the first time you have made its acquaintance. I have fought cripples with only one eye who were better than you. Why are you stopping? Can you not fence and listen? It is simple. You are to try to knock this small weapon out of my hand."

She extended herself fully, coming at him with fresh aggression in her attack, but his counter parry swept her blade clear and a lightning-fast riposte had the tip of his blade between her breasts.

"I do not need to tell you, I am sure, that had this been a real confrontation, you would now be dead,

Lady Kenna. If you have shown me your best, we may as well call it a day."

She renewed her attack with unsparing vigor, but it did no good, and she let her temper interfere and came at him with the fury of a wildcat. The room resounded with the ring of metal...*cling...cling...cling...clunk..."*

The *comte* stopped. "Lady Kenna, what was that last move? Does it have a name? If it does, I should like to know, for I have never seen it before, and I hope to never see it again.

"Show me something, Lady Kenna, for the love of anyone available."

She gave it all she had, and was pathetic.

He threw up his hands. "*Ça y est!* That is it! You parried but did not riposte. Is your foil made of straw? We are fencing, *mademoiselle,* and it is done *comme ça*— like this—" And for the second time in mere minutes, her foil flew from her hand.

"*Sacre bleu!* You must find a new interest, Mademoiselle Lennox. May I suggest painting unexciting little landscapes on the lids of ornamental boxes?"

She dropped her head, shamed to the core. "It is no use, Monsieur le Comte."

"Quitting so soon? I thought you were a woman of the sword. Where is your fighting spirit? Are you giving up without a struggle?"

She lifted her head and her eyes met his fully and frankly. "No, I am not quitting. I simply did not realize I would be so intimidated by you. I am better...much, much better than you have seen me. It shames me."

He considered her for a moment. "I never take unfair advantage of anyone, Lady Kenna."

"Monsieur le Comte, I did not mean..."

"Let me finish, my dear. I never take unfair advantage of anyone, and if you are intimidated by me, then we shall take steps to assuage your discomfort. We shall break for lunch, and afterward, you will practice with Josette."

Kenna said nothing.

Although she did not look at him, she knew the *comte* was watching her. "You won't be intimidated by her saber-rattling, will you?"

"I do not plan to be, but when you are bitten by the snake, you fear even the worm, Monsieur le Comte."

Three hours later Kenna and Josette took their positions on the *piste* and prepared for the bout. They crossed blades, Kenna holding hers lightly against Josette's, and the *comte* gave the word.

*"Allez!"*

The crossed blades slid against each other lightly, until Josette pushed against Kenna's foil, the gleam in her eye one of contemptible determination, as if she intended to make short work of this lowly Scot who dared to intrude upon her domain. Kenna allowed her to attack with haste and intensity, while she returned calmly, by keeping her distance and staying on the defensive.

Kenna knew she could lunge and attack at any point, but she was content to protract her resistance, yet she kept in the forefront of her mind that she should in no way underestimate Josette's physical or mental ability.

She remained cool and calm-headed, allowing Josette to dominate the beginning with her fiery Gypsy temperament, obviously confident that she could defeat Kenna in a matter of minutes.

Still, Kenna remained level, opposing with no counters, not even a riposte that would have given Josette an opening to take advantage of. Instead, she concentrated on deflecting every thrust and lunge that came in rapid succession, again and again. Above all, she did not look at the foils, but kept her gaze eternally focused upon Josette's eyes.

By taking no risks, and playing it slow, Kenna felt she had the advantage of stamina, for already she could see that Josette was showing signs of tiring. She could also see in Josette's eyes that she was becoming annoyed over Kenna's refusal to be drawn into a counterattack. Gradually, the annoyance gave way to anger, and Kenna knew the exhaustion of her opponent would hasten, and she continued to save herself until Josette lost control.

She did not have long to wait.

As she began to wear down, Josette made mistakes, which added fuel to her temper, and she began to pull out a few tricks—deceptive feints to lure Kenna into mistaking a false attack for a real one, but Kenna had grown up fencing her two elder brothers, who tried every underhanded trick imaginable to shake the burr of a little sister who wanted to hold her own with them.

*"Nom de nom!* Are you fencing or pretending to?" Josette asked.

"Strange that you should ask that, for I was contemplating asking the same of you. Please, do not defer to me, simply because I am a newly arrived guest in the home of the *comte*. You have my permission to end this by putting me in my proper place."

The fiery glare in Josette's eyes were a beacon that signaled the end was soon to come, and it did. Josette, clearly angry now, renewed her attack with tremendous vigor, and began to pay the toll for the heated rush, the rash self-belief, and the inflamed speed of movement she set, overconfident the match would be a short one.

And it was.

Realizing now she had seriously erred, Josette fell back, to conserve her energy, and Kenna saw in her eyes the exact moment when she became both dejected and discouraged. Kenna called the moment well, and moved in with a low feint, then twirled her point into *carte* as she lunged and brought the tip of her foil to rest at the pulse-point of her throat.

"Enough!" called the *comte*. "I have seen enough, Mademoiselle Lennox. It would seem you are a different woman than you were this morning."

Kenna smiled and stole a quick glance in Josette's direction, expecting even as she did that her gaze would be met with a glare of hatred, and the knowledge that she had made an enemy for life.

"Well done, little Scot!" Josette said, a genuine smile relaxing upon her lips as she came toward Kenna. "You have more than proved your mettle and thereby you are fully deserving of my respect. I salute you," she said, and brought her foil straight up, in a vertical line across the center of her face, the blade almost resting on her nose, and her thumb against the curve of chin below her lip.

"Excellent, my dear *mademoiselle,* most excellent. You displayed superb skill and tremendous mental agility that is a true accomplishment in one so young. Fencing is a sport of mind and body, and few can excel in both areas."

# Eleven

Jupiter himself was turned into a satyr,
a shepherd, a bull, a swan, a golden shower,
and what not for love.
—Robert Burton (1577–1640),
English scholar and churchman.
*The Anatomy of Melancholy* (1621).

"*Por Dios,* Montgomery, I have never seen you act so ridiculously besotted. She is only a woman, after all, and not some shrine to worship. This is fast turning into a pilgrimage," Alejandro said.

Colin gave him a knowing smile. "Oh, really? I happen to remember a certain *señorita* in Argentina, and how you led me across forested hills, humid pampas and flamingo-coated salt lakes. I almost killed myself drinking *maté* with gauchos beneath the shade of *ombú* trees, and nearly drowned in the River Paraná, and all because you…"

"All right. All right, point made. Forget what I said," Alejandro grumbled.

It was late afternoon and the sun was beginning its descent when Colin and Alejandro had their first glimpse of the lofty, pencil-shaped turrets that rose from the castle to dominate the hilltop.

After a rather steep ascent, they rode through a park filled with chestnut trees, and spotted a few deer from the road, before they reached the château.

"That," Alejandro said as they rode through the gates, "is a magnificent example of a feudal castle."

"When do you think it was built?" Colin asked.

"Its architecture suggests both the Romanesque and Gothic periods. The trefoil windows especially suggest Romanesque, with heavy Byzantine influence."

"'A heavy Byzantine influence'…you don't say! When did you become such an expert on castle architecture?"

"My family has lived in a castle for centuries, and my father made certain all of his children knew, not only its history, but that of many other well-known structures as well. He was a great historian, who had a particular interest in architecture. His designs were used to build several castles."

"Why did you never tell me that?"

"You never asked me."

"What else are you keeping secret?"

Alejandro laughed. "I shall not reveal all my secrets, for their power lies in the keeping of them. I prefer to divulge them one at a time, when the occasion calls for it. Otherwise, they would only serve to bore you."

They dismounted and handed the reins of their weary horses to a groom, before they climbed the stone steps to address a footman, in formal livery of blue, white and gold.

"Is the Comte Debouvine in residence?" Colin asked.

"*Oui, monsieur.* Do you have an appointment with the *comte* or his secretary?"

"No, but I would like you to give him this letter of introduction, and ask if he could receive the two of us."

With a click of his heels, the footman disappeared through the massive double doors. He returned a short time later and said, "Although the *comte* has no recollection of having had the honor of meeting you, he will receive you. Please, if you will come this way."

They entered a cavernous, flagstoned entryway, brightly lit by three chandeliers. Beneath the middle one stood a massive circular table, and in its center sat a large silver urn filled with greenery.

They followed the footman through an assortment of hallways and apartments before they came to a closed door, which the footman opened in a grand and flamboyant manner, and announced Señor Calderón of Spain, and Captain Montgomery of America.

They stepped into the *comte*'s large and impressively appointed library. A fireplace, alive with blaze and crackle, burned behind him. Shelves of books mingled with precious tapestries hung with gilt chains, and richly brocaded drapes were drawn back from leaded windows that gave a splendid view of the gardens. A fine Persian carpet threw rich splashes of color across the floor.

The Comte Debouvine sat behind a marquetry writing desk with bronze decorations, which was covered with neatly stacked letters and papers. The gray streaks in his dark hair were illuminated silver by twin candelabra gleaming with wax candles.

At the sound of the door opening, he looked up and dismissed his secretary, who, anticipating more work, had picked up his pen when Colin and Alejandro entered the room. "That will be all for now, Fornier. I will send for you later."

With a dignified nod, Fornier put down the stylus, closed the lid on a gold-and-crystal inkwell and left the room.

The *comte* rose from his desk to greet them. "Please, gentlemen, do sit down and tell me the nature of your visit."

The *comte* was dressed in dark blue velvet and a cream shirt with splendid ecru lace that fell in layers from the neck, and Colin was glad Alejandro had advised him to dress more formally than he normally did as a ship's captain.

"Monsieur le Comte," Alejandro said, "I have the honor of presenting myself, Alejandro de Calderón, and my good friend, Colin Montgomery, Captain of the American ship *Dancing Water.*"

"Welcome to France, gentlemen." He glanced toward the footman, who was still waiting by the door. "That will be all for now, Quirion. You may return to your post."

The footman departed.

"Now, gentlemen, I am eagerly waiting to hear what

has brought the two of you from Spain and America to Paris and my château."

Colin took over at this point, and explained their purpose for coming, how they had met and assisted Lady Kenna Lennox when she was desirous of leaving Scotland, and how he wished to speak with Lady Kenna, to hear how she fared on her journey from Edinburgh.

"So, you wish to pay a social call on Lady Kenna Lennox, based upon a chance meeting, at which time you chose not to help in any way other than to foist her off on the captain of a Danish ship?"

Colin was quick to reply. "You make it sound more callous than it was, *comte,* and I am certain if you inquire of Lady Kenna as to the nature of our encounter, she will speak favorably of us and agree to grant us a few moments of her time."

"Please continue on, Captain, for I have heard you wish to see how Lady Kenna fared on her journey, but man to man, is that the only reason you have gone to such great lengths to come to Paris?"

"I am sure you know that it is not the only reason, Monsieur le Comte, just as I am certain you know, man to man, what that other reason is," Colin said. "In all honesty, I was quite captivated by her, and her obvious distress and fear of some element unknown to us. In the time that has passed since seeing her last, I have oft wondered about her, and the reason she fled her home at Christmas, carrying nothing but two small traveling bags, and quite determined to keep her identity a secret."

"Which brings me to my next question," the *comte* said, "and that is, how did you learn her name and how did you discover her whereabouts?"

Colin related how he arranged for Captain Fischer to take her to Calais and to arrange passage for her to Paris. "Later, we discovered Captain Fischer's ship was anchored in Copenhagen when we arrived. I paid him a call and asked for the details as to where he arranged for her coach. He recalled renting it at the posting station. Luckily, he remembered the driver was the son of the proprietor. Once I reached Calais, I found the driver and learned the address where he dropped her in Paris. It turned out to be the home of Madame Guion, who gave me her name and told me of the letter of introduction she had to the Comte Debouvine."

"And that is it?" the *comte* asked.

"Yes," Colin replied. "I feel certain if you were to ask Lady Kenna, she would verify all I have said."

"There is no need," said the *comte*, "for Lady Kenna told me about you and Señor Calderón shortly after her arrival."

The Comte Debouvine came to his feet. "I have decided to send for Lady Kenna and see if she wishes to meet with you, and I do so for one reason only, and that is, you chose not to tell me that you advanced this Captain Fischer a considerable amount of money, and requested he secure safe passage for lady Kenna to Paris, which you paid for, and that you also requested she have the coach to herself. And now, if you will excuse me, I will have someone take word to her that you will be waiting for her in the Rose Salon."

After the *comte* departed, the footman returned to take them to the Rose Salon. A short time later, accompanied by the *comte*, Lady Kenna swept into the room in a green silk gown, her luscious red hair perfectly curled and coiffed.

Her eyes seemed to light up when she saw them. "Alejandro and Captain Montgomery, how good it is to see you again. I have wished many times that I would one day have the opportunity to thank you for all you did. Captain Fischer went beyond himself to make a journey taken for the direst reasons as pleasant as possible. I wish there was some way I could repay you."

"To see your face and the happiness displayed there is gratitude enough," Colin said. "We have had you in our thoughts constantly, and when we encountered Captain Fischer a week or so ago, we were quick to inquire about you. It is both a pleasure and a relief to see you looking well and happy, in such luxurious accommodations. I am glad your journey was a successful one," Colin said.

"Captain Montgomery, I am well aware of how much gratitude I owe you," she said. "Captain Fischer made certain I knew that it was not his largesse that made everything possible. He told me you gave him the money to pay the expenses for my passage to Paris. I am indebted to you. Please accept my inadequate but heartfelt appreciation."

"My pleasure, Lady Kenna."

"Lady Kenna," the *comte* said, "if you are content to continue your visit with these gentlemen alone, I am expecting a visit shortly from the Duc d'Avignon, and do not wish to bore any of you with his company, for the man has but two topics, himself and the weather, and I am sick to death of both."

When the laughter died down, the *comte* said, "Gentlemen, it has been an esteemed pleasure, and if you are so inclined, I invite you stay to dine with us tonight."

"That all depends," Alejandro said, "on whether you intend to invite the Duc d'Avignon."

Another round of laughter, and this time, when it faded, Kenna looked from Alejandro to Colin. "I promise to spare you that as well."

"In that case, we look forward to it," Colin said.

"Then it is settled," the *comte* said. "Until dinner, then." He was almost at the door when Kenna said, "Would you ask Josette to join us?"

"An excellent idea, my dear…an excellent idea indeed," the *comte* replied.

When the *comte* was gone, Alejandro asked, "Who is Josette?"

"I prefer to let you discover for yourself," Kenna said.

His brows formed two dark slashes over his eyes. "Ah, a mysterious woman."

Kenna laughed. "You have no idea, but I will give you a hint. Think of sad songs, fiery dances, heavy drinking and then smashing the glasses in the fireplace."

"An exotic creature… I think I am in love," Alejandro said.

"Worse things could happen to you," Kenna said.

"Alas, I am a confirmed bachelor," he said.

Kenna smiled coyly at Colin. "What married man has not sworn himself to that single state?"

They settled into conversation and managed to cover two topics before they heard the *tap-tap-tap* of someone coming down the passage. With a click, the door opened, followed by the faint rustle of crisp silk, as Josette entered the room. She looked slim and sleek in a fiery red gown, drawn up and bustled in the back. Her hair was pulled back, the black coils smooth and lustrous.

Colin and Alejandro rose to their feet immediately. When she noticed the two of them, Josette stopped, and with her accustomed solemn dignity, gazed upon the two newcomers who stood watching her.

"The *comte* sent word that I was to join you here," she said to Kenna, without averting her gaze. "No one mentioned you had guests."

Colin could see by Kenna's expression that she was a trifle annoyed by Josette's cold and cautious words. "Do come in and join us, Josette. I asked the *comte* to send for you. I wanted you to meet the gentlemen I told you about—don't you remember?—the ship's captain and his friend from Spain, who helped me with my passage from Edinburgh?"

Josette looked each of them over with an indifferent but guarded expression as Kenna made the introductions, which Josette acknowledged with a bow and a cordial, yet brief, "A pleasure, gentlemen."

She came farther into the room and seated herself. "I can see Lady Kenna has withheld information from us, for she failed to mention she had made the acquaintance of such a lovely lady," Alejandro said.

Josette ignored his flattery. "What brings you to Paris, gentlemen?"

"A desire to assure ourselves that Lady Kenna arrived at her destination safely," Colin replied.

"Now that you have seen the proof of it, how long will you remain in France?"

"A few days" was Colin's reply.

Alejandro laughed. "Are you the official timekeeper, *mademoiselle?*"

Kenna spoke quickly. "The *comte* has invited them to stay to dinner. They have traveled all the way from…" She paused and directed her gaze toward Colin.

"We came from Copenhagen, Mademoiselle Revel. Have you been there?" Colin asked.

"No," she said, in a curt, dismissive manner.

"You should go there sometime," Alejandro said, in his jovial manner. "It reminds me of you…beautiful but cold."

Almost immediately, Kenna leaped from her chair and grabbed a salver of macaroons from the *comte*'s table and thrust it in Colin's face. "A macaroon, Captain?"

Colin fought back a grin as he gazed into her lovely eyes. He took a macaroon, while he continued to fight the overwhelming urge to laugh. He recognized all the signs of a man walking dangerously down the path of the hopelessly besotted, something he had sworn never to do.

The salver disappeared, only to reappear in front of Alejandro.

"And you, *monsieur,* would you try a macaroon?'

"Why not?" Alejandro said. "God knows the room could entertain something sweet about now."

Colin watched Alejandro reach for a macaroon, but instead of taking one, he took the salver from Kenna and carried it to where Josette was sitting.

"And you, lovely *mademoiselle,* will you also have a macaroon?"

Josette shook her head. "No, I don't believe I want one."

He brought the salver closer. "Oh, but you must try a be-charming sweet, *mademoiselle,* for it is said they enchant even the most sour mood."

Her flashing eyes settled upon his face, and continued to look at him for a few seconds—long enough to make Colin quite uncomfortable, a feeling sensed by Kenna as well.

Unbelievable though it was, a smile played around the corners of Josette's mouth, and even from where he sat, Colin could see the birth of a spark of interest in that dark gaze, focused solely upon Alejandro's face. It was like witnessing a miracle, a fragile flower of peace that bloomed in a battlefield strewn with dead bodies.

For a moment, it looked as if both actors in this play had met their match, for Josette was like one suddenly struck dumb and turned to stone, staring at the macaroons, while Alejandro did not budge, but kept the salver perfectly aligned with her nose. And time did not march on, but seemed to have fallen asleep.

There was little doubt in Colin's mind that Josette was a woman who respected only those who stood up to her challenges, for she was intolerably cursed with a vinegary attitude directed toward the whole world. At some point in her life, she had learned to define power in terms of hostility and intimidation. It seemed she wanted to alienate people before they had a chance to decide if they liked her or not. Perhaps running people off was easier for her to accept than being rejected by them. What he could not figure out was, what made her feel that way?

After what seemed eons, Josette released an irritated sigh, whispered something, probably profane, and took a macaroon. This is a woman to be reckoned with, Colin thought, and when he saw Alejandro take a seat next to her on the sofa, realized Alejandro just might be the man to do it. He needed a woman to challenge him, one he could never completely control; for the moment she was completely tame, he would lose interest. Latin blood, Colin thought. It had to be all that hot Latin blood.

Colin had learned to expect the unexpected around Alejandro. That he seemed interested in this woman with the threatening, unkind brow was amazing, but it came as no surprise. He was obviously attracted to her, and if he could withstand the hot, scornful glances from her dark eyes, the bite of her sharp words, if he could be Petruchio to her Katherine—a task not envied, for it would take infinite patience and great strength to tame that wild heart of hers—then he might just win it in spite of all she did to drive him away.

Dare not, win not, Colin thought. Did anyone truly understand what went on between men and women?

"Would you care to see the château grounds?" Kenna asked. "They are quite lovely, with a fountain that is like a geyser, and shoots water into the air."

"I think I would like to take a walk. How about the two of you?" Colin asked, and directed his gaze toward Alejandro and Josette.

"I will wait for you in here," Josette said.

"I will keep her company," Alejandro said, and laughed at the vexed expression that spread across Josette's face.

"I do not mind waiting alone," she said.

"I know you don't, but I mind leaving a lady alone."

"Do what suits you," Josette said.

"*Señorita,* you have no idea just how much it does suit me," Alejandro said.

Kenna turned back to Colin. "If you don't mind waiting a moment, Captain, I will go after my cloak."

She wasn't gone long, and when she returned, Colin was waiting on the gallery that ran along the exterior wall of the château.

While Alejandro and Josette exchanged barbs in the Rose Salon, Kenna stepped through the glass doors. Colin was sitting on the balustrade. The music of the fountains followed them as they walked the graveled pathways. He paused near the steps that led down to the garden, where mazes and hedges were perfectly trimmed.

"Why did you come to France, Lady Kenna? I know you prefer to keep it a secret, in order to protect yourself, but you have nothing to fear from Alejandro or me. I have known your name for over a week, and no harm has come of it."

"Why do you want to know? Why should it concern you?"

"It probably shouldn't, but it does. I don't know what it is, but I do know there is something terribly out of balance in your life. There is a sadness about you, even when you laugh, and whenever I'm around you, I feel you are always looking over my shoulder—searching, but for what?"

She pointed toward a building just ahead. "That's the stable, and it is full of finely bred horses, including several from Arabia," she said.

"You do not speak of your fear because you are distrustful of me?"

"I am distrustful of everyone, Captain."

"Yet you trust the *comte* and Josette."

"I have to trust them."

"Why?"

She released a long sigh and stopped to sit on a bench beneath an evergreen tree. He sat down beside her, and observed how her hands were restless in her lap. He took one and pulled it through his arm. "Relax. I am here as your friend…someone willing to help you if you need it, or someone to talk to if you need that. You cannot go through life alone."

"I am not alone. I have a family in Scotland, and I have the *comte* and Josette."

"If you want to keep your reasons for fleeing Scotland a secret, I will respect that. I will also respect your silence on why you are living at the *comte*'s château. I am not trying to interfere in your affairs, but if your life is in danger, I think you are making a mistake if you think you can handle it alone." He looked off and did not say anything for a few moments, then with a shake of his head, he turned back to search her face in the late afternoon light. "I don't understand you. I've heard Scots were stubborn, and now I have seen the proof of it."

"Would that proof be coming from my stubbornness, or your grandfather's?"

That caught him off guard. "I see Alejandro has been talking."

"Not really. He only mentioned you had a grandfather who is a baron."

"Alejandro talks too much, but yes, I do. The two of us do not get along, which I am sure he also told you."

"Why do you not see things the same way?"

"He is a difficult man, as hard and flinty as the land, and colder than the north wind that sweeps in from the sea. It was his bitterness that drove my father to America, and he has never forgiven my father for that. Worse, he refuses to see it was his own damn fault."

"And he blames you for it as well?"

"My father is his only living son, but he would not come to Scotland to become Baron Fairlie, even if they gave him all of Scotland, and threw in Ireland, too."

"He cannot blame you for that."

"My grandfather can blame anyone for anything, including me. When he finally realized he would never convince my father, he began to work his magic on me. He tempted me with a title, and land, and all the trimmings that go with it. When that did not work, he tried the sympathetic approach…he was an old man, with no one to leave his title and holdings to. He wanted me to come so he could teach me the ways of gentry before he died. I declined and ended up on his list of undesirables. My father is, and has always been, number one. Last time I checked, I occupied the place right below him."

"That is sad to think people of the same blood miss so many opportunities of enjoying one another. Why won't you consider it? Is it because you could never see yourself as a Scot, or as Baron Fairlie?"

"Both. I am a ship's captain, and sometimes a privateer. I love the sea."

"You would never have a shortage of the sea in Caithness."

"I thought you said he only mentioned my grandfather was a baron. And now you say Alejandro told you my grandfather lived in Caithness, too. What else did he tell you?"

"Actually, you blame him unfairly. He did not tell me. He only mentioned having gone there with you once, and how it was the coldest place on earth, at least out of those he had visited. I asked him if it was Sutherland or Caithness."

"How did you know it would be one of those?"

"My grandfather lived in Sutherland, which I am sure you know, is next to Caithness."

"And that is where you are from? Sutherland?"

"No, I live in a small fairy-tale castle, at least small when compared to the *comte*'s château, but it is on the loveliest island in Scotland, in the middle of Loch Lomond. It truly is the most beautiful, the dearest place on earth. I am familiar with the north of Scotland, because my mother was from there. After my grandfather and mother died, I inherited his castle, but I have not been back there since I was a child."

"And now you are here in France, with a haunting secret, a look of sadness in your eyes, and trusting no one. I would like to help you, Lady Kenna."

"Please, call me Kenna, like my family does. I am only Lady Kenna because my father was an earl. If I were to marry, I would lose the designation altogether, unless I married someone with a title."

"Then that is what you should do, so you will always be Lady Kenna."

"I cannot think about such things right now. I am content to watch my sisters marry for the present."

She was watching him, and he knew she was thinking about what she would say when he began to question her about her family, so he purposefully let the subject drop. She would tell him when she wanted to…when she trusted him enough.

He was thinking of another subject to talk about when she came up with one on her own. "Did you know the Comte Debouvine was the greatest fencing master in all of Europe, until his retirement?"

There was something about the way she spoke the words that snagged in his mind, and he began to think about what the *comte*'s being a great swordsman had to do with her. Was it because…? No, surely not. The idea was preposterous, totally absurd. Whoever heard of a female taking up the foil?

He studied the face turned up to his, and even in the waning light, she was exquisitely beautiful, with an expression so open he wanted to crush her against him.

His next thought was he was absolutely insane. He hardly knew her, and he was acting like a lovesick swain. What was it about her—this little Scot who stood out among all the other women he had known?

He knew he was attracted to her for reasons beyond her physical beauty. He admired the straightness of her backbone, her fearless determination, the outward signs of an independent spirit uncrushed by the harshness and severity of English rule, and the consequences of it in the life she lived. He thought of her as the golden one—the one woman out of many—with her head high and her eyes full of sadness and sorrow.

He knew so little about her, yet enough that he respected her for her personal values, and her ability to be happy, in spite of the sadness of her past, and her determination to pursue that which was important to her, preferring to do it herself than risk those she loved.

He knew now that his thirst for her went beyond the normal physical attraction a man holds for a certain woman, although that was sure to cause him many sleepless nights.

And here she was, a dream come true, sitting quietly beside him, her hair glowing in the sun, skin pale as moonlight, and eyes as bright as evening stars.

He searched those eyes, so golden, so lovely and so perfectly fitting for her. He could see in their depths that she wanted to believe in him. He leaned forward and brought his lips to hers, and whispered, "It's all right. I think you are beautiful and desirable, whether you trust me or not."

He brushed his lips across hers, softly, and when she did not resist, pressed more firmly. "I have discovered there is something else I find more intriguing than your purpose for coming here."

"What is that?"

"You." He parted her mouth and tasted her, and drew her close against him. His hand stroked the soft skin beneath her ear, touching the curling wisps of hair, and then paused to stroke the sensitive skin of her earlobe. Lord, what he would like to do with her…the mere thought made him ache.

She was warm and soft, and melting against him, and he was filled with a desire to protect her from whatever devils nipped at her heels. He heard a soft, strangled moan as he deepened the kiss, and it set fire to his longing for her, the desire coiling tightly in his groin. His body was hard and trembling, and his hands yearned to do more than hold her. "I've thought a lot about kissing you on my ship that night, and there were too many nights that followed when I wished you were still there. I knew the minute Alejandro left with you that I was a fool to let you go."

"Why?"

"Because I wanted you."

"That is a bit frightening," she said, "like walking the plank or something."

He chuckled. "Walking the plank or something? I've heard it described a million ways, but never that way. I think I like 'or something' better."

"What do you mean by that?"

"One of these days, I'll show you."

"Does that mean I am safe for now?"

"Yes, especially now that you've told me the *comte* was the greatest fencing master in Europe." He paused, suddenly, for it hit him, just why she told him that little tidbit. "That is why you came here, isn't it? To be his pupil. You want him to teach you."

"I knew how to fence when I came here. I have since I was a young girl, but I wanted to be better. Good enough to cross swords with a man."

He started to chuckle but saw the expression on her face was stone cold, sober and serious. This was no laughing matter to her. "You are serious, aren't you?"

"Quite serious."

"I have never heard of a woman taking up the sword."

She laughed, in that husky, throaty manner that sent dangerous impulses to a part of him that did not need any help.

"Quite a few women have taken up the sword. Even Josette fences."

"Joan of Arc is the only one I've ever heard of."

"And she did not fight with the sword. She only used it to swat prostitutes with the flat side of the blade."

It was his turn to laugh, and then his thoughts turned

back to her. "You are afraid, aren't you? There is someone out there who wants to hurt you. Is that why you ran away to come here?"

She looked down at her hands, and he waited, giving her time, as the seconds ticked by.

At last, she sighed and answered him. "Yes, that is why I came here, but do not ask me any more. You know far too much already, and if he ever found you, he would kill you. He will kill anyone who gets in his way."

"My fear is for you, not myself. It does something to a man to see a woman in trouble."

"I can take care of myself, and with the *comte*'s help, I will be able to defend myself as well."

"And when you are good enough to defeat the *comte,* you will return to Scotland?"

"When I am good enough, yes, but I doubt there is anyone who could get the better of the *comte*. It would take a serious blunder on his part, or an accident of some sort for that to happen."

Footsteps came crunching up behind them. She gasped and turned, only to relax when she saw it was one of the footmen.

"Lady Kenna, Gaston sent me to find you. The *comte,* Josette and the captain's friend are waiting on you for dinner."

They started back, walking slowly, and when the footman disappeared, Colin said, "One last kiss before I go," pulled her behind a tree and kissed her again. Only this kiss was hard and demanding, where the first one had been soft and searching. He pressed her back against the tree, and he could tell she had never felt a man's body aligned against hers like that before. It was damnably exciting, but he knew he had to stop.

"You should not have done that. Someone could be watching."

"I wanted to tell you goodbye here, because we may not have another chance to see each other alone once we are back inside."

"You are leaving tonight?"

"We will spend the night in Paris and leave in the morning."

"Oh."

It was both pleasing and gut-wrenching to hear her breathe that one word in a way that allowed him to hear her disappointment. "I wish I could stay longer, but the ship and crew are waiting in Calais. If I leave them to their own mischief for too long, without myself or Alejandro there, I might not have a ship or a crew when I return."

He took her arm and pulled it through his, and walked her back to the château, the way a gentleman would escort his lady, and she was that.

"Will you be coming back?"

He paused long enough to grasp her by the forearms, and pull her close to plant a kiss on her forehead. "I was not sure of it until I heard you ask me that. Yes, I will be back. And I want you to promise if anything happens and you need help, get word to Monsieur Dessin, at Dessin's Inn. He knows how to find me. Promise."

"I will, I promise."

They stepped through the doors and joined the others for dinner, and by the time the evening ended, it was not easy for either Colin or Alejandro to ride away.

As they mounted their horses, Alejandro said, "I'm glad we are leaving tomorrow."

"Anxious to get back to sea, are you?"

"No, I am anxious to get away from a woman that scares the hell out of me.

"Ditto, my friend. Ditto."

# *Twelve*

Often the fear of one evil
leads us into a worse.
                    Nicolas Boileau (1636–1711),
                                    French writer and poet.
                                    *L'Art poétique* (1674).

In the week that followed, Colin Montgomery was too often in Kenna's thoughts, although her family was always at the center of her life and her heart. There were so many times when she felt herself weakening, when she wanted to get word to them, to tell them not to worry about her, but she was always conscious that the risk was too great, and protecting her family was foremost.

She had come very close to asking Colin to pay them a visit and tell them she was all right, but something—whether intuition or common sense—cautioned her against it. Lord Walter probably had men watching her relatives. If Colin went to them, it would put their lives as well as his in danger.

She could not, would not risk any of them.

The weeks passed and melted into months and Kenna continued to train with the *comte* every morning and every afternoon, except Sunday. She also continued to practice with Josette, but soon outpaced her to the point the *comte* stopped them.

"The difference in us is a matter of the difference in our objectives. Uninfluenced by emotions or personal prejudices, I fence for the sport of it, and sometimes for nothing more than the novelty," Josette said. "For you, it is an obsessive passion and a matter of survival."

It was at this point that the Comte Debouvine suggested it was time for her to fence with a few male partners, but only those who were considered to be the best. "I have selected three young men whom I know quite well, and their families also," he said. "I will have you working only with them, and I will swear each one of them to secrecy." His eyes took on a devilish gleam when he added, "It would also help if you could best them on a regular basis, for it is not like a man to boast that he has fenced with a woman. He is even less likely to do it if he has to admit she is better than he is."

"I do my best to win, always," she said.

"I know you do, Lady Kenna."

The *comte* arranged for her to engage some of the younger members of the nobility on a daily basis. Because they were all former pupils, they eagerly agreed because of the opportunity to work with the *comte* once again. However, when they discovered the reason for the invitation, they were reluctant—what young blade wanted to waste his time fencing a woman? But they were quick to change their minds once they engaged her, ceased to think about her gender, and concentrated on the foil that moved so swiftly, it was almost impossible to follow.

"I would like to provide you with a few more practice partners, but we must be careful here," the *comte* told her, "for we do not want word to get out about a red-haired lass from Scotland who is suddenly outfencing some of the best blades in Paris."

Now Kenna truly began to worry. She knew that the more her name was bandied about, the greater the chance that news of her could eventually get back to Lord Walter.

One afternoon, after her fencing class and after Josette had left, Kenna remained to speak with the *comte*. She placed her foil on the rack and waited until he did the same, then she told him about her fears that Lord Walter might find her as easily as Colin had done.

"Come, let us take a turn around the gardens. It is a grand day, and we are blessed that the air is dry after so much rain."

The gardeners were trimming the hedges of the maze, and had stirred up a hornet's nest, so they bypassed it and walked along the graveled paths, past the floating gardens and the beds of roses and irises, past the rhododendron and azalea garden, and sat for a while on a white marble bench in the Italian garden.

The *comte* was not worried about Lord Walter finding out something from Colin or Alejandro, but he said, "The thing I do worry about is, if Lord Walter is as devious and smart as you say, he might be able to back-track to the time when he first came into the lives of you and your sisters. We can assume that by now, he has made his way to Scotland and he has learned that you are not there. I am certain, based on what you have told me, that he is the kind of man who would want to see for himself. He would have personally made the trip to Inchmurrin Island to verify your absence. He has probably hired others to keep the island, as well as the homes of your kin, under surveillance. He has already learned the comings and goings of your family members, to the point that he is satisfied that you are no longer in Scotland."

"His next move will be to analyze everything until he feels he has a good idea where I am," she continued. "He is as cunning as he is deadly."

"Yes, he will be trying to think as you would. He lived in the same home with you and your sisters, which gave him ample opportunity to learn much about your behavior. He will use this to predict the future, based upon what's happened in the past. By your riding through the night, from your home to Edinburgh in order to save your sister's life, you have demonstrated your bravery and resourcefulness, as well as your tendency to seek friends and family in a time of need. It is in your favor that he has a big world to search."

"But not for long," she added.

"No, it won't take him long. In order to narrow the search, he will adopt the mathematical approach, and work on probabilities."

"Second-guessing me, thinking as I think."

"Exactly. He would surmise in the beginning that you probably would not go too terribly far from home, and that would eliminate America, South America, Asia, the Orient and such. Because of the Scots' conflict with England, he would rule that out as well."

"That would leave Ireland, or Europe," she said.

"Yes. I also think that instead of dashing off to those places, he would begin to eliminate countries. Because he lived with you, he surely knows that you speak French, so that would put any English-speaking or French-speaking countries at the top of his list."

Her hands began to tremble, and the secure, peaceful feeling she'd had since coming here vanished, and worse, she knew it was gone for good.

The time for preparation was drawing to a close.

Soon it would be time for the meeting and the final confrontation. Would she be good enough to beat him, and smart enough to outwit him?

The *comte* put a hand to her cheek. "Do not look so despondent. All is not lost. The worst you can do is give up."

"I know, but it is disheartening and terrifying at the same time. Here I thought I had it all planned out. I thought I was so smart and capable of taking care of myself." She put her hands over her face as the emotion began to overpower her. "Oh God, he knows…he knows!" she said, trembling at the fading away of her false security. Then she gained control, and spoke in a detached manner. "He already knows where I am. I am certain it did not take him long to decide I came to

Paris, and once that was realized, he could come up with your name rather quickly."

He nodded. "Ah, yes, because of your connection to Sophie de Bourbon."

In the months that followed, Kenna concentrated on each of the new partners she fenced with. She was focused, determined and driven beyond any ambition or drive they possessed. One by one, she either came to best them frequently, or they quit rather than face humiliation of being beaten by a woman, until there were not very many left who would even agree to a match.

When she was not fencing with them, she would practice her moves, and work to strengthen her body, and frequently would fence with the *comte,* until she soon could count more than one time she had won the match against him.

As she knew it would, the time came when her time as the *comte*'s pupil was at an end. It happened on a day they had a match planned between her and the *comte.*

Kenna was in the gallery when the *comte* entered, still a youthful figure for his age, and the epitome of grace and elegance in his black pants and white shirt.

They took their foils and checked the round adjustments that were made to each sharp, steel point, so no blood would be drawn during a hit. Satisfied, they took their positions on the *piste* and the match began, with the *comte* scoring the first hit to Kenna's left shoulder. The second hit went to Kenna. When they started for the third time, Kenna had the advantage of youth, but the *comte* had the years of knowledge and skill behind him. The fight went on for a long time, until Kenna tested him with a riposte, and he had no time to parry, before the tip of her foil caught him just below the right clavicle. A second later, she saw a bright red stain on the *comte*'s white shirt.

Horrified, she looked at the tip of her foil and saw the protective cap had fallen off. She rushed to see to his wound, full of apology.

"Oh, *cher Maître*. What have I done?"

He chuckled. "Done? Why nothing that is not done on a daily basis in every fencing school. It is nothing that has not happened to me many times," he said, with a glimpse at the oozing wound. "You see? It is a superficial cut and nothing to fret about, my dear Kenna," he said.

But, to Kenna, it was much more than a superficial wound. It was a sign…a blood sign that her time in France, her time with the *comte,* was up.

"Please, do not look as if this were the end of the world. You know I have given you a nick or two and drawn blood. Tomorrow you will have forgotten all about it."

"No, Monsieur le Comte. It is over."

"Over? You don't intend to let a little cut stop you."

"It is a sign…confirmation that it is time for me to return to Scotland."

As she knew he would, he did not try to argue or second-guess her, but respected her intuition and her feeling that the time they both dreaded had come. "I cannot stand in the way of your appointment with fate. Have you some idea when you plan to leave, or is it something you will have to contemplate?"

"I think I should go right away, as soon as I can pack."

"I have something for you to consider. Since we have accepted the invitation of the Duc and Duchesse de Pontaillac a week from tomorrow, what do you think about that as a leave-taking celebration? You can go the next day, or the day after, if you prefer. What say you?"

Kenna's intuition was telling her strongly that she should leave immediately, and that the drawing of the *comte*'s blood was a prophetic herald that pointed to the future…the hour that was to come for the settling of a score with an old enemy.

But when she started to speak of her feeling, she allowed herself to be swayed by the hopeful look in the depths of the *comte*'s blue eyes. She knew he had come to care for her as much as she had come to love him, and many times in the past year he had mentioned his dread when her days as his pupil would come to an end.

Still, her heart and her head wrestled.

"It is only one week," he said.

There was such hope in his voice, and she recalled how she had felt that day when she first came here, with so much riding on whether or not he would agree to help her. How could she, then, not acquiesce to his request?

"Very well, *cher Maître*. I shall make preparations to leave after the Pontaillacs' ball."

He kissed her forehead, and then took her hand in his. "Come with me into the gallery. I have something for you."

She went with him, and was surprised to see him move a large carving of his family crest. Behind it was a locked door about a foot square. He withdrew a key from his pocket and unlocked it. He withdrew a dark blue velvet sleeve, tied at one end with a velvet tassel.

Curiosity curled around her like the tail of a cat.

He untied the tassel and withdrew a magnificent sword.

Truly, it was beautiful, with the exquisitely modeled head of a woman. Her long hair curled in spirals around the hilt, down to the blade. The image was finely featured and emeralds gleamed in her eyes.

"Take it. It is yours."

"Oh, I could not, for it is a priceless piece."

"Oh, it is that. It was my father's sword, and his father's before him, and on back many generations. No one knows exactly how long it has been in our family, but the legend says it was made by the god Vulcan, for Mars, the god of war, son of Jupiter and father of Romulus, the founder of Rome. It was said to have magical properties, but I have never witnessed such, and neither did my father." He handed it to her. "But you will notice that there is one thing magical about it."

"Its weight," she said, awed, for it had no more heft than her foil.

That night, Kenna went into Josette's room and told her about the sword and her hit that drew the *comte*'s blood, as well as the reservations she still had over her agreement to remain at the château until after the Pontaillacs' ball.

"I know it was an omen that I must leave here as

soon as possible," she said, her mind racing ahead. "It is time for me to go. I have learned all I can. To stay longer would endanger both of you."

Josette, with her Gypsy blood, held strong beliefs about premonition, signs and such, but she had been raised with the kind and gentle ways of the *comte,* and taught the value of truth, honor and trust. "You know I believe in presentiment, but I also believe in honoring your word. You agreed, Kenna, and that is the end of it."

Kenna sighed. "You are right, of course."

The subject was dropped, and the conversation drifted naturally to the subject of Colin and Alejandro.

"You liked him, didn't you?" Kenna asked.

"*Like* can have many meanings," Josette replied.

"You know the meaning I am talking about. You cannot hide it from me. I was there. I saw the way you looked at him as if he were a side of beef and you were coming off a long fast. I saw the sparks flying from the heat of all that hot Latin blood and temperaments intermingling."

Josette laughed. "You aren't allowing yourself to get distracted from the reason you came here, are you?"

It was a sober reminder. "No, that is never far from my mind. I will see you tomorrow."

"Are you going back? It is early yet, and we have not had dinner."

"Tomorrow I have a match the *comte* arranged for me."

"And you always take a light meal in your room the night before a match," Josette remembered.

"Of course, otherwise I will drink wine with the two of you and my head will feel as if it is full of sawdust the next day."

"I shall be in the gallery tomorrow, to watch you."

As it turned out, Josette was not the only spectator the next day.

After her match with Anselme, Comte Freneau, Kenna, the *comte* and Josette were quietly talking with him and two of his friends, Raoul, Vicomte de Sainte, and François, Vicomte de Duperrey, when the footman entered and spoke with the *Comte* Debouvine.

A moment later, the *comte* turned and said, "Please excuse me for a moment."

Kenna did not pay much attention to his departure, but she was stunned when he returned a short time later accompanied by the Duc de Bourbon…the same Philippe Henri Louis Marie de Courtenay—Duc de Bourbon, Marquis de Marigny, Comte de Rochefort, Vicomte de Rohan, with whom she had shared her coach the night she traveled to Paris.

"Lady Kenna, we meet again at last," the *duc* said. "I can see by your expression that you are surprised to see me."

"I am stunned, Monsieur le Duc. How did you know I was here?"

"I shall have to claim responsibility for that," the Vicomte de Sainte said. "The Duc de Bourbon is a cousin of mine, and when he told me about the night the Comte de Lorraine was wounded and the lovely Scottish lass who kindly shared her coach, I knew it had to be you. I am sorry to admit, I forgot myself and mentioned your name, and that you were a pupil of the Comte Debouvine."

"It was meant to be," de Bourbon said, "and fortunate for you, Lady Kenna, for I have been most put out over not learning who you were, so I could thank you properly. I understand you will be at the home of the Duc and Duchesse of Pontaillac next week."

"Don't tell me they are cousins of yours."

He gave her a flirtatious smile. "Second cousins," he said, and everyone laughed.

Including the *comte,* who put his fatherly arm around Kenna. She had rarely felt happier than at this moment, wrapped in the joy of laughter and the love of friends.

# Thirteen

Caesar said to the soothsayer, "The Ides of
March are come," who answered him calmly,
"Yes, they are come, but they are not past."
                              —Plutarch (circa 46–120),
Greek historian, biographer and philosopher.
*Parallel Lives,* "Life of Caesar"
(1st century to 2nd century).

On the eve of the ball at the château of the Duc and
Duchesse de Pontaillac, Kenna was in her apartment
looking at herself in the large, gilt-framed pier glass
that stood between two windows of the same propor-
tions as the mirror.

It was the first time she had worn the silk gown
embellished with flower embroidery—a gown far
grander than she had ever owned. She had to admit
that when it came to fashion, the French were masters of design and workmanship. The dress was far
too lavish for her, she decided, considering her reflec-

tion in the mirror. It belonged on one of the ladies at court.

Kenna was about to remove the gown when Josette stopped by to see if she was ready.

"Your gown is beautiful," Kenna said. "I have never seen you wear white before. It is so stunning with your coloring."

That was true, for the white gown, embroidered with deep red roses along the plunging neckline and more roses around the hem of the skirt, was breathtaking. It was different and quite dramatic.

Josette was walking around Kenna, looking at her gown.

"Don't say anything. I know it is too much. I'm going to change."

"Oh, my…that is exquisite," Josette said. "If the queen is there she will be jealous."

"I told you, I'm not wearing it."

"Don't be silly. You will turn every head in the room. I have never seen anything quite like it…and the use of red thread on a white gown is sumptuous."

"Truly, I had already decided it is too much gown for me. Look! Over there!" she said, pointing to the bed. "I have already laid out the blue satin. If you will help me unfasten the back I will change quickly."

"I'll do no such thing." Josette went to the bed, snatched up the blue gown and stuffed it in the trunk. "The white is perfect, and you look like a princess and, since it may be the only chance you'll ever have to be a princess, don't ruin it."

She walked to the door. "Well, come on, the *comte* is waiting."

"Are you sure I don't look like Catherine the Great in this dress?"

"You look more like an angel in that dress…like St. Brigit, the patron saint of Ireland, for it is said she had red hair.

"You look like every man's dream, and you will see what I mean once you are there. Of course, every woman in the room will hate you."

"Oh, now, that's a wonderful thought. I don't want to be hated at my one and only social outing in France."

"Don't worry. It's a nice kind of hate. They always hate me. Envy is better than being overlooked."

Kenna was not fully convinced that what Josette said was true, but when they arrived at the ball, Josette on the *comte*'s left arm, and Kenna on his right, the envious glances of the other women said it all.

At the top of the stairs, they paused while the Comte Debouvine, Lady Kenna Lennox and Mademoiselle Josette Revel were announced. For a moment, Kenna stood staring down into the massive ballroom, decorated like the inside of a pasha's tent, with the entire ceiling draped in bright colors, the fabric tied back with golden ropes for guests to pass between as they stepped through the doors onto the balcony.

Two Ottoman *tugh* bearers stood on each side of the stairway. Kenna could not hide her fascination with the *tughs,* or Turkish horse-tail standards, they held, each a bundle of red horsehair fixed on a wooden staff and topped with a finial.

As they began their descent and the violins began to play, she saw several men in long, flowing robes carrying trays of figs and dates. By the time she stepped off the last step, at least a dozen young men were gathered around them.

While they made their greetings to the *comte,* Kenna opened her fan and whispered behind it to Josette, "You were right. It is nice to be envied, if only for once in your life."

"And to have it happen in a tent in Morocco," Josette whispered.

"I was thinking Turkey," Kenna whispered back.

"I think you are both wrong," a masculine voice said from behind them. "My guess is *Arabian Nights.*"

They both turned and Kenna recognized the Comte de Lorraine, and the Duc de Bourbon smiling down at them.

"I think I like your suggestion best of all," Kenna said, "for it evokes a richer, more evocative image in my mind. I can almost see shifting sands, handsome bedouins in flowing robes astride camels, racing across the desert in long, loping strides."

"Careful, or someone might abduct you and keep you as his prisoner."

Kenna laughed and spoke to the Comte de Lorraine. "I am not worried about that happening with you and the Duc de Bourbon to protect us. May I say that you are looking much better than when I saw you last, suffering from a broken arm in my coach, Monsieur le Comte?"

"I feel much better," he said. "I am perfectly healed, thanks to your generosity in sharing your coach with us, Lady Kenna. I had hoped to see you again, so I could thank you in person."

"It is thanks enough to see you looking so fit and healthy."

"I almost wish I was the one who broke his arm that night," the Duc de Bourbon said. "I have been waiting by the stairs all evening, afraid I would miss your arrival. May I say that in that gown, you would be impossible to miss? You are enchanting tonight, dazzling Parisian society with your beauty, and I am not the only one who thinks so."

Kenna smiled as she gazed into the vivid blue eyes of the *duc*. "Good evening, Monsieur le Duc. You are looking rather splendid yourself in your dashing uniform." And that was true, for his livery was all gold and white, embellished with enough braid and looped rope to dress every window at Versailles.

"Splendid enough to dance with me?" he asked.

"To the envy of every woman in the room, I am certain," she said. "Now they will all dislike me for taking you away."

"They would envy you whether you danced with me or not, for it is your beauty and gracious way that has their tongues wagging. Not to mention your gown… exquisite on you with your coloring, by the way."

The next moment, she was inside the tent, dancing with the Duc de Bourbon, her thoughts on how it would surprise Sophie when she told her she had danced with a relative of hers.

She caught sight of Josette dancing with Jules, and she thought what a handsome couple they made, with their dark heads together. She looked around the room for a glimpse of the *comte,* and found him standing just outside one of the draped doors that led to the balcony.

Just at that moment, she caught sight of a servant, wearing the robes of a Bedouin but with no tray of figs and dates.

He stepped through the doors where the Comte Debouvine stood talking to two men and then he turned his head toward her for a split second before he turned away, but it was long enough for Kenna to suck in her breath, for the eyes were Lord Walter's eyes.

No, she thought, as a feeling of panic gripped her. It cannot be. I was mistaken.

"I hope it is not another man who has captured your attention."

Kenna turned her gaze back to de Bourbon. "It was another man, and one I care a great deal for, but he is like a father to me, and he has passed his sixtieth year."

"The *comte* has said your presence has gifted him with a second daughter."

Kenna was about to respond, when suddenly there was a great commotion on the balcony. A woman screamed. Shouts erupted, and several men in uniform dashed through the door.

"Oh, my God!" a woman shouted. "Someone has stabbed the *comte!*"

Kenna felt her heart stop, and when she turned she could no longer see the *comte.* "No!" she screamed. "Dear God, no!" She wrenched herself away from Philippe and fought her way toward the balcony. She no more than made it through the door when she spotted him. For a moment, the *comte* remained erect, his eyes registering surprise. Then a shudder coursed through him, and with a bubbling moan, he collapsed and dropped to the floor.

Paralyzed for a moment, she could only stare in horror at the Comte Debouvine, lying on his back, with a dagger in his chest.

"Let me through!" she cried, pushing people away until she reached his side and dropped down next to him. Tears streamed across her cheeks as she lifted the *comte*'s head and held it in her lap. "Someone find a doctor!" she shouted. She leaned close and kissed his forehead.

With her skirt, she wiped the lips flecked with froth and blood. "Hold on, *cher Maître*. We will have a doctor soon, and then we shall take you home."

His face was terribly pale. His eyes were wide with astonishment, and already his lips seemed parched and dry. She could barely hold back the wrenching sobs that threatened when she saw the scarlet stain that covered his entire chest. She recalled how she had drawn his blood, the day he had gifted her with his sword.

A cold shiver rippled down her back, for she knew it had been an omen, a portent of what was to come.

*If only I had followed my instincts, I could have prevented this.*

She stroked his face. "Do not give up, *cher Maître*. Use the strength you have so often given to me."

"It is time," he whispered. "I had hoped to see your great success, but I know it will happen, and if God is willing, I will see it from above."

Josette was suddenly beside them, and dropped down on the other side of the *comte*. Like Kenna, tears rolled down her face. "Do not leave me, Monsieur le Comte. You are my everything."

He touched her hand. "Do not fret so, Josette. Everything will be as it has always been. I made certain of it many years ago. I have no heirs, and upon my death, the château is yours, *ma petite*."

"I do not want the château if you are not there. I cannot live without you! You cannot leave me!"

"My daughters," he said, struggling to get the words out, for there was blood foaming from his mouth with each gurgling breath he took, "you have brought me great joy."

He turned his head slightly to look at Kenna. "Do not doubt your ability. You are ready. You have nothing to fear. I will be gone, but I will be with you."

His last breath bubbled forth, and his noble head fell to one side. Kenna felt someone lift her, and heard the strong voice of the Duc de Bourbon. "The doctor has come."

"It is too late," she sobbed, and felt his arms go around her as he pressed her to his chest, and she cried on his splendid uniform of gold and white.

The *duc* and the *vicomte* escorted Josette and Kenna into the study of the Duc de Pontaillac, and stayed with them while the *comte*'s body was removed.

"I don't know why anyone would do this," Josette said, her body shaking with sobs. "The *comte*'s very soul was beautiful. He never had an enemy. Never!"

"But I have one," Kenna said. Her tears had already

stopped. They had ceased the moment she realized that what had happened here tonight was because of her. "I have an old enemy, and I am the one who caused the *comte*'s death. If I had left last week, none of this would have happened."

Josette had Jules's kerchief and she dried her face with a sniff. "You do not know that, Kenna."

Kenna turned anguished eyes upon the face of her friend. "I do, Josette. I do know it…here," she said, and pounded her heart.

"Stop it!" Josette said.

"It is true! I feel his evil presence surrounding me. The nightmare has begun. Lord Walter has found me, and I am doomed."

Josette slapped her. Hard. And Kenna's head snapped back.

Jules's arms went around Josette, and he held her back against him, so she could not strike Kenna again.

"It is all right," Kenna said. "I deserved it. After what happened tonight, I don't deserve to live."

De Bourbon's arms tightened around her. She felt his warm breath against her neck as he said, "Shh…do not speak so."

Kenna pushed at him. "Don't you understand? It was my fault! It should have been me," she cried, emphasizing each word with a fist to her chest. "It should have been me."

Josette struggled against de Lorraine's iron grip. "If this *bâtard* would let me go, I would slap you again!" she screamed. "You mock him by speaking as you do! His last words were to you. He gave you his beloved sword, or have you forgotten? He said you were ready, that you had nothing to fear. And if this Lord Walter is the one who did this foul deed, then you owe it to the *comte* to cut his murdering throat. And if you don't, by all that is holy, I will!"

Kenna reached across and took Josette's hand. "I am indebted to you, Josette, for the slap, and your words were what I needed. Please forgive me."

Josette's lip trembled and her arms went around Kenna. "We are all that is left of this wonderful, giving man. We will see this through together."

In place of tears, Kenna felt nothing but cold, hard hatred for her archenemy. "I swear before God, and before all of you, that the *comte*'s death will not go unavenged. I will find Lord Walter, and I will settle the score for my father, my brothers and our beloved *comte*."

Josette lifted her head, and Kenna saw that her tears, too, were gone, and in her eyes burned a fire of vengeance. When she spoke, her voice came like cold spikes hammered into solid steel.

"Your fight has become my fight. I shall go with you…"

As the last letters of his epitaph were being hammered into the marble of the Debouvine family crypt, the wax candles were burning in the Rose Salon of the château, around the velvet-draped casket containing the inanimate body of Bastien François Marie Lievin, Comte Debouvine.

Neither the sad, mournful sounds of tears from the maids, nor the chanting prayer of the priest, nor the sad melancholy that echoed through the château like the lugubrious notes of a cello had the power to divert attention away from the decisions that had to be made immediately following the *comte*'s demise.

In the *comte*'s library, the Duc de Bourbon, Comte de Lorraine and Vicomte de Bignan sat quietly talking with Kenna and Josette.

Kenna, so vibrant and rosy-cheeked the day before, was now an ethereal, pale beauty, her former fire now turned to ice. In the candlelight, her skin took on the look of transparent opaqueness, so frail and fragile it seemed. The only glimpse of the woman she had been the night before was the graceful, regal elegance with which she conducted herself. No one could see that deep in the secret chambers of her heart she hid her sorrows, bitter rue. "He was of noble blood, and an important man, beloved by so many," Kenna said. "He must have prayers and a mass, then a proper funeral, before he is interred in the family crypt."

"I understand that," the *duc* said, "but we cannot take the risk of allowing you to attend the *comte*'s funeral. When the mass begins, the two of you will already be on your way to Calais. In your place at the mass and burial, we will have two of the *comte*'s maids dressed in black with dark veils to impersonate you. Father René Delon, Gaston and the footmen will make it known that you are so grief-stricken you cannot speak with anyone, and will beg they respect your request for privacy until some time has passed."

"When will we leave?" Josette asked, her own

dusky beauty now quite pale, the curved cheeks drawn, and the dark lips trembling with each forced word.

"You will be on your way to Calais with us tonight. I do apologize, but we must go on horseback, because it is faster and much safer," the *duc* said.

Josette dabbed at her eyes with her kerchief. "It seems a sacrilege. He deserved so much more than that."

"What he deserved," the Comte de Lorraine said, "is for the two people he loved most in the world to survive, and right now that is what we must concentrate on. The longer we delay, the greater the risk to your lives. We have to get the two of you out of France, secretly if possible, before your friend Lord Walter can strike again."

The *duc* seemed to be pondering something, for he seemed caught in a moment of quiet consideration.

"What are you thinking?" the *vicomte* asked him.

The *duc* seemed to have trouble expressing just what was in his thoughts. "I was only wondering, that is... well, my question is, are we *certain* it was this Lord Walter person?"

Kenna wasted no time with her quick reply. "I am sure it was Lord Walter. Mere seconds before he plunged that knife in the *comte*'s chest, he turned his head and looked straight at me, as if he wanted me to know he was there. I would know those eyes anywhere."

"What I don't understand is, why would he take the *comte*'s life when it is yours he wants?" the *vicomte* asked.

"Oh, my friend, you do not know him as I do. To kill me quickly as he did the *comte* would not give him the satisfaction he desires. I must be tormented. He wants to play with me as a cat does a mouse. Killing me would be too easy, and he would not find satisfaction in my death coming so soon. He must make me suffer, for that feeds something inside him. He wants me to know he is here, and he will enjoy knowing I will live in terror each second until he decides to end my life."

"Sinister monster, isn't he?" said de Bignan.

"You have no idea," Kenna replied, and she felt a gush of sorrow that filled her eyes and twisted her heart with a painful ache. She breathed deeply, pushing the pain aside, so she might focus on the evil being who was no longer confined to his den, but roaming freely, thanks to the English king, who like Lord Walter, was both cunning and wicked.

After a few parting words, they dismissed themselves to get a few hours' rest and prepare for the long ride ahead. De Bourbon, de Lorraine and de Bignan were to reside in the guest apartments of the château, so they would be close at hand, should anything go wrong.

As they walked down the dimly lit passages, no one seemed to notice the presence of so many more of the *comte*'s men, standing guard.

They stopped by the Rose Salon to pay their last respects to the *comte*, and to speak a few words with Father René, who offered them prayers and condolences. The salon was now more like a dim cathedral than a greeting room for guests. The lovely, tall windows had been darkened with black velvet drapes, and the haloed light of four large tapers cast eerie shadows from the four corners of a catafalque, a raised platform hung with black, on which rested the *comte*'s coffin.

Numb and filled with a black abyssal darkness within, Kenna moved to stand beside the *comte*, his face as pale and waxen as the candles that illuminated it. She kissed two fingers and placed them on his cold, silent lips. "Farewell, beloved *comte*, father, *Maître* and friend. Now it is time to say goodbye to the gilded pageantry of the past, and to face the future, not with happiness, but a measure of calm resolve. Your murder will be avenged, *Maître*, or I shall join you in death."

# *Fourteen*

In trouble to be troubl'd
Is to have your trouble doubl'd.
— Daniel Defoe (1660–1731),
English novelist and journalist.
*The Farther Adventures of Robinson Crusoe*
(1719).

It was almost noon and the sun had already burned the dew from the road that led to Calais. Down this dry, dusty road came a weary cavalcade, sitting astride well-lathered horses. The noble but dust-covered group of travelers, composed of three men, two women and several guards in the service of the Duc de Bourbon, came trotting down the dirt road and turned onto the cobbled streets of the city.

The travelers caught the eye of many of the shoppers on the street, for there was something both majestic and melancholy about the well-dressed group.

The neat figure of the Duc de Bourbon was a mirror of elegance in his tan breeches and perfectly fitted chocolate-brown coat, all quite indicative of his affluence. He rode a fine gray gelding with a spirited gait, and sat well in the Flemish saddle padded with blue velvet, with enclosed stirrups that covered the top part of his boots.

The Comte de Lorraine was dressed in brown breeches, with a dark blue coat. He was not as tall as his friend, but well put together, and in possession of an extremely attractive face, in which dark, alert eyes took note of everything they passed. His saddle was similar to that of the *duc,* and his horse was a good-natured chestnut, with a smooth gait.

The Vicomte de Bignan rode a black horse that began to prance sideways and nervously champ his bit when they entered the city. The *vicomte* did not seem to notice, neither did he see many of the women on the street casting interested glances at the tall man with the princely face and blond hair.

Kenna and Josette rode side by side, one on a bay and the other on a sorrel, their quiet repose the embodiment of the beauty of womanhood, with a refinement that put them well beyond the attainment of the average man on the street.

Yet, the contrast between the two was striking, one dark and exotic, with black hair, long and straight; the other fair of skin and face, with rosy-red curls tucked beneath the hood of a blue cape.

They turned down a street that sloped toward the harbor and clattered over the cobblestones before they drew up in front of an inn, whose sign swayed in the breeze, but not so much that one could not read the name, Dessin's Inn.

When the party stopped, two of the *duc*'s men, who had ridden ahead, came outside to inform them that rooms had been procured for everyone.

A stable boy came out to help with the horses, and one of the soldiers told him to take only the horses of the women. "Leave the other horses here, for now," he said.

The Comte de Lorraine and Monsieur le Vicomte had already dismounted to help Josette and Kenna out of their saddles.

Jules lifted Kenna from the saddle, and held her for a moment when she was on the ground. "Your legs may not work at first," he said to her.

She put a hand on his dusty sleeve to steady herself. "Faith! You are right. So many hours in the saddle and such a fast pace...I am stiff as a statue."

Kenna was about to thank them for the escort, and to tell them that there was no need for them to remain in Calais, when the Duc de Bourbon said, "We are staying here, Mademoiselle Lennox, until we see you safely aboard a ship."

He turned to the man who had procured the rooms. "You made certain they are clean?"

"*Oui, Monseigneur,* I inspected them myself."

He was not able to say more, for the proprietor, who introduced himself as Monsieur Dessin, came out and said, "Monsieur le Duc, our rooms are so immaculate, a king would not be disappointed."

The *duc* turned to Kenna. "It has been a long ride,

and you must be tired, because I am accustomed to such as this, and I am exhausted. Three of my men will remain here, on guard, while the others get a bath, a hot meal and some much needed sleep. I want the two of you to get the same."

He turned to one of the guards. "See that everyone has something to eat and there's enough hot water for everyone to have a bath. Once you've done that, ride down to the harbor and see what the choices are for early passage out of here."

Kenna and Josette shared a private room on the second floor, a handsome chamber that overlooked the same garden Kenna had gazed upon over a cup of tea, the year before. She almost expected to see Captain Fischer walking up the street. How long ago that all seemed to her now.

She turned away from the window and joined Josette at the small table, which held an assortment of delicious-smelling food.

They were so hungry, the meal did not take more than a quarter of an hour to devour. Now they sat talking quietly while they waited for maids to fill the tubs with hot water.

Suddenly, the rattle of hooves drew them to the window, and they saw the *duc*'s men riding back from the harbor, their confident expressions telling Kenna that they had met with success. France would soon be in the past.

She breathed a sigh of relief, for she knew it must have been quite difficult to arrange passage for the two of them. Precious few captains were willing to take the risk of being sunk or captured by the English, who continued to patrol the waters between France and Scotland, as they searched constantly for Jacobites, enemies of the Crown, who were making their escape after Culloden.

Only twenty-one miles separated France and England across the Strait of Dover, so it was easy for the English to patrol the area. If a ship was lucky enough to evade them and make it farther north, the girls' chances of escape improved greatly.

She let her gaze travel down the cobbled streets, past tree-lined squares and ancient ramparts, until she saw the harbor and the naked masts of ships that tugged at their anchors with the receding tide.

There were several vessels anchored, in readiness to sail when the wind served and the tide was in, and the area seemed to be clear of the English ships seen earlier, prowling the French coast.

Below the window, they could hear the men talking. She identified the *duc*'s voice. "It will be getting dark before too long, and I would like to have this thing decided before we retire for the night. I hope you were successful."

She did not know which of the men answered, "Monsieur le Duc, it was disappointing to learn all the larger ships were sailing for Bordeaux or the Mediterranean ports of France. I was beginning to wonder if we would be able to find a brave smuggler or a privateer willing to line his coffers in exchange for two female passengers. *Mon dieu!* Is everyone afraid of the English?"

"It would appear so. Were you able to book passage?"

"*Oui, Monseigneur,* the captain of a Swedish ship, the *Ingeborg,* bound for Stockholm, agreed to stop at Kirkwall, Scotland, where you will be able to find a ship to take you to Caithness or Sutherland. She leaves at noon tomorrow, when the tide is expected to be at its highest."

"Excellent," the *duc* said. "I will inform the ladies."

Josette turned to Kenna. "Where is this Kirkwall?"

"It's a town in the Orkney Islands in the far northeastern part of the Highlands. The Orkneys belonged to the Norwegians for centuries."

Josette's only comment was "Hmm…"

The voices died away, overcome now by the raucous cries of vendors calling out as they passed, hawking their wares and arguing among themselves.

The next day, the sun rose through a bank of apricot-tinted clouds, and lent a jade-green sea all its lovely hues. As the hour approached eleven o'clock, a boat carrying Josette and Kenna approached an East Indiaman, the *Ingeborg,* riding at anchor while her crew scampered about readying her for sea.

It was emotional to bid goodbye to the Duc de Bourbon, the Comte de Lorraine and Vicomte de Bignan, who all made Kenna swear she would send word to them when they arrived safely. "And so we will also know where you are in order that we might pay you a visit when you least expect it," the *duc* said.

Kenna bid each of them farewell, with a kiss to the

cheek and tears in her eyes. "I would not have made it this far, if God had not put the three of you in my life. I hope someday to be able to repay you."

"You can repay us by staying alive," the *vicomte* said.

The *Ingeborg* was a large merchant ship on her return voyage from China. She was sailing to Stockholm, and then to her home port of Göteborg, on Sweden's west coast.

Her captain was a stern Swede by the name of George de Frese, whom Kenna and Josette never saw smile, except when they boarded the ship and he learned they had no luggage except for their small traveling bags.

"I advise you to stay in your cabin. Your meals will be brought to you. We are expecting rough seas."

They watched their departure from the portholes in their cabin, as the ship, in full sail, negotiated the narrow channel into the sea. Sometime later, they were thankful Captain de Frese advised them to remain below, for the ship was rolling in the billows, plunging one way and then the next, as it fought its way through the rough seas.

By the time land disappeared, Josette was already beginning to feel bad, and Kenna advised her to lie down, for she feared Josette was experiencing the first twinges of seasickness. Josette eyed the hammock swinging back and forth and declared, "It makes me feel worse just to look at it moving back and forth. I can't sleep in that thing. I doubt I can even get into it."

Recalling her own experience of climbing into a

hammock for the first time, Kenna was sympathetic. "It is a bit tricky at first. After landing on the floor a few times, I think I finally got the hang of it on about the fifth try."

Josette had worse luck, and after several attempts, gave up completely and announced, "I cannot sleep in it because I cannot get into it."

"How about sitting down on it while I hold it still, then see if you can get one leg in, and then the other."

Josette did not look as if she thought that would help, but she was turning pale and had to be feeling worse, so she agreed to try. "One leg at a time, right?"

Kenna nodded, and gripped the hammock with both hands and held it tight as Josette sat down. So far so good, Kenna thought, and waited for Josette to get one leg in place. "We are almost there," she declared, "now do the same with the other leg."

Josette did and the hammock flipped over and threw her on the floor.

Kenna, her finger resting on her chin as she went over the previous procedure, tried to decide what went wrong. "I think it might be your petticoats getting in the way. Why don't you take them off?"

Petticoats off, Josette tried again, and this time she made it.

"You see? Perseverance always pays off," Kenna said. "How are you feeling?"

"A bit banged up, and my stomach is queasy."

"Just lie still and try to sleep." Kenna tiptoed toward her own hammock, and was relieved to get in on the first try. She settled herself and closed her eyes.

She was almost asleep when she heard Josette call her name. "What?" Kenna replied.

"You won't believe this," Josette said.

"I won't believe what?"

"I need a chamber pot."

The rough seas lasted all afternoon. With waves rising high as a hillside, the ship tossed and pitched, but Kenna did eat the evening meal, and managed to spill more soup than she swallowed, but it was enough to ease her hunger and make her sleepy enough that she immediately crawled into her hammock.

It was the same the next day. The ship seemed to hover, suspended on the crest of a churning wave, then would suddenly glide swiftly down the other side, to what felt like immediate doom.

Once, Kenna was looking through the port window and saw another ship riding the crest of a huge swell, then completely disappear. Kenna waited, perpetually it seemed, before it suddenly appeared again on another huge wave.

At one point, Kenna truly thought it was all over for them, for it seemed to her that the waves would rip the ship apart. But, miraculously, the ship managed to stay on top of the waves.

"If we are lost, we are lost," Josette said, "and I would as soon not know about it. Do you have any of those biscuits left from your breakfast? Perhaps eating one would help."

Kenna gave her the biscuits, and she ate three of them and began to feel better. After a while, they played cards to help pass the time, or as it turned out, Kenna spent the afternoon watching Josette cheat at cards.

The next day, the storm passed and the sea was relatively calm, except for another bout of rough seas off the coast of Scotland, as they passed Dunnet Head. Kenna knew this because she recognized the sheer hundred-foot cliffs, and she stood at the window, awed by the pure beauty and power of the sea as it hurled geysers of spray that exploded on impact when it collided with the solid rock of the cliffs.

Later that afternoon, the *Ingeborg* sailed as close as the ship could get to the gray old town of Kirkwall. Since there was no harbor here, the ship dropped anchor, and the two women were rowed to shore by two men in a skiff, who complained mightily about the number of herring boats bobbing at anchor. Half an hour later, they found themselves standing on a sandy shore that lay flush along the west side of Broad Street.

The bottom half of their skirts was wet, along with their shoes, for the men did not bring the skiff close to the sandy beach, nor did they offer to carry them to dry ground.

They studied the landscape…or lack of landscape, for the island seemed to have a severe shortage of trees or shrubs. Not even a blade of grass could they see for some distance in any direction—nothing but mile after mile of savage island, desolate and forlorn.

"It reminds me so much of Paris," Josette said, her wistful words embroidered with melodrama.

Such melodrama, that Kenna burst into fits of laughter, for seconds before Josette spoke she was thinking it wasn't much of an island or a town, which sounded awfully apologetic even to her.

They watched the *Ingeborg* make ready to set sail once more, and recognized the figure of Captain de Frese shouting out orders on deck. It was the first sighting they had had of the captain since they'd gone on board.

"Accommodating man, wasn't he?" Josette said. "I shall add Swedes to the list of nationalities I would not want to marry."

"Is it a long list?"

"I can fit all of them on one piece of paper if that is what you mean."

"That isn't so long…considering," Kenna said.

"I write small."

Kenna laughed again, and studied Josette's face for a moment. She was thinking how far they had come since the day of their first meeting, when she would have sworn this woman could not befriend anyone, and yet, here she was, as dear to Kenna as a sister.

They took one last glance and watched until the *Ingeborg* was nothing more than a tiny dot on the horizon, before they turned away and walked along Broad Street, toward the center of town. Kenna was reminded that neither she, nor Josette, had mentioned the death of the *comte* since the onset of their journey. She supposed that for them both, it was too fresh and raw to talk about, as each of them grappled with the loss in her own way. Even now, thinking about it caused her nerves to prick and left her heartsick.

The wind was starting to pick up. Kenna tilted back

her head to glance at the sky, which was beginning to turn darker as the clouds sped by. Earlier she had seen a few gulls and a cormorant or two, but now all she glimpsed were a few ragged auks that looked as if they had been battered by the wind.

"We need to find somewhere to stay," she said, and picked up her traveling bag. "Those clouds are promising something we don't want any part of."

They hurried into the small town, mindful of the black and turbulent sky overhead, as it began to churn and boil, driving the clouds before it.

From peat fires came the aromatic tang of herring being smoked, as they passed stone houses along the narrow streets of Kirkwall, with their thatched roofs and spiraling curls of smoke rising from their chimneys and seeming to flatten on the horizon. Every so often, a shop was wedged in among the stone houses that lined the street.

The wind was becoming more blustery, so they picked up the pace and entered the first inn they came to. It was called St. Magnus Inn, for it was near a twelfth-century cathedral of the same name, or so the proprietor told them.

"St. Magnus is really a cathedral in miniature, for it is only fifty feet long, and twenty feet wide," said Grímr Scartaine who, like most of the Orkney Island residents, had a name of Norse origin.

In spite of his grim-sounding name, Grímr was quite a friendly, congenial person, with a long, drooping mustache and a wrinkled brow that made him appear rather walruslike. By far the most impressive thing about him was the speed with which he provided them with a clean room, and he managed to have something to eat sent to their room.

The room was quite plain and simple in its barrenness, and rustically furnished. There was naught hanging on the walls—not so much as a picture or a peg—but it was spotlessly clean.

Kenna inquired about acquiring passage on a ship to the north coast of Sutherland, where her grandfather's home, Durness Castle, stood on a cliff overlooking the sea.

"A ship, you say? Well, now, ships come in and out of here all the time, but none of them operate on a schedule, you see. Don't mean to sound discouraging, you understand. You might be able to gain passage to the mainland in a week or so."

"There's no other way?" Kenna asked.

"Herring boats, but no fisherman would allow a woman on his boat for any reason...nor would ladies like yourselves want to be. Come out smelling like herring, you would."

By the end of the third day of sightseeing and playing cards, Josette was so sick of the island and the game, she was no longer inspired to cheat.

Kenna was beginning to wonder if they would be forced to winter here. Then finally, toward the end of their second week, Grímr knocked on their door and said there was a gentleman below to see Kenna.

She opened the door. "A gentleman? Did he give you his name?"

"No, he said it was a surprise," Grímr said seriously,

but there was a mischievous gleam in his eye that made Kenna suspicious. Was Grímr playing some kind of trick on two unsuspecting newcomers—one that was an old Orkney tradition, perhaps? Or, was there truly someone down there who knew her? No, she thought, that sounded preposterous. "Thank you, Grímr. I will be down in a few minutes," she said, and closed the door.

She did not move, but leaned back against the door thinking about how strangely Grímr was acting. Who could possibly know she was here? Surely not Lord Walter.

Her gaze fell upon Josette, who was looking at her with an interesting sort of curiosity, before she asked, "Is something wrong?"

"No," Kenna said, shaking her head. "I find this all a bit odd, that's all. I cannot imagine anyone knowing our whereabouts."

"Not even Lord Walter?"

"I thought about that, but there would be no reason for him to connect me, even remotely, with the Orkney Islands."

"Who could it be, then?"

"I thought for a moment that Grímr might be playing some kind of local joke on us, but that seems too far-fetched. Still, something isn't right about all of this." She paused. "What do you think?"

"I think you either go down and see who it is, or you stay here and wonder. As I see it, there are those two simple choices—go or stay. You are clever enough to figure that out, so why are you trying to make it complicated?"

Josette always managed to reduce everything to its simplest form, Kenna thought as she replied, "I suppose I make it complicated because cleverness and stupidity get on so well together," Kenna said. "Is that reason enough?"

Josette was smiling now. "Go down if you want, or don't go down if you are wary or uneasy about it. What is it to be?"

"I fear my curiosity overpowers my bewilderment."

"Is that a yes?"

Kenna smiled. "Yes."

Josette rose to her feet. "Very well, I shall accompany you," she said as she caught up her cloak. "Take your cloak and we can take a walk down those boringly familiar streets before we come back upstairs."

The public room was filled with pipe smoke from several men puffing away as they sat around tables playing backgammon. The dense tobacco vapors caused Josette to have a fit of coughing.

Grímr hurried over to them, stroking his walrus-tusk mustache. "A thousand pardons, my ladies. These old men insist upon frequenting my public room each Thursday afternoon. I have done everything short of drowning them, and still they come back here every week. What is a man to do in that situation?"

"Let them stay here and smoke," Kenna said, thinking that sounded a lot like something Josette would have said. "Where is the gentleman you said asked for me?"

Grímr smacked himself on the forehead. "Forgive me, my lady, I completely forgot. He stepped outside to get away from the smoke."

"At least he has some semblance of intelligence," Josette said, "and enough sense to get away from this wretched fug."

Grímr opened the inn door for them and they passed through before coming to an immediate, and abrupt, halt on the other side. Both were too stunned and over-whelmed at the shock and surprise of what they saw, that neither could find the words or her voice to speak.

He was here, and so achingly familiar from that impossible-to-blot-out image she carried of him in her mind. It was a picture she would never forget; a memory he created the first time she innocently walked into his life that day in Edinburgh, aboard a ship called *Dancing Water.*

And impossible though it was, he was here now, in Kirkwall. She would never forget the way he looked, with his black cape swirling around his feet, placed wide apart, the wind tugging it back just enough to expose the merest whisper of a white, tucked shirt, in a manner wickedly pleasing. It intrigued her and made her wonder just what else lay hidden beneath that cape.

He was eloquent, shrewd, handsome, annoyingly desirable and a thief of hearts: hers.

She noticed from the corner of her eye that Josette apparently had recovered from her shock, for she and Alejandro were talking quietly as they started to walk up Broad Street.

Josette and Alejandro? Two hot bloods…a Gypsy and a Spaniard? Her logical side said no. Yet, there was another part of her that said it could be: only time would tell.

Her thoughts were drawn back to Colin, who walked toward her, a welcome sight indeed. He could not have been more desirable or more attractive if he had been dipped in chocolate.

"It has been a long time," he said.

*Too long,* she wanted to say. "Yes, it has been a long time. Why are you here now?"

"I told you I would come back to see you, the last time I was at the château, or have you forgotten?"

*I remembered everything you said and every day you did not return.* "How did you know where we were?"

He grinned and shrugged his shoulders. "Curious, are you?"

"You knew I would be, just as you know you would be curious in my place."

"A man does not like to give away all of his secrets, but the truth is, I went to the château to see you…I was very sorry to hear about the *comte.* He was an outstanding man, and I know how much he meant to both you and Josette."

"It was devastating. Even now, I have difficulty not blaming myself for what happened."

"I knew you would shoulder the burden the moment the *duc* told me what happened, but you know you are wrong to consider it your fault. I have a feeling the *comte* would tell you the same thing, were he standing here right now."

She was careful to keep her features expressionless and her emotions hidden, for she had still to learn the reason why he was here. "I am certain he would, and

I understand everything you say, but the simple fact is, I was the reason Lord Walter was in France, and even now, just to think of that night fills me with chaotic emotions. To lose the *comte* leaves a gaping hole of emptiness in the lives of too many people. He was greatly loved and admired, you know, and his worth extended far beyond his being the greatest fencing master in all of Europe. I miss him terribly, and I must stop speaking of it. I never knew there were so many strings that could be plucked in the human heart."

She paused to study Colin's face, drinking in the sight of his intense blue eyes. He was a beguiling presence who seemed to dwarf everything else in her life, the epitome of tall, dark and handsome, with his graceful stride and easy manner. She was thinking he was a beautiful piece of God's perfect workmanship, but how he had arrived here was still so puzzling. "Who told you I was in Kirkwall?"

"Gaston thought I might find out more about where you went if I spoke to your friend, the *duc*. So, I did."

She had not had time before to study his strong profile. It was one of the powerfully desirable things she felt drawing her to him. "The *duc* was obviously helpful."

"In more ways than you know, for he suggested we find a way for me to bring your clothes to you, as well as Josette's."

Her expression brightened. "And did you bring them?"

"Right down to the last corset."

Feeling a slight touch of awkwardness, she glanced

quickly away and heard him chuckle. She asked him another question, before he had time to comment. "How were you able to remove our belongings, without Lord Walter becoming suspicious, if he had men watching the château?"

"I believe Josette gave Gaston instructions before she left, that he was to give all the *comte*'s clothes to the church, to be distributed to the poor. We simply made it look like the *comte* had a lot more clothes going to the church than actually were. Once it was delivered to him, Father René had your baggage sent to a church in Amiens, mixed in with a load of supplies that were going there. We stopped by the church on our way through Amiens and brought it with us to Calais. It is on board the ship now."

"I am relieved to know it, for the other night, Josette dreamed we were shipwrecked and had nothing to wear but leaves."

"You shouldn't tell me that, for now I am tempted to toss everything overboard."

"This is a near treeless island, in case you have not noticed."

"Even better," he said.

This time it was her turn to laugh. "Do all Americans talk as you do, with such levity and charm?"

"No, I'm the only one…at least I would like you to think so."

"Very well, I will humor you in that regard."

His smile was seductive and so wickedly dangerous, she felt her knees go weak. "I understand you have been waiting here for passage to Sutherland."

"We are in most desperate need of a ship. Do you know where we might find one?"

"I know where you can find a lot of things that you need," he said, looking her over seductively, "including a ship."

She laughed. "You are incorrigible. You never miss anything, and certainly not an opportunity to be a bit wicked, do you?"

His eyes gleamed with merriment. "No, but only because I know you like it."

"Bah! My fancy is not captured by such."

He moved closer to her. "Let us test the validity of those words, shall we?"

Before she could answer, he drew her around the corner of the building so they were hidden from the view of anyone on the street. The next thing she knew, he had captured her face in his hands and drawn it upward so he was gazing deeply into her eyes, which sent a corresponding shiver rippling down her spine. His arms went around her and he drew her close, and held her tightly against him. Of their own volition, her arms encircled him as well, and the moment they did, she felt the hard press of him against her.

Instead of being shocked, she found it terribly arousing, and she saw no reason to pretend she was insulted or that she was not attracted to him. He was still watching her, and without realizing, at first, that she did so, she lifted her hand and stroked the curve of skin beneath his high cheekbone, before continuing on to let her fingertips trace the fullness of his lips.

She could feel his breath on her cheek, and then suddenly he was kissing her, a deep, searching kiss. He cupped her face, teasing her earlobes while his mouth continued to assault hers, probing, seeking, questioning and highly erotic. Passion shot through her like a cannonball, laying waste to everything, to the point that she felt her knees buckle and the answering tightening of his arms, which slipped around her to keep her there with him. She never knew it was possible to feel desire in so many different parts of her body, for it seemed like a well-coordinated machine that was grinding away and making great strides to reach a goal that yawned like a great abyss in the distance.

And the words of Dante came creeping into her mind… *Abandon hope, all ye who enter here.*

Thankfully, for both of them, he chose that moment to break the kiss. "I wish I had either a stronger conscience or a weaker one, because you are both so innocent and damnably seductive."

He was smiling down at her, and then kissed her lightly on the nose. "I was not sure if you would kiss me back or slap my face for taking such liberties in broad daylight."

"If I had slapped you, I would not have gotten my kiss, now, would I?"

His laugh was thunderous. "You are a pert and saucy wench, I will grant you that."

She was wishing he would grant her a lot of things, but she couldn't tell him that, of course. All she knew was, she enjoyed kissing him immensely, and was thinking of little else at the moment. Her heart pounded in a manner that kept interfering with the rhythm of her breathing. It seemed that whenever she was around him, everything went slightly off kilter.

He captured her hand in his and held it to his lips, while he pressed a kiss to each of her fingertips.

"Would it be...?"

He waited a moment, then asked, "Would it be what?"

"Scandalous," she said.

"How do you mean?"

"Would it be scandalous if I told you I have thought about being with you like this many times since I saw you in France? I found myself praying that the curse of Lord Walter would be lifted from me, so I might allow myself the luxury of responding to you in the way I feel inside, not in the disciplined, self-denying way I know I must follow. I understand that this outrageous exposé contains thoughts that could be damaging to my reputation."

"Only if they were used by someone with an intent to hurt you, which I would never do. You are a woman of strong and sincere emotion. To open your heart to another is never scandalous. There are more choices to consider in a romance between a man and a woman than silence or scandal."

She placed her head against his chest, and allowed her hands to wander freely over the tight musculature of his back, much in the same manner his hands did to her. It had been so long since she had felt safe and peaceful enough not to search about for a sign, a presence, a shadow, an old enemy that could disguise himself and step out of the darkness and drive a dagger into the heart of another human being.

She knew she was walking on boggy ground and that she could be sucked under at any moment. She wanted to see where this mutual attraction would go, but she could not. She must be on her guard. She must never allow anyone else to suffer death in her place again.

She had to see this for what it was, two people who might have loved each other had they met at a different time. He was like no man she had ever known, and she realized she was beginning to fall in love with him. But she would never tell him, any more than she would let her tender feelings for him progress to full bloom.

She would allow herself only this one time—until they reached Durness Castle—to feel alive, young and carefree, and to open her heart, but when they reached Durness, she would send him away, and out of her life.

She sighed and hugged him tighter, enjoying the thought that for now, he was here and he was hers. There was such strength beneath her fingers, and she could feel a surge of power flowing into her from him. It left her feeling restless, and desirous of all he could show her.

When she gazed into his eyes, she felt an instant connection with him, as if they had known each other forever. She would almost swear he knew her thoughts. "Will you kiss me, just this once, like you would if we were the only two people left on earth?"

She had expected a wild, passionate mating, but his lips touched hers softly, and with much tenderness, and then, as quickly, they were gone, and she felt the emptiness inside as acutely as the cool kiss of air where only a moment ago had been the warm weight of his lips against hers.

"I care for you," he whispered against her mouth, "too damnably much, and it has happened way too fast."

The visual kiss of her skin sent an eddy of pleasure across her, and she wondered what it would be like to lie with him and feel the drugging weight of his body move over hers. How would his hard muscles play against her own feminine softness? What would it do to her to know the touch of tempered-steel thighs pressing between hers, offering the exquisite promise of his body, the refined cruelty of its denial?

His lips came again, and this time they covered hers tenderly and moved with slow, sweet languor, a kiss that was gentle, yet swept through her with brutal effect. She responded to him as if her body could not get close enough to his, or her mouth feel the probing heat of his kiss long enough.

Paralyzing, dizzying seconds ticked by, like smoke rings, each one looping into the other, like a chain that held them one to the other.

The future seemed to well up inside her, tinted with purple hues and full of rainbow bubbles that threatened to carry her away, and for a thin slice of time, she knew that if he were to ask her to sail away with him she would have gone.

But the present has a way playing the bully, by elbowing its way brutally against the fragile links that connect the future with the past. The moment was shattered, and her hopes of ever knowing what it would be like to make love to him fell like tinkling glass around her feet, and she knew, sooner or later, this thing between them would end.

The sound of voices passing by reached them, and reality set in. She tilted her head to look at him, and was surprised to hear him say, "It's not over, no matter what you think. This is one thing that will not end before it has begun. Remember that."

He offered her his arm and they went around the corner and started down Broad Street, in the opposite direction to where Josette and Alejandro had gone earlier.

"I wanted to walk this way, so I can send a couple of my men back to the inn to get your things. Do you have it all packed?"

"Yes, all three dresses. It took ever so long to do."

"Brat," he said, and laughed. "Does anyone ever get the best of you?"

"Josette does all the time," she said, "but I always find a way to get even."

She noticed a skiff, its bow resting on the sand. Three men were waiting beside it. "Are those your men?"

"Yes."

"Go ahead and speak with them. I will wait here." What she did not tell him was how much it pleasured her to watch him walk in that long-legged, loose-hipped way he had of moving that made her ache with desire for him and filled her with a sweet languor.

"We've been looking for you."

Kenna turned around at the sound of Josette's voice

and she smiled at Alejandro. "I am sorry I did not have an opportunity to speak with you earlier. It is good to see you again, although I must say it took me a while to get over the shock of seeing you and Colin here. Kirkwall does not have the same draw as Paris."

Alejandro looked her over, and then did the same with Josette. "I could never agree with that. From where I stand, I see it has a great deal more to offer."

Kenna had to confess the compliment was well received, but her attention soon settled upon Colin, who was laughing at something as he stood talking to his men. She knew she would never grow tired of looking at him, or listening to the uplifting sound of his laughter, and while she drank in the sight of him, she was dreamily recalling every moment of the kisses they shared, all the more precious because of their scarcity.

# *Fifteen*

Journeys end in lovers meeting.
—William Shakespeare (1564–1616),
English poet and playwright.
*Twelfth Night* (1600-1608), Act II, Scene 3.

It was late afternoon by the time everyone was aboard *Dancing Water,* ready to set sail for the last leg of their journey to Durness Castle.

Up on deck of the sloop, Kenna and Josette sat upon a huge coil of hemp rope. This put both of them out of the way, yet gave them the opportunity to enjoy secondhand the excitement of preparing the ship for sail.

She considered it her good fortune to not only see Colin, but be able to watch a man who tackled his work with dedicated enjoyment. This unique experience helped her understand why an adventuresome life appealed to him. The sea holds a place in every Scot's heart, she thought, so it must be something he inherited from his father and grandfather.

It was easy to see it held a place in his heart. She knew too well life at sea was not all romance, for it could be a mystical, sometimes miserable existence, where motivation came from the sound and sight of the ocean; the power of a ship skimming over the waves.

She observed how he moved aboard ship with as much grace and assurance as he did on land, whether standing at the helm or climbing the rigging, which he did with the skill and agility of an acrobat, for he was quick and nimble, with a sense of balance that bespoke a body in perfect harmony with itself.

Her reverie was suddenly interrupted by a shout from the top of the mast that a large sloop was anchored off the coast, and had launched two rowboats that were coming straight toward them.

Kenna was happy the weather was warmer today, and the wind not as strong. Colin wore neither his cape nor his jacket, but seemed perfectly comfortable in his customary white shirt, tight brown pants and tall boots. She was thinking he looked quite splendid, but she put the thought away, for at that moment, he appeared right in front of her. He looked much better up close.

"I must order both of you to go below and stay there." And then, as if he knew how much Kenna would chafe at being confined to quarters, he smiled down at her, and his tone softened. "I regret the inconvenience, but due to the approaching boats, it will be necessary for both of you to remain out of sight. I have instructed Mr. Cooper to escort you to my cabin, where you will at least get a glimpse of the boats through the windows.

Mr. Cooper will remain there with you until it is deemed safe for you to return topside."

He gave them a courteous bow, then Mr. Cooper asked that they lead the way. He fell in step behind them, until they reached Colin's cabin. He unlocked the door and ushered them inside. "The captain said to make yourselves comfortable. I will be standing guard outside the door. Should you need anything, you've only to knock."

Kenna looked around the cabin and recalled that day in Edinburgh when she first saw Colin sitting behind his desk, quite inebriated but still charming. As she looked around the cabin, she decided nothing had really changed, except her.

When they heard the click of the door behind them, Kenna and Josette made for the open portholes, to observe the approaching boats and speculate about what it all meant.

On deck, Colin had his eye to the glass. There were nine men in all—four crewmen in each boat, and another man who was probably a ship's officer. It appeared each of the boats also carried a chest. All the men were armed, but not heavily.

Colin closed the glass and handed it to Alejandro. "They are nine men in all, plus two sea chests. If she was flying colors, she has struck them. The ship's name I could not make out. I saw nothing to give a clue as to why they are coming toward us. It is a 'wait and see scenario.' Tell the men to arm themselves, and send Mr. Cunningham below to ready the cannons to fire on command, and pray like hell we don't have to give that order."

It turned out to be a French brig, the *Marie Claire*, hired by Spaniards at Cadiz and then sailed to Veracruz and Havana. "We were on our way to Sweden, when we were fortunate enough to outrun two British war ships, only to encounter a British man o' war half an hour later," the captain explained. "They engaged us in a fight and we were heavily damaged, with a cracked main mast. We were fortunate that it was late in the day when they went at us, so it grew dark quickly. We managed to escape into the night, and made it this far before the rough seas further damaged our mast and it gave way and toppled into the sea. But luckily the current brought us in far enough that we could drop anchor."

"And your reason for coming to my ship?" Colin asked.

Captain Pierre Antoine Laurent seemed quite ready with an answer. "Please believe me, Captain, I have no interest whatsoever in the cargo of the *Marie Claire*, which belongs entirely to the Spaniards. Our cargo consists of sixty-five chests of silver, five barrels of cochineal, fifty-seven of indigo, one case of vanilla, sixty cases of sugar, and thirty-five hundred cow hides. I have brought with me two chests full of silver, one of which I will give to you, Captain, if you will take us wherever you are going."

Colin agreed and the two chests and nine men boarded *Dancing Water.* At the helm, Colin said to Alejandro, "Get word to the men to keep an eye on our guests. I don't trust the bastards. I think they have designs on sending us to the bottom of the sea and sailing off with my ship and the Spanish silver."

"Why did you agree to take them with us?"

"I would bet this ship that they have their big guns trained on us, and if we don't agree they will blow us out of the water. At anchor like this, we are like birds on a fence. I figure we have them outnumbered, and if they try anything, we have the better chance of over-powering them and may end up with two chests of silver instead of one."

"We could do with two chests of silver," Alejandro said.

Colin ignored that. "Make sure the men stay armed, put a double guard at my cabin door and tell the women to lock it from the inside."

Alejandro started off and Colin called him back. "One more thing, tell Mr. Higgins to put their rowboats in tow, and try to have a serious face about it."

With an unfurling of sails that immediately caught the breeze, they set sail. They were approaching the *Marie Claire,* riding at anchor, when Captain Laurent came to speak to Colin.

"*Monsieur le Capitaine,* if I might have a word with you." The words were barely out of his mouth when he swiftly extracted a dagger from his pocket and pressed it against Colin's ribs.

"A slight change of plans, *Monsieur le Capitaine.*"

"You are so right," Colin said, at the exact moment Alejandro came up behind the Frenchman and, with a tap to his head, put the Frenchman down for a nice nap. Colin's crew then kicked into action and made equally prompt dispatch of the eight men that had accompanied Captain Laurent.

Once they were out in deeper water and past the *Marie Claire,* Colin said, "Load the captain and his men into their boats. They should be back aboard their ship in time to greet the British man o' war when she comes looking for them."

It wasn't until they sailed around the tip of John o' Groat's that Colin allowed the women back on deck, and then wished he hadn't, for he was hit with a round of questions from both of them, which he politely answered by pointing them in Alejandro's direction.

They sailed on past John o' Groat's not far from Dunnet Head, and through the Pentland Firth, with the northeast point of Scotland on their left and the Orkney Islands to their right, heading toward the Atlantic Ocean.

Kenna overheard Colin tell Mr. Porter, "The sea is unusually smooth, and the wind dead aft. I think this would be a good time to have a look at those chests our French friends left us. Pick enough men to move the chests over here."

Mr. Porter gave him the respectful "Aye, aye, Captain," and departed. They watched several men move the chests, before Josette, already beginning to feel the queasiness in her stomach, decided to return to the cabin so she could lie down before the worst of the seasickness was upon her.

Kenna insisted upon going with her, so she could see her comfortably settled. "Then I will come back on deck."

"Stay here and see what is in the chest," Josette protested. "If they start giving away jewels, grab a handful for me. Don't worry. I'll be fine."

The deck was alive with men moving and others talking among themselves as the chests were pushed and shoved, and sometimes carried into place, while the men grunted and breathed heavily with the effort. Kenna, meanwhile, found it pleasant to lean her head back, for she loved the feel of the wind-scented sea spray on her face as the ship skimmed over the tops of the waves like a soaring gull, and while the canvas sails flapped overhead as they caught the wind. When Kenna closed her eyes, the sounds on deck seemed magnified, and she tried to associate what she heard with what she imagined was happening.

Her reverie was broken when Josette said, "I decided to come back." She sat down beside Kenna.

Kenna opened one surprised eye and then the other. "Are you feeling better? That was awfully fast."

"No, I still feel the same, but I want to see what is in those chests."

"Mr. de Calderón, will you open the chests and let us see if we have Spanish silver or a load of rocks," Colin said.

Alejandro broke the locks on both chests, and threw back the lid on the first one.

A synchronized gasp rose from the crew. Kenna and Josette could not see over the heads of the crew, so Kenna stood on top of the rope coil to see what caused such surprise. The chests did not contain silver. "They are full of gold," Kenna cried. "Filled to the top, they are."

"*Sacre bleu!*" Josette said, prompted now to clamber up beside Kenna to have a look for herself. "Dare we hope the captain shares with us some of his rich bounty?"

"Don't go spend it just yet" was Kenna's advice.

It had grown awfully quiet on the ship, while everyone stood silently staring at enough gold to rival that of King Midas.

With all eyes on the two chests, Kenna thought for a moment that if anyone dared dip as much as their little finger in either one, they would probably find themselves tossed overboard. The moment stretched painfully thin, and something was sure to snap, unless someone spoke up soon.

That someone turned out to be Alejandro, for he came right out with the question every man there wanted an answer to. "What are we going to do with all this gold?"

Kenna focused on Colin with eyes of stern disapproval. Yes, she thought, what are you going to do with all that gold, Captain Montgomery? Would he buy himself a shipping line with it? Or build a mansion in America to house his beautiful wife and a dozen offspring? Or would he have a ship built that would put all the royal barges in the world to shame, and simply spend his life sailing from port to port, with a different woman waiting for him at each stop?

She hated to be so cynical, but she had seen too many times what money did to honest people. Wealth was too often a place where vipers bred. It brought out the worst in people. She knew it was quite possible an argument could break out, and perhaps fighting, too, along with it. As for her, she wanted no part of the scavengers that would come in after the kill.

She turned, ready to go back to the cabin, when Josette caught her by the arm, and when Kenna looked at her to see why she stopped her, Josette tilted her head toward the gathering, indicating Kenna should look there for her answer.

Kenna's gaze barely had time to settle on Colin when he spoke. "Mr. de Calderón, you will see that every man on the ship receives twenty gold pieces, and that includes yourself. The rest we will leave with my grandfather, Baron Fairlie, who will see that it is distributed to the poorest Highlanders, including the widows and orphans of those lost at Culloden, and passage for those who lost everything and want to emigrate. It will be deposited safely in the bank, and Baron Fairlie will contact the lairds of every clan to meet in Inverness, so we may come up with a list of those who need and deserve it most."

Kenna was stunned, and on the heels of that came shame. She had judged him falsely, and based it upon nothing but her own cynicism. When had he ever shown a side of himself to her that was not honorable and just? She had judged him…wrongly judged him, and she was sorry for it to the depth of her being.

She realized that the crew seemed pleased with his decision, and most of them took time to tell him so, for they had seen firsthand the devastation that was the Highlands. She could understand now why his men held him in such high regard. He was obviously a man who lived his life according to his values, with a fine respect for intelligence, justice, responsibility and consideration for those less fortunate.

She watched him move among the men, as Alejandro counted out their gold coins, and admired his smooth and easy way. It left her with the feeling that he was comfortable with his skin and everything beneath it. He was friendly, easy to be around, quick to laugh, slow to anger, with a fondness for humor. And those striking blue eyes—with the fine mind behind them, and a good heart a few inches below…

Colin spotted her sitting on the coil of hemp and started toward her. He realized when he reached her that although she was there, her mind was somewhere else. He did not speak but was content to wait her out, and see how long it was before she wanted to include him, if at all.

It took her longer than he expected, before she realized he was standing there. She jumped, and looked up to meet his gaze. He saw there an expression he had not yet noticed in her eyes and he gave her a quizzically puzzled look in return.

He sat down beside her. "I was wondering where you were, or if you were even going to come back and join the here and now."

She turned her head to look out over the vastness of water, as if she was considering something, before she turned back and said, "If you must know, I was chastising myself for thinking you would hoard the gold, and then, when I heard what you said about taking it to your grandfather to distribute to the poor Highlanders, I realized I could not have been more wrong, nor more unprincipled, in judging you. You have proved you are not only aware of the Highlanders' plight, but you are also sympathetic to it. I can only say, it made me feel incredibly small."

It was his turn to remain silent and look off, for he was equally surprised that she would think poorly of him, and even more so that she would admit it and cast herself in a less desirable light.

"I know you are angry. You have a perfect right to be, for no one likes to be misjudged and accused falsely."

He shook his head. "To the contrary. I was thinking how it is quite remarkable that you told me. Not many could admit such, or serve as their own judge and jury, and pass down a severe sentence along on themselves, as you did. Admission of a wrong is never easy."

"I am sorry I misjudged you, and hope you will forgive me for it."

He grinned at her. "I seem to remember a time when a half-frozen lass appeared out of a snowstorm and landed smack in the middle of my ship. I think I did a pretty good job of misjudging her...although I did justify it a bit by being head-splittingly, knee-wobblingly drunk at the time. I figure the two cancel each other out, but if it is forgiveness you need, then I will forgive you, but only if you will do the same for me. Agreed?"

"Agreed," she said, and matched his smile with one of her own.

She was watching him and he could almost hear the grinding of her mental gears, and he nearly laughed out loud at the way she wrinkled up her nose and squinted her eyes and asked, "Are you married, or have you ever been married?"

Well, now, that *did* knock the wind out of his sails. To say her question surprised him was a bit mild, for it took a moment for it to settle, and when it did, he gave a shout of laughter.

"I find I am always trying to decide just where it is that you are coming from. My mother always told me that I would save myself a lot of grief if I remembered a woman's mind did not work the way a man's did. She also pointed out that I had a mother and three sisters I could observe and use to hone my skill in dealing with females. I always thought I did a fair job of it, but your question has cast a dark cloud of doubt over my ability now. What made you ask a question like that? Do you honestly think I would have shown my obvious attraction to you if I had a wife twiddling her thumbs back in America, waiting for her philanthropic husband to come home? Do you see me as a man who corrupts people by encouraging them to behave immorally, especially in an unrestrained and self-indulgent way?"

"Well, that was certainly a mouthful, but no, I was trying to learn more about you. I had a feeling you weren't married, but I thought it best to be certain. One can never be too careful about these things."

"Why? Were you thinking about asking for my hand?"

"Don't be silly. I have no designs on you whatsoever. However, if you were married, I would not be sitting here now, talking to you."

He watched the way her cheeks grew slowly red,

and how the faint throb of a pulse at her throat became more prominent.

To ease her embarrassment, he said, "No, I'm not married, but I do come from a nice, loving and big family. Does that help?"

"Your parents, are they alive?"

"Yes, both of them. My father, Alexander, is a farmer by blood and a lawyer by vocation. I grew up on the banks of the Potomac River. My parents still live there. My mother, Henrietta, was a Claiborne before they married, so I have a large number of relations on her side. I think you know that my father was born in Scotland, and left there because he fell in love with my beautiful and gentle American-born mother, and he did not get along with his father."

"Who is Sir Hugh Montgomery, the twelfth Baron of Fairlie, and lives in Caithness."

"Good memory, you have. As for the rest of my family, I have two brothers. Davidson, who is younger, is unmarried and probably always will be."

"Why do you say that?"

He laughed. "He is an astronomer and scientist… now, what woman would want to spend the rest of her life gazing at stars and living in a house that smelled of sulphur?"

"Tell me about the rest of them."

"My brother Henry is the oldest of my siblings. He is a Presbyterian minister, married with four children. My oldest sister, Winifred, whom we call Winny, is married to an idiot, Charles Marcus Prudhomme De-Witt the Fourth, who deserves a whole chapter to himself, so I won't go into how he is unequivocally an idiot, just now. They are blessed with three little idiots, and one little angel, who doesn't seem to belong there—stork error or something." He chuckled. "My minister brother always frowns when I say that, so I keep saying it just to irritate him."

"I would have never pegged you as the type."

"Oh, I was a little hellion in my younger days. My mother prefers the term 'imp.' As I was saying, my sister Winny and her husband, Charles Marcus Prudhomme DeWitt the Fourth, live in Maryland, which is not far enough away. My sister Julia is two years younger than I, and is engaged to an Italian count, Conte Andrea Visconti, whom I genuinely like. They will live in Bologna after they wed. And the youngest member of the family, Emma Helene, is busy being distraught because she isn't being courted, and mourns the fact that she will be an old maid. I might add, she was born beautiful and hasn't changed, and she is only fourteen."

Kenna smiled at that. "You are fortunate to have such a lovely family, and even more blessed that your parents are still with you."

"Yes, I am, and also blessed that they are extraordinarily remarkable parents."

"You are close, like a small clan."

"I had not thought of it that way, but it is an excellent analogy, for like clan members, we share a common ancestor, the same last name, and we are headed by a chief. And we stick together…even to the point of tolerating the idiot Winny foisted upon us."

When she stopped laughing, she asked, "If I were to ask your family to tell me one thing about you, what would it be?"

He smiled, not even having to think about that one. "My parents always said, 'Colin was born ready to lead others.' I was told that from an early age I was an organizer. My mother said I commandeered the nursery and held my siblings prisoner, and wouldn't let them come down to dinner until they lined up and marched, single file, with me in the lead, of course."

"You did not outgrow it, I see."

"Apparently not, for I seem to have a natural urge to give structure and direction wherever and whenever. I remember when I was twelve, I tried directing my father's workers and almost caused a revolt."

"Where did you get your love of the sea, and why privateering?"

"I think I told you that I grew up on the banks of the Potomac River in Virginia. When I was twelve I had my own sailboat and sailed up Chesapeake Bay, which I thought was wonderful. I forgot to tell my mother, which wasn't so wonderful, and my father sold my sailboat because of it. I suppose the biggest reason was my uncle, who is my mother's brother, Henry Claiborne, is in shipping…*big* shipping. I spent a great deal of time with him and my cousins when I was growing up. I suppose over time I developed a love of the sea, but I like to think I was born with it."

"Your uncle is a privateer?"

He laughed. "Hardly. He is too dignified for that, and he scolds me severely about it each time I go home."

"What made you become a privateer?"

He gave her a serious look. "I'm not a full-fledged privateer, you understand."

"Yes, you are only a privateer when it suits you."

"Exactly. I only become one when the circumstances arise, as they did today with the French captain."

"When was the first time?"

"You might say I fell into it. I captained a ship for my uncle and took a cargo to Edinburgh a few years ago. While I was still in Edinburgh, making ready to set sail for home, I was approached by four Jacobite gentlemen who wanted me to take them to France. I agreed, and on the way, we were attacked by a Spanish ship. We won the battle, I commandeered the ship, dropped the crew off in Portugal, sailed her home and gave the ship to my uncle."

"But, *Dancing Water* doesn't belong to your uncle, right?"

"No. This sweet little craft is all mine."

"It is a beautiful vessel."

"Beautiful and fast. She draws such a small amount of water there is hardly a place she cannot go. One hundred and sixty tons, armed with eight six-caliber brass guns, two howitzers aft, and two six-pound cohorns on the taffrail."

Kenna looked up at him and intentionally crossed her eyes, and he wanted to kiss her so much at that moment it took every ounce of his resolve to keep from doing it. Instead he laughed. "You know, my father always told us if we crossed our eyes like that, they might get stuck that way."

"Do you still cross your eyes?"

"No, I never learned how, except by putting a finger up and bringing it toward my nose, like this, and following it with my eyes until they cross. I was the only one in the family who couldn't do it. Lots of teasing on that one."

Colin noticed Alejandro signaling to him, and he was sorry to have to end the conversation with her. "Alejandro wants me to relieve him at the helm, so he can go below and play with his maps and charts." He stood and picked up her hand and kissed it, not on the top, but by turning it over and kissing her wrist. "I have enjoyed this visit with you."

He noticed the evening sun was striking her in a way that made her look as if she belonged in a holy shrine. "You are beautiful with the sun setting fire to your hair like that. If you continue to tempt me, I may decide to make you my sea wench and sail away with you."

"I'm not the easiest sea wench to get along with. I am certain you would be returning me in less than twenty-four hours."

"Don't tempt me, lass, to prove you wrong." With a smile and a quick nod, he departed.

After he was gone, she remained sitting on the coil of rope for quite some time, lost in the reverie of her own thoughts...thoughts of Colin...of Durness, her grandfather's castle, the family she missed, the *comte*'s death, and the new life that awaited her a few miles down the coastline.

And as always, she thought of Lord Walter and wondered where he was right now.

Being back in Scotland was difficult for her, for it was home and synonymous with family. She wondered what new babies had been born, and if her younger sisters were in love, or perhaps married. And her biggest concern, after the loneliness she felt over her separation from them and how deeply she missed them, was would they ever forgive her for leaving as she had?

She realized there were good things that had come out her decision to leave Scotland. The dear face of the *comte* rose up before her, and Josette's, too, and the *duc*'s, the *comte*'s and the *vicomte*'s, and Alejandro's. Colin she placed in a class by himself, for her feelings for him were different, and more fragile. She was glad they met again in Kirkwall, and pleased someone of his stature and strength was taking her to Durness.

Alejandro came toward her and seated himself in the spot Colin had vacated. "Tell me, where is your friend, Josette?"

"She is probably as sick as two dogs about now."

"Do you mean, *mal de mer?*"

"Oh, yes. She was sick most of the way coming from Calais, so she went straight to bed when we set sail. I think I should go check on her."

"Come back and tell me how she is doing."

Kenna smiled and put her hands on her hips. "And why should I be doing that, Señor de Calderón?"

His eyes sparkled. "I prefer to keep that a secret from both of you."

"You best be careful. Josette is not someone you want on your bad side."

He laughed. "She is only that way because she has not met the man who can love her the way she was meant to be loved."

"And that man is you, right?"

"Could be," he said. "But we will have to wait and see."

Kenna found Josette was just waking up when she entered the room. Kenna could tell by her expression what she needed; she grabbed a basin and handed it to her.

After a few minutes, Josette gave it back to her. "I am dying," she said, "and I will never get on another ship, which means I cannot return to France, unless I sprout wings. I don't understand why you don't get sick."

"I think I'm too stubborn."

"Don't make me laugh, it makes my head hurt. Arrrgghh…" she said, and lay back in the hammock. Kenna noticed her face was a peculiar shade of pea-green.

Colin turned the wheel over to Mr. Porter when he saw Josette come on deck, with a wobbly walk and a pale face.

He stopped to speak to her for a moment, and inquire how she was feeling.

"As if I've been run over by a herd of horses, but thankfully the worst is over, I hope." She glanced around. "Where is Kenna?"

"She went to see about you and did not come back. She must still be in the cabin. I'm going down and will see where she is."

"You better be glad the *comte* isn't here. He would have a problem with that, you know. He was quite protective of her."

"Are you trying to tell me he would not approve?"

"No, only that he would not be quick to decide. Once he sensed your interest in her, he would have to figure out if you were worthy of his trust, or if you were good enough for her."

"And you? What do you think?"

She drew her finger down the side of his face and laughed. "I think Kenna will make up her own mind, independently, and not based on another's bias."

"I cannot ask for more than that, can I?"

She gave him a flirtatious look, then laughed. "I think I feel up to a cup of coffee," she said, evading his question with aplomb.

Colin watched her go. She had a nice walk...a *really* nice walk, and an even nicer swing to her hips. He shook his head. The man who desired her would have his work cut out for him, in a big way.

He turned around and saw Alejandro was watching her as well. Colin shook his head. Would the two of them be a good combination, or would their hotblooded ways end up pushing them apart? It was too early to tell, he decided.

Kenna came on deck, and stopped to talk to him. Alejandro caught up with Josette, and soon the sound of his laughter drifted over the ship.

Kenna had a cup in her hands, and spent some time looking over the side of the ship before Colin came to stand beside her. She sipped her tea, and the two of them began talking about her time in France, and Lord Walter's horrible impact on her, her family and her life. They talked about the reason she went to France, and the family she missed so much; how difficult it was to go to Durness Castle without seeing any of her sisters.

"When was the last time you visited?"

"Goodness, I don't know...I was quite young...nine or ten, perhaps younger. What I remember most was my grandfather, a giant of a man, with obvious Norse blood. He was my mother's father, you know, and all I remember about him was his red beard and bright blue eyes that always seemed to be shining like little lights, strung together with mischief."

"So that is where you get it," he said.

She smiled but remained silent.

"Who owns the castle now?"

"I do. My mother was well entailed and possessed many properties...at least enough to see that each of her daughters received something of their own."

"Who has been taking care of things since your grandfather died?"

"The MacKays have a strong clan. They have kept it in order for me, and once a year, one of them comes to Inchmurrin to give me a report on it. My father managed that part of it until he died."

"After such an absence, I hope there is still a stone left."

"It will be in decent shape. The MacKays would not allow it to fall into ruin. Family pride, you know."

"Oh, so that's where it comes from…MacKay pride and red hair?"

"There is red hair in both my mother and father's family," she said with a hint of stubbornness in her voice. "The MacKays and the Sutherlands."

"Oh dear," he said.

"What do you mean, oh dear? You had best be careful, for some ancestors come back as ghosts to haunt those who are disrespectful."

"I meant no disrespect to your ancestors. I was only thinking some of our children will undoubtedly have red hair…perhaps all of them."

"Oh, it is children we will be having, is it? And spoken as if I have no say in the matter at all." Her eyes sparkled like fire, and there was raw passion in her voice. "Our children! Bah! And more fool you! Are you daft? You must be to talk that way. Why, I have only met you, and here you are planning to have children with me, as if all it takes is a simple declaration. You had best be revising your plans for the future, for there is no marriage with you in mine."

"You can have a say in the matter of children. You can name them."

"You can go to the de'il! I believe you call it *devil* in America, although I do not know why you don't recognize the name. I am certain he must be a close relative of yours."

Colin watched her stomp off, amused at how easily riled she could get about certain subjects. She was both passionate and fierce, a lot like her beloved Highlands, so wild and uncharted, with ironbound cliffs, swirling whirlpools, hard winds and rough seas, and yet she had in her a reserve of romance, which saw her through life's hardships and perils, so she could find beauty and happiness in the thunderous crash of breakers, the haunting silence of desolate moors.

There were not many like her, who could accept the life of a resident recluse, in a lonely castle that hugged a cliff at the farthest end of Scotland, and find satisfaction in a meal of nettle soup and cold lobster, surrounded by people timid as sheep and ignorant as limpets, and through it all, stick like a burr.

# *Sixteen*

Half to forget the wandering and the pain,
Half to remember days that have gone by,
And dream and dream that I am home again.
—James Elroy Flecker (1884-1915),
English poet, playwright and novelist.
*Collected Poems,* "Brumana" (1916).

*Durness Castle, Cape Wrath, Scotland*

The sky was growing darker, which made it difficult to see Alejandro and Colin where they stood together at the ship's bow. Kenna and Josette sat with their heads tilted back, studying the vast blackness overhead, amazed at the clear sky and abundance of stars. They placed bets as to which of them could identify the most constellations, and discovered they were both equally terrible at the task.

At last, the need for sleep sent them belowdecks for

the night. Josette dropped off almost instantly, but Kenna remained awake for a long time, gazing upon the moonlight that stole quietly into their cabin, while her thoughts focused upon the gaping jaws of the unknown that lay ahead.

When she fell asleep at last, her slumber was shortlived, for the frequent banging of the sheet blocks on the foredeck ended any ideas she or Josette might have had about a quiet night. Cruelly jerked from deep slumber into groggy wakefulness, they both shot into a sitting position at the sound of a loud, booming crash.

"What was that?" Josette asked.

Kenna listened for a moment. "I don't know, but it sounded frightfully close to the ship," Kenna replied, then added, "way to close."

"It sounded like a tree crashing through the roof during a storm," Josette said.

"I know, only we don't have any trees out here, so it had to be a part of the ship. I hope we haven't lost a mast. I'm going to have a look." Kenna slipped out of bed and took up her cape.

"You aren't going on deck, are you? It could be dangerous."

"If so, I will come back. I only want to find out what happened, and whether we should remain calm or jump into the briny deep."

"Well, that is a pleasant thought," Josette said. "Thank you very much."

Kenna smiled to herself. "You can think upon that while I am gone."

Kenna encountered Colin the moment she stepped on deck.

"I was coming down to check on you," he said.

"It is comforting to know you didn't jump overboard and leave the rest of us to fend for ourselves."

"If I went overboard, it would be with you tucked safely under my arm."

His words were touching by virtue of the fact that there were two kinds of truth, one that revealed, and one that warmed the heart, and by his declaration, he had done both.

"What happened?" she asked, gazing toward the place where most of the crew had gathered.

"A sail lashing fell through the open hatch," he said. "There is quite a bit of damage, but it's nothing life-threatening."

But her line of thinking was taking a different direction. "It is an evil omen," she said, and suddenly felt bereft and full of apprehension.

"Don't worry your superstitious self about it. We are fine…the ship is in no danger. The worst part is, once we drop anchor, we will not be able to leave until the repairs are made. The best part is no harm will come to you."

"How do you know that it won't?"

He wrapped his arms around her and whispered the answer against her hair. "Because I won't allow anything to harm even one of these priceless red strands on your head."

She knew misfortune would come whether he let it or not, but there was something comforting in hearing

Colin speak so. It made her feel all warm and sleepy inside, and for the first time in many years, safe.

Colin was rubbing her back, and she found she liked it enough to allow him to continue, until he suddenly said, "Oh, lord…"

She pulled back. "What's wrong?"

"I just realized that you don't have anything on beneath your cloak, other than your nightgown."

"I was asleep when I heard the crash. Do you expect me to sleep in my clothes?"

"Just the opposite. I was thinking a gown was too much."

"You are too much," she said, and moved away from him, but he caught her and led her into a dark corner behind the mizzenmast, where it was dark and quiet and hidden from view.

Her breathing quickened. "I should go back."

He pulled her closer, and she felt as if she was stepping into the unknown, but she followed, blind and trusting. She knew she should not go with him, yet knew that she wanted this as much as he, for it had been so difficult being around him, on his ship like this, and never having a moment alone to share her need with him.

Fabric rustled in darkness as her cloak brushed against him, when he stepped closer. Half hidden by the surrounding darkness, she could see little more than deep shadow and shades of light. His arms went around her, and he eased her back until she felt something solid against her spine. His hands were on her face, her throat, her shoulders and then skimming lightly over her breasts to encircle her waist. He held her as if afraid to let her go, and the thrill of knowing it left her breathless and wanting more.

She opened her mouth and drew in a breath of air, only to feel the shock of the penetrating warmth of his kiss. She felt every point of pressure of his body, knew the places where he was hard and soft, while her own body throbbed with unfamiliar yearning. She did not push against him or pretend she did not want this as much as he. They were simply two people who met as equals, in desire, honesty and lack of pretense.

She was warmed by the thought that he wanted to be with her like this, and that he had yearned to have a moment to share the loving caresses, the stolen kisses that every young couple strives to have, and finds so difficult to achieve. She was weakened by the nameless desire that gripped her. She felt emboldened by the absence of shame, and the thrill of being secreted like this, of being in the dark with him, as if he were a stranger that came to her like a thief, who stepped out of the shadows of the night. The urge to be with him coursed through her, silent, swift and as deep as an underground river.

She had a vague thought that she should return to her cabin, but the perfume of seduction came, like a quickened breath, and held her here, and she stayed where she was. He kissed her again, more firmly this time, a kiss that held a question she was afraid to answer.

New awareness. Unknown yearning. Burning desire. A flowing inward, into herself, and she was swept along by a spiraling curl of need that was warm, and growing warmer, until it melted, as a candle left too long in the sun.

She knew the warm texture of his mouth, his taste, the smell of his breath, the curl of sensation at his touch, and the spirit of the night came into her and swept her back, far back, into the primitive world where two people stood, naked and full of new knowledge in a long-lost garden, and she knew she wanted to be like that with him—naked, in love and unafraid.

The kiss was long, longer than her thoughts of resistance, but not as long as her desire for more. Everything about him, his ship, the very idea of being on it was surreal to her, as if she stood in a room of mirrors and saw her own reflection on a ghost ship, in the midst of an ocean with mysterious currents that pulled her under. Nothing seemed real. Nothing except the kiss that left a burning reminder imprinted on her lips.

Her hand came up to spread over his chest, a mute show of resistance that was born of the need to touch him, and the moment she did, she found her fingers captured by his and drawn downward to press upon his need.

He broke the kiss and leaned his forehead against hers. "I want to hold you and touch you all over, but I know that we cannot, so we will have to be satisfied with the little moments we can capture. Your mouth is sweet, like nectar," he whispered, his lips touching her mouth, then lower to kiss her throat and shoulders.

Kenna shuddered. "I should go back now." She had difficulty talking for her breathing kept getting in the way.

"I don't think I can let you go. You don't know what it's like to stand at the wheel and watch you, knowing you are so close, and that I cannot hold you."

He kissed her again, and Kenna knew this had to end soon, while they still had the strength to make the choice, and the knowledge of it hit her like cold water, for now she was afraid…not of Colin or what he might do, but of herself, and what she wanted to give him.

"Please," she whispered, "we cannot stay here any longer. I don't want one of your men or Alejandro to see us like this."

"I know, and yet how do I let you go?" He released her and stepped back. "Stay here. I will get the men on deck to help me clear some of the debris from the mast. You will be able to return to your cabin without being seen."

"I hope so," she whispered, "but it is difficult to hide a fire."

His hand caressed her cheek and she turned her head to plant a kiss against his palm. "It will be daylight soon," she said. "I will dress and return in time to watch the sunrise."

"I think you don't want to miss the first glimpse of your grandfather's castle."

She smiled. "That, too," she said, and waited until he had the men working, and then she went below-decks.

Later, as the sun came up, she returned, fully dressed, with her hair tucked up in a braid. He watched her walk, and wondered if Josette had been teaching her how to use her hips to torment a man, because he had not noticed that about Kenna before. It was part of her charm and her attractiveness, to discover, day by day, new revelations about her.

He smiled when she took her customary place on the coil of rope. It occurred to him that he would never be able to gaze upon that spot again, without thinking of it as *Kenna's place*.

Josette joined her half an hour later and the two of them sat quietly talking as they watched the sun rise over the water, turning everything a glorious shade of ruby married to bronze.

Alejandro appeared on deck and mentioned to Colin. "The shoreline is smooth." When Kenna inquired as to what he meant, he replied, "It means I don't see anything I recognize. There are no prominent landmarks. A great deal of sailing is done by landmarks you identify on shore."

"Oh, you are right. I never thought of it from that perspective," she said, studying the coast. "With no promontories or the like, it is impossible to tell precisely where we are, or to gauge our progress."

"Unless I break out all of my fancy equipment and take measurements." And with that, he turned and went back down to his world of maps and charts.

After that, Kenna and Josette waited quietly until Alejandro came on deck again, to gaze carefully up and down the shoreline. "Good," he would say, and then he would turn and go belowdeck again, leaving Kenna and Josette to stare at each other with amazement.

Josette was clearly in a state of confusion resulting

from an inability to understand or to deal with something, but Kenna had no idea what that was. She was certain, though, that it was connected to Alejandro in some way. A clearer understanding of it came with Josette's next words: "The man moves to another level of existence when he is working, for everything else around him seems to disappear. He certainly makes a concentrated effort to focus on his area of responsibility, and here I thought him incapable of such," she said.

After viewing this odd behavior several times, Josette said to Kenna, "I am beginning to find this truly irritating."

"Alejandro, or his frequent trips on deck?"

"Both," she said, "for every time he says *good,* I can neither concur nor argue with him."

"Hmmm…" was Kenna's only response to that, for she spotted a familiar town, and felt her excitement mount. "It's Tongue," she said. "It won't be far to Durness Castle now."

"Tongue?" Josette asked, in a squeamish way. "You mean tongue, as in the mouth?" She shuddered. "What a frightfully awful name for a town…or for anything, for that matter."

"Except a tongue," Kenna said.

Josette shook her head and spoke, as if thinking out loud. "What have I done…going from Paris to Tongue? I must be out of my mind."

"Then be happy we won't be sailing up the estuary to visit it." Kenna was laughing now, for in truth, Tongue did sound awful, and when used in the same sentence with Paris, it sounded quite rustic and backward, which it was. "The good part is, we won't be living there."

"Where will we be living, then? What is the name of the town?"

"There isn't a town, only a big castle on a cliff."

"How far to the nearest town from the castle?"

"That would be Durness, which is a tiny village, smaller than Tongue. You can judge the distance yourself, for Durness is not far from here."

They passed the winding channels and pastel colors of a *benbecula,* or ford, which was the part of the river or tide pool, shallow enough to cross to the other side. Overhead, terns were screaming and diving in a burst of energetic activity.

"A terrible noise," Josette said, watching the raucous birds. "What are they doing?"

"When the tide starts to flow into the sea pools the terns feed upon the eels, and they aren't quiet about it."

"I had no idea it was so primitive and wild here."

"You have only seen the top of the tree."

"It gets worse?"

Kenna answered with a knowing smile.

Josette pointed toward land. "Is that your castle?"

"No, that is the ruin of Castle Varrich. The next thing we see should be Durness, which is very close to Durness Castle."

A moment later, Durness appeared just ahead. It was a tiny village, with a sprinkling of stone cottages. They did not stop at Durness but sailed on past, Kenna's heart pounding wildly. The same could not be said for Josette, who exclaimed, "I have yet to see a *real* city, or even a town. You do have them in Scotland, don't you?"

"Yes, but not many in the Highlands, and almost none this far north."

"It is quite different from France, in both the land and the architecture...or lack of it."

"The Scottish lowlands are more like what you are accustomed to. Here, wood is used sparingly, because trees are scarce. The cottages are made of sturdy rock, the roofs are steep, with a higher pitch. Even the castles look strong and massive, cold and enduring. French and English houses look like they are made from papier-mâché—they are like toys. If you sneeze, they would collapse. They would never withstand our wind or our winters. They would crumple and blow away. And those flat-chested streets...walk them in your sleep, you could."

Kenna looked on amazed as Josette lost herself in a laughing seizure.

"I think it is the desolate scenery that is getting to me," gasped Josette, wiping her eyes. "I feel as if I'm approaching the village of the dead. Is this how insanity begins? You simply start laughing and cannot stop? *Mon Dieu!* I fear they will find me thirty years hence, old, withered and dry as a mummy, my eyes gleaming with madness, all utterance pure gibberish, and I will sit and grin at everyone, with an expression of cunning on my face, while I drink my milk from a wooden bowl."

Josette struggled up and said, "*Sacre bleu!* I am so

weak I cannot stand. Between you and the *mal de mer,* I have lost what little strength I had. I am forced to go to the galley for a roll and a cup of tea."

Colin, who had been observing them for some time, considered Kenna thoughtfully for a moment, then he, too, threw back his head and laughed.

The ship was a noisy center of activity now that the deck had been scrubbed and the planking was dry. Overhead, in the crosstrees of the masts, men were scrambling like spiders to prepare the canvas for when they reached their destination and dropped anchor.

Colin was on the foredeck of the ship, his hair a bit disheveled by the wind, as he talked to Mr. Carlisle, who was asking, "I was wondering, Captain…should we cut the rest of the mast through, so we can remove it once we reach drop anchor?"

Kenna observed how Mr. Carlisle, who had only one eye, had it focused firmly on Colin while he waited for a reply.

"Let me have another look at it, Mr. Carlisle." And the two of them walked off together.

Alejandro was talking to an older man who was mending a sail near the gunwale, and nearby someone called out to "use a rolling hitch, not a clove hitch, you dunce!"

"Well, that's a romantic way to express oneself."

Kenna smiled at Josette, who looked better than she had earlier. She was holding a cup of tea and sipped it slowly.

"You look like you feel better."

"Much better. I like this slower pace we have taken since the mast broke."

Overhead, a sudden burst of good-natured laughter came from the men aloft, and they turned to watch Mr. Porter climb the rigging in his loose-bottomed denim trousers to arm the lead, which Kenna had learned meant to take a sounding of the water's depth.

Unconsciously, Kenna let her gaze search for Colin, and she found him at the stern, but he was difficult to see clearly because she was dazzled by the sunlight's reflection off the brass bell near where he was standing. She remembered seeing it being lovingly polished the day before by one of the older members of the crew, whose name she had yet to learn. By the time the glare from the bell was gone, so was Colin, and a new search located him standing to the fore of the mizzen in a deep discussion over a map Alejandro was holding.

Colin had changed clothes and now looked handsome and distinguished as a ship's captain, dressed in dark blue pants and a jacket of the same color. The effect of it and seeing him in his own world so far removed from hers had a strange and sobering effect on her, for she knew their journey and time together were almost at an end. Once she stepped off the gleaming decks of *Dancing Water,* the fairy tale ended. The security of knowing she was protected and out of Lord Walter's reach would vanish like sea spray, and the young, lighthearted woman he had kissed in the dark shadows would cease to exist. The moment was bittersweet, for she would always remember this man and the time she had had with him, and she would always carry the pain of regret that her circumstances did not allow this attraction they had for each other go further.

Once the soil of Scotland was firm under her foot, there would be no room for Colin or romance in her life. She swallowed and forced back the tears that banked in her eyes. She could not become maudlin or sentimental now. Now she must focus upon one thing: staying alive.

They were almost there, so she moved closer to the railing and stood on tiptoe, to lean out over the rail, in hopes of catching her first glimpse of the magnificent sight of Durness perched on top of a jut of rock, as it looked out upon the Atlantic Ocean, where the loch reached the sea.

A redthroat cried overhead, but she did not bother to look.

She did not know that Colin had returned until she saw Josette turn her head and smile, and then Kenna felt him close behind her, and without thinking, she leaned back into him, while she turned her face to the sun. She could feel the penetrating heat upon her skin, and felt, too, the warmth and the comforting embrace of Colin, holding her firmly at the waist, as if he was only helping her maintain her balance, instead of doing what she knew he wanted, to take her in his arms.

It was a nice feeling…to have a man be so close to her, and she felt a sense of loss when he excused himself, for they were about to drop anchor.

By the time it went rattling over the side and hit the water with a *plop,* the morning mist had burned completely away, to reveal the same sunny day on land that they had enjoyed at sea. Now Kenna stood at the railing beside Josette, who was bursting with questions, while Kenna did not want to talk at all.

She felt strange....

All around her, the air felt weighted and heavy with silence, and the shadows of the past reached out, beckoning and calling her to this ancient place, in the same way her ancestors had been drawn to it centuries before.

She saw the proud face of Durness bravely facing the Atlantic, and the memory of worn stones and roofless towers came forth, haunting in a way that made her wonder. What was it that was disturbing her? Did it come from that part of her she inherited from her parents, the ancient beliefs and ideas that dwelt innately within? Or, was it something as yet unknown?

My mother was born in that stern, imposing place, she thought, as were her ancestors for centuries before. Like Castle Lennox, Durness was built as a fortress, but unlike her beloved home, it was somber and as welcoming as a cold shoulder. The wild, bleak setting was the perfect backdrop for the high window slits that peered down at her like narrow, suspicious eyes and the massive gates, closed to unwelcome guests. Its many shot holes and gun ports bespoke a turbulent past in a way words could never do. All it needed was a brooding hero and a resident ghost or two.

Who knows, she thought, perhaps in time, we shall have even that. "One would have to be determined, or insane, to go there," she said, thinking out loud.

Josette did not answer her right away, and when she did, it was not what Kenna expected her to say. "Even when you are with someone, you are separate."

Colin returned with Alejandro, who took the liberty of putting his arm around Josette, which caused Kenna to suck in her breath with surprise.

Josette laughed and asked, "What? Did you think I would knock him overboard?"

"Yes," Kenna said. "Yes, I thought just that."

Any other time Kenna would have laughed with the rest of them, but her emotions were riding high, and her mind wandered from excitement, to uneasiness, and then to melancholy.

Colin must have sensed this change in her. "Are you going to be all right with this? You know you don't have to stay here...you can change your mind. I will take you wherever you wish to go. Just say the word and we will be under way."

She was tempted. Oh, Lord, was she tempted, but she had come too far and worked too hard, and she would never have a future if she did not take this stand. "No, I cannot leave. I foolishly let a moment of melancholy get to me. I did not realize it would have such an impact upon me to return to both Scotland and Durness at the same time. Did I look like a lost soul banished to walk the moors for eternity?"

He stepped closer and leaned over the rail, so that their elbows touched. Behind them, the rattle of a boat being lowered announced their time together was diminishing.

Without looking at her, he said, "When I first saw you standing here, you looked like a solitary figure in a painting... Mona Lisa with the inscrutable smile, coy and enigmatic. The Italians have a word for it, you know."

"What word is that?"

"*Sfumato,* a smoky style that creates a dreamlike mist or haze."

"Leonardo…"

"The most skilled Renaissance practitioner of *sfumato,* according to my sister."

"You didn't tell me you spoke Italian, or that you were an artist."

"That, I'm afraid, is my only word of Italian, and the only time I pick up a paintbrush is to dip it in varnish and daub the ship. But she paints, and when I was younger, she had a remarkable talent for talking me into posing for her, then forcing me to endure long and dreadfully boring explanations on the subject. Once, she had me in a dress and a mobcap, until my father saw me. She had to find a new model after that."

"I am sure you were adorable," Josette said.

Kenna delighted in the discovery that she not only liked this man, but also seemed to be forming a fond attachment for his family. Colin, she decided, was good for her, for the moment he appeared her spirits lifted. "Are you ready for us to go ashore?"

"Oh, yes. No one could understand how anxious I really am."

# *Seventeen*

Forewarned is forearmed.
—Anonymous.
Proverb.

With her feet firmly on the sand, Kenna paused to look at the castle on the bleak cliff looming before them, and something about it made her shiver. It was also a strong reminder of the reason she was here. Now she knew all her gaiety was left behind, on the ship.

"How do we get up there?" Josette asked.

"There is a track that winds around the cliff to the top," Kenna said. "It's only steep in a few places."

"There is not another way?" Colin asked.

"Yes, one that is used to bring in supplies, but it is farther to walk. This is the best way if you are on foot."

The four of them started out, and when they reached the foot of the cliff path, they had to go in single file with Kenna in the lead. "I will go first, since I have been here before, even if it was a long time ago."

As they drew closer to the castle, what had been a cool morning seemed much warmer. They paused to take their breath, and to catch a closer glimpse of the twelfth-century fortress that cast its massive shadow over them. They could see now the grotesque gargoyles, terrifying guardians of the outer walls and towers, perched on the balustrades staring over the Atlantic, grimacing and crouched, as if ready to spring from their perches and pounce downward to chase intruders away.

Kenna knew gargoyles were only grotesque carvings of human or animal figures found on large structures, where gutters ran along the spine of the gargoyles and the water ran out through the mouth and fell to the ground or streets below. The gargoyles on Durness were more like monsters, half man and half beast, frightening, demon-looking creatures carved from stone.

She could remember visiting here as a little girl, and lying awake in her room in the dark of night, hearing the rain gurgle its way through the spouts as it gushed out. Her mother would tell her the gargoyles would not hurt her, that they were only ugly so they could frighten away evil spirits. Even now, the memory of it was like a spectre, white and ghostly in her mind.

It frightened her then, and with a shiver, she realized it still frightened her now.

They stumbled along, stepping over the rough

stones to wind along the cliff, when suddenly something hurled from above clipped Kenna's shoulder before it slammed into the dust by her feet.

Colin grabbed her and fell back against the cliff, with his body covering hers, as more bits of stone fell like rain upon them, one hitting Colin on the back.

When it was over, Josette had small bits of stone down the neck of her dress, and Alejandro escaped with nothing more than dust on his clothes.

Kenna's hair had fallen down over her shoulders, and was now sprinkled with shards of gravel. Colin pushed her hair back and dusted the debris from her face. "Let me see your shoulder."

"It is nothing bad."

"Let me be the judge of that."

She pulled her hair to one side, and slipped the shoulder of her dress down far enough to expose a large red splotch, oozing blood. He took a kerchief from his pocket and placed it over the wound, then impersonally rearranged her dress. "That should hold it until we get to the top."

Their gazes locked and an electrifying moment passed between them. "Keep still and let me do something with your hair," he said, and turned her around. Before she knew what to expect, she felt him yank something and she yelped, "Ouch! What are you doing? Pulling my hair out?"

"I was taking the ribbon out of the tangles. Now, be still and stop your mewling." She could feel him braiding her hair, but not the way his hands trembled as he did it. "There," he said at last, "that's better."

She put her hand behind her to pat the braid and found it surprisingly neat.

"Where did you learn to braid a woman's hair?" Alejandro asked.

In unison, both Colin and Kenna answered, "From three sisters."

Kenna rubbed her shoulder as she began to search the area around them.

"What are you looking for?" Josette asked.

"I am trying to find what hit me."

"This," Alejandro said, kicking his foot against a chunk of stone. "It's just a gargoyle that came loose and you happened to be in the wrong place when it happened."

But Kenna realized that it wasn't just a coincidence. She knew she would have to be very, very careful from here on. "It is an omen, and that does not bode well for me," she said.

"Nonsense," Colin said. "It was an accident, nothing more."

"Let's go on," Kenna said, ignoring his comment. "I don't want to stand here arguing until another gargoyle falls."

"Can you make it to the top?" Colin asked her, "Or do you want me to carry you, although there is always the chance I might trip or drop you."

"I have managed to get this far and I see no reason why I cannot keep up with you, even with a wound," she said, and realized she sounded curt, which had not been her intention.

Colin merely nodded, his eyes cold as he turned away.

As they started up the track, Kenna took one last glance up the side of the cliff and searched among the towers that frowned from aloft, searching for the grim stone monsters that had sent one of their own hurtling down to crush her skull, and had come close to doing just that.

The sun passed from behind a cloud and a beam of light struck her eyes, and she saw grinning monsters laughing and dancing over the steep rooftops. She turned her head and rubbed her eyes, and when she looked back, all she could see were the frowning gray gargoyles, carved from stone more than six hundred years ago.

They reached the top of the cliff, but the excitement of her return to Durness Castle had deserted her. Nothing could bring it back, nor shed a favorable light upon the circumstances of her return, nor make her disastrous destiny look more promising than that final moment when she would step into the murky darkness where shadows dwell, and meet for the last time the man waiting there for her. But for now, she focused on Durness Castle, which was to be her home, no matter that it glared down at them like a giant, menacing creature, part castle, part cathedral, part Middle Age fortress.

Colin banged the massive iron knocker, and they were greeted by a slightly humpbacked man who introduced himself as Ewen MacNab, and informed them, "I am the butler and sometime gardener, as well as having a few lesser titles. And who may you be?"

"I am Lady Kenna Lennox, Ewen. I don't know if you remember me."

His little gnomelike face seemed to light up from within. "Yes…yes…" he said. "I do remember you, but you were a wee mite then."

He invited them in, remarking that it seemed silly to do so, "It being your castle, and all," and he apologized there was no one to meet them at the beach when their ship arrived. "The castle operates with a small staff," he said, "enough to keep up the repairs and have the castle functioning as a castle should, but with no one in residence, there is no need for a larger staff."

They stepped into near darkness, and even after their eyes adjusted to the dim light, it was still gloomy, with only a few candles that guttered and flickered in sconces along the walls.

Colin and the others, she noticed, stood quietly to one side, offering her no support, comfort or assistance, seeming content to merely observe.

Kenna felt like some beggar who had come asking for alms, for even her friends seemed to desert her as she stood, her dress torn and her hair dusty, uncertain about her future or her presence here.

Ewen seemed to take no notice, however, and ushered them into the great hall, whose only light was the fire that had burned low in the huge fireplace, and become a bed of glowing coals.

As Kenna continued into the room, two brindled monsters leaped at her with such force she was knocked down, which put a capstone on a day that had progressed from bad to worse.

It ended better than she thought when she felt a wet nose against her cheek, for the monsters turned out to be the castle's two resident deerhounds, who demonstrated they were more prone to face-licking than dragging intruders about by the throat. Still, in spite of her well-placed cuffs and loud entreaties to be released from their adoration, she had to suffer the ignominy of a face washing until everyone stopped laughing and Colin helped her to her feet, saying as he did so, "You have now added a nosebleed to your mounting list of indignities and injuries."

"If you are finished with being the chameleon and switching from friend to foe at whim, I would like to invite you to go back to your ship and polish the decks and scrub a few brass bells until you feel a civil mood approaching."

"That would be scrub the decks and polish the brass bells," Alejandro offered.

Kenna ignored him, drew a deep breath and gave Colin a hot look before she said, "And when you go, be sure to take your flippant friend, Echo, with you." She was too angry to notice much, but she did catch what she thought was a faint smile that appeared momentarily on Colin's lips.

Ewen returned with a tray and served hot tea and biscuits, which did much to quiet the flare of tempers recently displayed. It was good to sit down after the arduous climb, and the tea was welcomed by all of them.

Kenna noticed everyone had grown so quiet since her outburst, that she was beginning to feel she was in the room alone. It did not take a great deal of intelligence to understand it was up to her to break the silence. "I apologize for the state of our arrival. It is not exactly as I would have planned or wished it to be. It isn't a very welcoming sign, I know, to have half the roof hurled down on you before you set a foot inside, and then be chastised by Countess Gorgon."

"Well, you did have a stupefying effect on the conversation, if that was what you were after," Colin said. "Gorgonized to speechlessness, we were."

"It did not bother me," Josette said. "I was born to a nomadic, unconventional way of life. Superstition and wanderlust runs in our blood. Living in Scotland seems not so different from being a Gypsy—we tenaciously cling to our identity, and come from a strong clan system. We are also more than familiar with unwelcome receptions. Ergo, I feel quite at home among gargoyles and gorgons. Paris is dreadfully dull compared to this."

Kenna glanced at Colin and saw his face was impassive, which made her lift her chin with determination. She would not let him know of the fearful anticipation that twisted like knots inside her, and caused her to become waspish. "I cannot say I am pleased with the homecoming, but I am relieved that you are all taking it with good humor."

"Don't you think you should let someone look at your shoulder now?"

Kenna rubbed the sore spot, forgotten until now.

A log fell in the fireplace, and a cool draft swept down to bring a spark of life to the flames, but they soon died away, swallowed by the glowing coals, leaving nothing behind but a chill that seemed to wrap itself around Kenna and settle in her heart. Consumed by sadness and filled with disappointment, she felt neither of these as acutely as the despair that sliced away at the courageous confidence she had had before leaving the ship.

Colin, she noticed, had come to his feet and was leaning against a table, his arms crossed, regarding her with a level gaze. She could almost feel him picking and prodding at her brain, trying to understand her. Faith! She was incapable of understanding herself.

She wondered if Colin waited for her to say something more, but she had made such a mess of her earlier attempts, she decided silence was better than another mistake, so she said nothing.

Finally Colin pushed away from the table. "Alejandro and I need to find someone who can loan us a couple of horses, so we don't have to make that grueling trek back to the ship." He stepped close to Kenna and lightly touched her shoulder. "You do need to have that cleaned," he said, "and if there's no one here to do it, I am up to the task."

"That won't be necessary," she said. "I can take care of it myself."

"I will help you with your shoulder," Josette said. "I forgot to mention that we Gypsies are also famous for our healing skills and potions."

"Just don't filthy it up with a bunch of cobwebs and snakeskins," Colin said. "I've grown too accustomed to having her underfoot."

Josette waited until Colin and Alejandro were almost through the door before she said, "I promise to save all the cobwebs and snakeskins for you."

Alejandro turned and blew her a kiss, but Colin offered no response. A moment later he was gone.

# Eighteen

To have begun is half the job:
be bold and be sensible.
—Horace (65-8 BC), Roman poet.
Epistles (circa 20 B.C.)

Kenna's return to Durness did nothing to stir any household emotions—neither bitterness nor its opposite. And in her mind, Kenna felt the staff received her with the typical Scottish stoicism that she had come to expect.

By the next afternoon, their numbers had grown considerably, due to Ewen's determination to bring Durness back to life; the castle literally bustled with activity—there were servants cleaning and cooking, but also there were men scurrying about outside, although she had no clue what they were all doing.

It was enough to trust Ewen, as her grandfather had done and who knew more about Durness than anyone. It was a good feeling to know both she and Durness were in capable hands.

She thought about Colin, and how she had not seen him or Alejandro all day. She did know that Josette asked Ewen to saddle a horse for her, and had ridden down to the ship, while Kenna retired to her grandfather's study to pore over years of papers and ledgers, in hope that she could gain some idea of how things were handled here, and what shape everything was in. She knew Durness belonged to her, but she had no real sense of just what it was, exactly, that she owned.

She was relieved to discover someone had been keeping extremely good account of the financial aspects connected with Durness, and she learned there was a large account with the bank in Inverness and another fairly large amount in Aberdeen's bank. A herd of sheep still grazed the moors, and three fishing boats belonging to Durness were being managed and cared for by the MacKay clan members.

She also came across an account book for her grandfather's now defunct distillery, and she made a mental note to find out where it was located, so she could see the status of it, and whether or not it could be put back into operation.

She put down her pen and stood to twist a few kinks out of her back. Her shoulder had been throbbing all day, and she hoped that was not a bad sign.

With her hands on her hips, she walked to the window and looked down into the courtyard, where Ewen and two young boys were washing several horses that looked to have good bloodlines and were well cared for.

She allowed her gaze to travel over the landscape

and caught sight of the sun riding the crest of a hill in the distance...so far away, and such a big world.

And Lord Walter was in it...somewhere. And he was looking for her.

She did not hear the door open or close and had no idea anyone had even come into the room until she felt the press of a warm kiss on her neck. "Mmm," she moaned with an exhaled breath. "I have not seen you since early this morning, and I was beginning to think you decided to leave without saying goodbye."

"Never. You know I wouldn't do something like that. Not even when you were at your worst, which you came close to yesterday, by the way."

She smiled. "I know. It wasn't my best day."

"An understatement, surely."

She turned from the window and rested her palms on the stone ledge behind her. His hand came up to cup the side of her face. "Such loveliness to be shackled with such a burden." His hand slipped lower to rest on her upper arm, near her injured shoulder. "How does your shoulder fare?"

"Sore as the devil, it is today."

"Nothing more?"

She shrugged. "It throbs."

A frown settled between his brows. "And is it still as red as yesterday?"

"I don't know. I did not have time when I arose to look at it."

"You should take better care of yourself." His hand moved to the front of her dress and hovered lightly over the buttons. "I better take a look. If you start to get red streaks in the wound, it is not good."

"It will be fine."

"So said the mouse in the lion's mouth."

She had to smile at that one. "I am sure it is fine. Truly, I am."

"You don't know that. You said yourself you had not looked at it." He loosed the top button and her eyes flew to his and remained there, for he held her trapped like a wild and skittish animal in his gaze. He loosed the second button, and then the third.

He pushed the dress away from her shoulder and drew it halfway down her arm. He studied the abrasion and touched it in a place or two, causing her to grimace.

"This place here, where you have the worst cut…it is starting to crust over, but it needs to be cleaned out."

"Why?"

"It festers."

She was barely listening, for she had more important things to worry about. He must have sensed her disinterest, for he was determined not to let the subject drop. "Josette should be able to do it, but if not, I will, unless there is someone else here that can perform the task."

"And what will happen if I leave it as it is?"

"The wound is infected already, and if you do nothing, the flesh will abscess, and, believe me, you do not want that."

"I will see to it then."

He started to pull her dress back in place, but his hand touched her skin, and rather than withdraw it, he left it there. Without taking his eyes from her face, he began to caress her neck and the smooth curve that sloped down to her shoulder.

She swallowed at the sudden dryness in her mouth, and when his hand slipped downward to rest between the swell of her breasts, her breathing became heavy, the sound of her heartbeat loudly audible in her ears. He tucked his fingers inside her chemise and moved his hand back and forth along the line of it, his knuckles crossing over both breasts as he did so.

Her head lolled back to rest against the window and her eyes closed. Her breath was coming hard and fast, as he continued to stroke her with the same movement of his hand that followed the edge of her chemise.

And suddenly he stopped.

She was about to open her eyes, when she felt him push both shoulders of her dress down to her waist. She swallowed against the dryness a second time and began to breathe through her mouth as she felt him undo the buttons of her chemise, pushing it back to allow her breasts to spill free.

"Lord above! Your breasts are more beautiful than I imagined they would be. Perfectly shaped, firm, and so heavy in my hand."

She could not speak, and she dared not open her eyes, but she did gasp with pleasure when she felt his thumbs circle her nipples, rubbing and teasing them to hard peaks. The next thing she knew, he put his hands round her waist and lifted her to sit on the stone ledge. He took her in his mouth and she could not stop her hands from threading through his dark hair to cup his head and hold him to her. Her body thrilled to his touch again and again, while he kissed first one breast and then the other, as if he could not decide which one he liked the best. It was driving her over the edge of what she could bear, for the ecstasy of it, the exquisite feel of the warm, wet roughness of his tongue, teasing and biting until she writhed and felt him press his body against her, pushing her legs apart.

With a groan, he captured her mouth with his, and kissed her hard, deeply and with abandon, groaning and caressing her, telling her with his body what he could not say with words. She knew she should push him away, but she could not, nor did she want to.

She wanted his hot mouth on hers, and his warm hands to touch her at his leisure, wanted him to show her, to teach her all the things she had never put a name to. From their first kiss, he had awakened her in a way she never expected. It was as frightening as it was thrilling and she needed it enough to surrender to him, by allowing his hands and his mouth free rein.

Kenna, who had never before known wrenching desire, or felt herself in the throes of passion, was now imprisoned by the wants and the needs of both, but only with this man, who was now master of her body, to do with as he would. She not only cared for him more deeply than even she would admit, but she also trusted him, and that, she knew, was a very dangerous combination.

And one she would think about tomorrow.

She melted against him, unable to stop the little groans that came from deep in her throat, and she learned that he did not want her to be quiet, for each time she moaned, it seemed to impassion him more, until she knew he was as tightly trapped in this coil of desire as she was. She was vaguely conscious of his hand sliding down her leg, and she felt a sudden draft of air as he pushed her skirts upward, his hand moving as if it knew where to go, until she felt the touch of his palm slide across her, and knew the feel of his naked skin against hers, and it left her wanting to push against him and open herself to him in a way that was so strong, it frightened her.

It was an instinctive recoil born of this fear that made her try to draw her legs together, but he must have known what she was about, for he deepened the kiss and brought his body closer, making it impossible for her to close her legs now, and dear Lord, she did not want to. Not really.

She gasped and her eyes flew open when she felt him touch her intimately and she heard him whisper, "Damn, I've never touched anything so close to heaven. How perfectly you are made, so warm and wet, and you feel like velvet." He kissed her eyes and stroked her until she knew she was his to do whatever he desired.

He stroked her a few more times, then he groaned with a shudder, and the next thing she knew, he was pushing her skirts back down. His hands came up to cup her breasts. "So beautiful, so heavy, and all mine."

He kissed each breast and then drew her chemise up and buttoned it. He followed that by raising the bodice and the shoulders of her dress, until all her clothes were back as they were before.

But, inside, she would never be the same. Everything had changed. New awareness blossomed now, next to the strong, almost overpowering craving for him to finish what he started. She knew it was hard for him to stop, and she doubted if she could have done what he did. Now the secrets of lovemaking were revealed and she had bathed in the exquisiteness of it, yet she yearned to feel his hands on her again, knowing that once would never be enough, just as she knew there was more to it, more to come, for she felt the knots of desire still writhing inside her, left unsatisfied.

He lifted her and brought her feet back to the floor. "I did not come in her with the intention of doing that, and if I offended you, you have only to tell me to go and I will hobble away on my crippled ship tomorrow."

She put her arms around him and placed her head against his chest. "I don't want you to go...ever, but I know this is not the time, if there is to be a time for us. I desire you, Colin Montgomery, more than I ever imagined a woman could desire a man. I loved to feel your hands on me. I was not shamed by it because it felt right and I cannot see the wrong in that."

"Lord above, how was I so fortunate to find such a woman? Men would kill for a woman like you...beautiful, passionate, open, warm, loyal and graciously, honestly giving."

He turned away from her and murmured an oath, running his fingers through his hair. "You pack a powerful punch, Lady Kenna, and I am still reeling from the impact of it."

She laughed and he joined his laughter to hers.

When it died away, she felt the featherlight touch of his kiss upon her lips, and it traveled through her like fire, quick as a jagged flash of lightning.

"I find you adorable. Too adorable, and I am not certain what to do about it."

"Then do nothing. If the feeling is true, it will remain, and if false, it will go, and there will be no need for explanation."

"So much wisdom. How could so much beauty come with brains?"

She could have remained here with him for the rest of the day, all day, but the sun had gone down, and she was standing near the window, and the cooler evening was beginning to bring a chill to her backside. His beautiful blue eyes were mere inches away, watching her in a way that made her believe him when he said she was adorable.

She wanted to be adorable for him, always. And she would never tire of hearing him say she was so.

He kissed her softly. "I still adore you, even if you don't believe me."

Her heart believed him. It was her mind that was skeptical, but then it always was. Her heart and her mind...they were like identical twins that never agreed on anything. If one went right, the other wanted to go left. If one said yes, the other said no. If he said she was adorable, her mind scoffed, telling her he said that only to get what he wanted.

But, oh, her heart believed.

She could hear it saying so with each little beat: I am falling in love with you, Colin. I am...I am... She could hear it thumping in her ears, and the words poured from the center of her heart, making her believe they were destined to be together since the beginning of time.

But her head said she was a fool to tell him such, and for once, she agreed. Not because she did not want to tell him, but this was neither the time, nor the place. She had a rendezvous with Lord Walter that would not wait, and she could not weaken her resolve with Colin and keep it strong for Lord Walter, for to do so would compromise her and leave her weakened, and that meant one thing: defeat.

She looked at the ledgers on her desk, and back at him. "My accounts await me, and you have a mistress dancing in the bay that needs your attention."

He kissed her lips, not with passion but with understanding. "Sweet Kenna, do not fret so. I did not come here to upset your world any more than I think you intended to upset mine. We cannot change what has happened...what is happening between us, but we can control it. At least, Lord help us, I hope we can. I want to protect you and take you away from here, but I know that would only drive a stake through the beating heart of our affections for each other. I cannot have you, but I can be with you, and whenever you need me, you've only to send word."

He left as quietly as he entered, making no sound as he closed the door behind him. Kenna stood in the same spot for some time, trying to deal with the flood of emotions that raced through her.

Later that evening, when she began to feel normal

again, she was in the great room when she looked up to see Colin enter. As soon as she saw him, an odd flare of warmth shot through her. After what had happened between them earlier, she was embarrassed to be caught smiling like a fool, so she turned her face away and gave a stray hair a tuck to get it back in place.

There was no one else in the room and not a sound could be heard, save the occasional snap or pop of the low fire. The light coming in the windows touched his dark, shining hair with glints of burgundy, and the skin over his high cheekbones glowed.

She caught the way he looked at her, for it told her he was well aware of her scrutiny, and she saw the humor in his intense blue eyes.

"I thought you were still down at the ship."

"I have only this minute returned. I was looking for Alejandro."

"He was in the courtyard with Josette."

"What are they doing out there?"

"Archery."

"Alejandro? Are you sure?"

"I saw it with my own eyes. Why does that seem so strange to you?"

"Alejandro has never shot a bow in his life."

She grinned. "I know. He managed to hit everything in the courtyard except the target."

Colin shook his head. "When a man becomes infatuated with a woman, he does strange things."

Her brows went up. "Oh? I was not aware of that. So, tell me Colin Montgomery, what strange things have you been doing of late?"

It was his turn to grin. "A man has to keep some secrets, otherwise you would probably have me out there shooting arrows like an idiot."

Before she could respond to that, he said, "I will go and look for him, and hope I don't get an arrow in my backside doing it."

The sound of her laughter stayed with him, long after the sight of her was gone.

The next morning Kenna supervised the maids in the unpacking of her trunks, while two doors away, Josette did the same. They were both still thankful that the *duc* had devised a plan to get both their things to Scotland.

When she opened the last trunk, Kenna found the sword the *comte* had given her lying on top, and when she removed it from its velvet sleeve, the wide-eyed maids looked at one another fearfully, until Kenna assured them they were in no danger. "It was a gift to me from a very dear friend," she told them. "He is dead, and the sword is more precious to me now than it was before."

The maids smiled and went back to work, but Kenna knew she would be the topic of discussion in the kitchen tonight, when the staff sat down to dinner together.

She left her room and went to see how Josette was doing with her unpacking, and found everything tidied away. As for Josette, she was lying on the bed, with a dreamy look on her face.

Kenna sat down beside her. "You aren't falling in love with Alejandro, are you?"

"No, but if I was, would that be a problem for you?"

"Of course not. All I want is for you to be happy."

"I am happy, and I am also surprised, for I did not expect to be, at least not so soon after the *comte*'s death. I am glad you insisted I come with you. If I had remained at the château, I would have grieved myself to death."

Josette's gaze went to the end of the bed, and Kenna knew she noticed the sword Kenna had placed there before she sat down. "I'm glad you brought it. It is good to have a part of him here with us."

"I know."

"You have not worked with your sword for several weeks. The *comte* would not be pleased."

"Where will I find a fencing master here?"

"You do not need a fencing master. The *comte* said you had learned all he could teach you. If you want to practice, I will fight with you like we did before."

"I don't know…you always got so angry."

"You were not my friend then."

"Excellent! But we will need to get a sword for you."

"I brought my sword with me, just as you did."

Kenna stood and picked up the weapon. "I will find a place tomorrow. It will be good to pick up the sword again."

"It will also help save your life, or have you allowed a false sense of security lull you into complacency?"

"No, I have not done that, but I was a bit overwhelmed when we first arrived. I will see you at dinner," she said, her tone cold and final.

# *Nineteen*

A man may drink and no be drunk;
A man may fight and no be slain;
A man may kiss a bonnie lass,
And aye be welcome back again.
    —Robert Burns (1759-1796),
    Scottish poet and songwriter.
"There Was a Lass, They Ca'd Her Meg"
            (1788).

For the next two days, Colin and Alejandro spent most of their time on board *Dancing Water,* and their work was paying off. With no timber the size of a mast available, they had to work with what timber they could find to brace the mast, after which, they wrapped it with rope from top to bottom. They then ran cables from it to the outer extremities of the ship, to hold the mended mast straight and in place. It was not repaired, but it was mended enough that they felt it would get them to where they needed to go to have a new mast built.

Because they were away from the castle, Colin did not have much time to be with Kenna. It wasn't the way he wanted things, but he knew she had much to take care of, and she needed to start her training again. He knew he was a distraction for her. Part of him wanted to stay nearby to protect her; part of him knew she would resent that.

He informed the crew to take the rest of the afternoon off, for tomorrow they would prepare the ship for sailing. He calculated they had one more day here and then they would be gone. Soon, Colin would have her repairs finished, and there would no longer be a reason for him to remain in Scotland.

Kenna was someone he cared about, and he cared a lot. He wanted to pursue this attraction they had for each other, and see if it led to something permanent, or if it would eventually die out. There was a price to pay for this pursuit, though, and it was the slow torment that left him feeling as if he was standing on a razor-thin edge of sanity. He not only had Kenna to worry about, and the clock that was eating up the minutes he had with her, but also the ever-mounting desire thundering through his veins. All in all this was fast proving to be a trying afternoon.

For most of the day, he carried in the back of his mind the memory of being with her the day before, an image of how he imagined her naked—of her generous, rose-tipped breasts, a nipped-in waist, and the flare of feminine hips. And that caused a flare of something else. With a sad sigh, he damned himself for a fool for pushing away the thought. Some trade-off that was—the image of her naked body in exchange for the sudden shrinking of his erection.

In spite of what Kenna said, Colin was not sure there was a distillery at Durness Castle, for they had just spent a good part of the morning searching for it and had thus far come up with only a small room for brewing beer. "If there was a distillery here, where is it?" Colin asked.

"I don't know, but we will find it."

"Doesn't Ewen know where it is?"

"He said my grandfather shut it down before he came to work for him."

"Well, he should still know where it was."

"I know, and I cannot decide if he truly does not know, or if he does not want me to know where it was located."

"That doesn't make much sense, though, does it?"

"No, but it doesn't make much sense that we cannot find something as big as a distillery."

They walked together toward the sole entrance in the north wall, at the base of the tower, where there were two cellars at one time. One cellar was made into the great hall, but they were having no luck finding the second one.

The steps to the first cellar that led to the great hall were to the right. Colin opened the double door and paused to study its construction.

"This is ingenious," he said. "Look at this. See how the doors were designed so they opened to the outside and blocked access to the stairs."

"Smart ancestors," she said. "I must have inherited that from them. Remind me to show you the beheading pit, with a beheading block," she said. "It lies on the other side of the castle."

"Nice ancestors you had."

"We have a turbulent past, you know. I hope that the unfortunate ones who ended up there truly deserved it. It is a gruesome thing to have in close proximity to one's home. I want to have it dismantled."

"A sensible idea. In the meantime, I will strive not to anger you."

They inspected the kitchen and storage rooms, then the laundry, and found nothing. She was disappointed and it showed on her face. "I know it has to be somewhere."

"Perhaps it was blocked over at some point in time."

"You could be right, and since we cannot find it, I suppose that is why. That means we have to see every place it could have been." They walked down a long corridor and passed several places where it looked like windows were once there but had been blocked up with stone. Kenna stopped. "Look at this," she said, pointing to the shape of a window that had been filled in. "There are several of them along this corridor."

"It looks as if they closed off a section of the cellar. Perhaps they did not need it, so sealed it off."

"Or, perhaps it is where my grandfather had his distillery."

They walked toward the end of the corridor, but instead of going out the doors, they continued on to the end, where a long table stood in front of a window. To the right they found curving stairs that led down to a door. Colin broke the padlock and they entered through the narrow arched doorway.

They entered a cavernous room and stepped back in time to the ancient world of alchemists. The scent of peat and malt permeated the room, blended with a hint of smoke that clung to the smoke-darkened stone walls.

Colin took out his tinderbox and a lit a candle with the flint and steel, and used the candle to light one of the torches hanging from a metal bracket on the wall. The glow of candlelight revealed the clutter that had accumulated over time. "It doesn't look as if it has been cleaned in a century," she said. "Some of these things look ancient, as if they have been here since the castle was built."

A table along one wall was covered with an assortment of jars, vials, pestles and pottery jars with lids that she was afraid to lift.

"Why?" he asked.

"I don't know, but each time I think about opening them, I get a cold chill."

He laughed at her trepidation, while he studied some shelves on one side of the room that did not look sturdy enough to hold all the wooden boxes, moldering books, rolled scrolls of parchment, with a scattering of tins, beakers, vials and flasks, that it held.

She rubbed her arms, roughened by goose bumps. "This looks like the den of an old Celtic crone," she said.

"Or Merlin's abode in a cave," he said.

"Doesn't it feel creepy in here to you? I feel as if all

we need are some ground bat wings, and a ewer of bog water."

He chuckled. "If we're going that far, we might as well add a few frog toes, blind worms, lizard legs and a raven on a perch," Colin said.

"Hmm, I have learned something else about you," she said. "You read *Macbeth*."

"I did, but I am surprised I remembered any of it, other than the first line—'Double, double, toil and trouble.'"

Kenna finished it for him:

"Fire burn, and cauldron bubble.
Fillet of a fenny snake
In the cauldron boil and bake;
Eye of newt, and toe of frog,
Wool of bat, and tongue of dog,
Adder's fork, and blind-worm's sting,
Lizard's leg and owlet's wing,
For a charm of powerful trouble,
Like a hell-broth, boil and bubble.
Double, double, toil and trouble;
Fire burn, and cauldron bubble."

"I am amazed you memorized that," he said. "Why?"

She shrugged. "You know Macbeth was a Scot. Well, my father thought his bairns should all learn several passages from it. Naturally all seven of us chose the witches' lines as one of them."

She looked around the room. "I can picture what it

must have been like in here. Can't you just imagine it? I can see them now, entirely isolated from the outside world, like medieval monks, veiled by the silence of their vows. They would walk along these same vaulted corridors, across the polished stone floors to the barley room. As if they were the sole guardians of some mystical secret, they protected the centuries-old scrap of parchment…an ancient recipe taken from Arab alchemists for a mediaeval elixir, which my ancestors transformed into whisky."

"Your imagination," he said, "is overwhelming."

"Come on," she said, and they looked along the walls, where silent torches once gleamed and sputtered from dozens of metal brackets. Farther over, they discovered dozens of remnants of guttered candles lying in dust on tables. An old brass brazier stood in the corner.

She gave it a closer inspection. "We had a brazier like that. It burned sea coal. I wonder what tales the shifting shadows in this cellar could tell, what secrets still lie in here, waiting to be revealed?"

She spied two cupboards in the wall and she went and put her hand on the handle. She glanced back at him with a mischievous look on her face. "I hope bats and ravens do not fly oot."

She opened the cupboard and found a large, cracked, leather-bound book. She lit two more candles, and watched as the light of the feeble flames crept forward as slow as the wispy veils of fog that came in with the tide.

She opened the book. It was written in Gaelic, so she

translated it for Colin. "It says that in 1294, some of my ancestors dedicated themselves to live in seclusion, self-sufficient and isolated from the rest of the world. Here they were able to get peat, and could grow most of the grains needed for their secret recipe.

"According to this, in the year 1244 a Spanish ship wrecked on the rocks below the castle. There were only three survivors, who were brought into the castle. Two of them died, but the third, an Arab, survived. When he was well enough to return to his home, he gave them an alchemist's recipe for an elixir he called the Water of Life.

"They locked it away and forgot about it. It wasn't until half a century later, when bad weather and failing crops threatened the lives of all the residents of Durness, that they turned to the ancient recipe."

"The recipe was for whisky?"

She read on. "The Egyptians practiced the distillation of perfumes three thousand years before the birth of Christ. The word *alcohol* comes from the Arabic word *al-koh'l.* Koh'l, it says, is a dark powder from pulverized antimony and was used as an eye makeup." She paused. "Do you know what antimony is?"

"I think it's a sulfurlike compound."

"The rest of it says the distillation of *aqua vitae,* or water of life, spread across Europe, especially Ireland and Scotland under its Gaelic name of Uisge Beatha."

"Is that all?"

"Almost, but the rest of it is not so important. It says all the distilling utensils, and the *bere,* which was a preferable type of barley, was imported from Ireland beginning in 1650."

She closed the book and a cloud of dust arose, which set both of them to coughing.

Kenna returned the book to the cabinet. "I wonder who wrote that, and how long ago it was written."

"Come over here," Colin said, and she turned to see him at the opposite end of the cellar. It was darker at that end, so she carried a torch, and saw the old still that was mentioned in the book. It was probably copper, but it needed cleaning to be certain. What really excited her was, it was all there—the four parts—the vessel, head, arm and the worm.

They opened a door and found wooden casks stacked along one wall, and farther over were what she called "Ancient Celtic copper cauldrons. *Celtic copper cauldrons,*" she said. "It is a phrase that tangles and tickles the tongue."

"Now, here is something interesting," he said, and she followed him to a door with another huge padlock. "This door leads outside."

She studied it a moment. "How do you know?"

He pointed at the keyhole. "I can see daylight through the original keyhole."

"Aah, I was wondering how they carried all their supplies up and down those stairs."

They walked back to the center of the room. She stopped beside the long table that ran down the center and leaned against it, suddenly aware of the way he was looking at her.

Her first impulse was to tell him to put the thought out of his mind. There were more important things to be done than falling in love with him, and she itched to tell him so, but she knew it would lead to an argument, and she was not up to one right now. She was trying, really trying to keep everything pleasant until his ship was ready and he was gone. She clamped her mouth shut in order to be sure she did just that.

She did not know how long they stood there, neither of them speaking, but at some point, he must have grown tired, for he moved over to the table and leaned back against it. She followed the long line of his legs down to where his ankles crossed. A woman could do a whole lot worse than a man like him.

A lot worse.

They stood side by side, leaning back against the table, and said absolutely nothing, each aware that their bodies touched lightly at the hip. She wondered if he was going to kiss her, and she knew she would let him. Not only let him; she wished that he would do just that, and more. She wanted to know how it would feel to lie with him in total abandon, to give him the freedom to teach her all he knew about a woman's body. She swallowed audibly. Along with the mental yearning, strange things were happening to her body. She knew it was desire, and she did desire him.

Yet, neither of them spoke as they looked upon the leavings of those who had used this room a long time ago.

"I guess it's going to be me," he said at last.

"I do not get your point—if you are making one."

"I am talking about what we are both thinking."

"I don't know what you mean."

"You are not that dense, but you are too stubborn to

give an inch. You were thinking what I was thinking, only I will admit it. You want me every bit as much as I want you, but you are an obstinate wench," he said. He took her face in his hands and touched his lips to hers, silencing forever the intended retort that waited on the tip of her tongue.

He held her close to him, closer than she could ever remember being held. How perfectly their bodies molded to each other's, as if they had been joined somewhere, or at some point in time, then split asunder, only to find themselves perfectly aligned once again.

Her loosely piled hair fell around her shoulders, and she could smell the scent of heather from the soap she used to wash it. She wondered if he caught the scent of it as well.

She could be so strong when it came to bandying words with him, but she was too weak to resist him when they were together like this.

But, she reminded herself. I cannot deal with him in the midst of all that's happening in my life right now. He is a distraction, which is the last thing I need. Even so, she debated the issue with her subconscious mind: He has to leave soon. *Then why not enjoy the time you have with him? Let him teach you what you want to know, teach you what it feels like to have his hands and his mouth worship your body. Let him give you the things you can only imagine. And when he leaves, you can keep the memory.*

As if sensing her thoughts, he turned slightly and took her in his arms and began kissing her with soft, nibbling kisses, then spoke warmly against her lips. "Why can you not trust me, or at least meet me half-way?"

His voice was gentle and soft, and she knew the words came from his heart. Burning tears blurred her vision. She wanted him to always be here for her, wanted to bask in the security of his protection. She desired these things, but she could not tell him how she could want one thing and do another. She could not bear the thought of him, or anyone, losing their life in order to save hers.

She had started this battle when she intervened on her sister's behalf. In doing so, she had saved Claire's life and endangered her own, but it had not ended there.

Lord Walter took Claire's rescue as a fair exchange: Kenna's life for that of her sister. They had traded places now; she was the hunted. "It isn't that I don't trust you. It is simply that you do not belong here. Not now. This is not your war."

"The hell it isn't. Your war is my war."

She was about to tell him differently, but changed her mind. She did not want an argument, a discussion or a debate. What she wanted was to feel his arms around her.

She was under a powerful spell that took her breath, shook her composure and left her open and yearning. She could feel Colin's unbearable nearness and warmth. She wanted him to touch her. She did not need to get involved with him, she reminded herself. And in frustration, she pushed away from him and walked to the other end of the table, where she stopped and opened a book lying there.

It was a poor substitute for a man like Colin and she regretted her impulsiveness. She might as well give in, she thought, because it was going to torment them until they were both crazy.

She wondered if she had spoken those words aloud, for he moved down the table and stopped behind her. He pressed closer and his arms tightened around her. She released a faint moan and her head fell back against his chest.

Suffused with weakness, she was too filled with yearning to stand. He was kissing her neck—his breathing quick and heavy. She moaned, louder this time, when she felt his hands dip down the front of her gown and lift her breasts, exposing them so he could torment them with the sensuous movement of his thumbs. He kissed her neck again, his breath hot and erotically arousing, as he moved his lips over her skin, deliberately slow, deliberately sensual, deliberately seducing her. The heat from the fire within her clawed its way upward, to wrap scorching tentacles of flame around her, winding itself tightly. She gasped and her breathing increased, until she felt as if she might suffocate from it.

Everything within her was intense, tight and waiting.

Colin whispered in her ear the things he wanted to do to her, the things he wanted her to do to him. Her mouth parted and she felt her breath coming in short pants. Her skirt slipped over her hips to the stone floor. One hand was on her breasts, the other slid over her stomach to find the opening in her drawers.

She gasped at the intrusion, the strangeness of it.

"You have tormented me since I first saw you, to the point that I have thought of little else, save having you here like this." He held her in his power now, for he knew her body better than she, and each time he touched her she felt herself flowing out to him.

"You are like a flower, soft, delicate, kissed by dew. I am charmed by you. Infatuated. Would that I could do more, that I could show you the way of it."

He did not speak again, and if he had, she doubted she would have heard him, for her own rapid pants sounded like a rushing wind in her ears. She groaned, and felt a gathering of tension, a delicious sensation that enveloped her. His hand touched her again and again until she was mindless, her head rolling from side to side, her legs parting more, granting him access.

Something was happening as pressure built within. Strange noises came from her throat; she thought she could die from the pleasure of it. And then she felt her body shudder again and again in a wild, escalating spasm in perfect harmony of the sensual beat of the music below. She held back the cries that pushed at the back of her throat to be released.

And when she thought she could not hold them back any longer, that she had to give birth to the scream in her throat, he turned her and crushed her against him with powerful arms, while he kissed her, and kept on kissing her until her arms went around his neck, and she caught a little glimpse of heaven.

Afterward, Colin held her, occasionally kissing her neck but saying nothing. His silence burned into her, hot and searing. She was hurt to think she came close to making love with him, when Colin had not even mentioned the word or anything close to it. About the only thing she knew was, he desired her. That was not love, and it was not what she was willing to settle for.

"I must get back," she said.

"Don't go. Not yet."

She was embarrassed to have gone as far as she had, and it caused her to speak with indifference. "It has been a very long day as you know. I am tired. I want to retire, and I think I have dallied here with you overlong," she said, her tone flat and a little icy.

"Dallied? Is that what you call it? Dallied?"

The word seemed appropriate to her. What else could she call it? He'd made amorous advances without serious intentions and she had let him. She deserved what she got. She was a fool to grant him such liberties. Next time they were together he would expect more, and the time after that, until it became a regular thing, and when he tired of her, or when it came time for him to leave, he would do so, without so much as a hint of sadness.

What comes easily goes easily. "Yes, that is how I see it and what I choose to call it. Do you have a better way to express it?"

"Why does it have to be reduced to one word, diced and chopped to oblivion? You make it sound like a topic for debate."

"We are debating it, are we not?"

Colin was silent for some time, and although she did not look at him, she knew his eyes were on her. "What made you change so suddenly?"

"Perhaps I saw myself as something I neither approve of, nor like."

"You are a passionate woman with feelings. Is that so wrong?"

"I do not want to be hurt, Montgomery, and I cannot face Lord Walter with my mind distracted and my heart broken. It is as simple as that, and if that sounds cruel, so be it. I must remain focused. Surely you can understand that."

"It does not have to be that way. I can take care of you and I can take care of Lord Walter. Why can't you let me?"

"Because I can't. I don't know why, but I can't. I have always seen this as my fight. I have already lost someone dear to me by letting my guard down and thinking I could live a normal life, and I lost sight of the fact that I will always fail in that regard simply because Lord Walter is not normal."

She threw up her hands and walked away, her brain too jammed with words, thoughts, emotions, wants, desires...all that was missing was something to club him over the head with. Just why couldn't he understand?

She turned back to him. "I don't want to disagree anymore. I don't want to argue. You have your ideas and I have mine. Neither of us is right or wrong. We are just different people. Our ideas are different. Even our genders are different. We come from different backgrounds, different cultures, different everything. We were not meant to agree on everything. But we should be able to get along if we try. If only for a little while. Can't we decide to at least be friends while you are here?"

He did not say anything, but there was a spark she would call hope in his eyes. And then he surprised her again, when he pushed away from the table and said, "I'm hungry. Do you want to go to dinner? That should be a subject we can agree on."

She smiled. "I am always agreeable when it comes to food."

He returned her smile. "I will remember that."

They began to snuff out the candles, and doused all the torches but one, which they carried toward the same door where they had entered. Colin opened the door, and Kenna waited in the corridor while he doused the torch and replaced it in the metal bracket.

They passed along the corridor, and when they were beside a long medieval bench, Colin grabbed her and pulled her down to sit beside him. "Once we are back in the castle, I won't be able to have you all to myself," he said, in a husky, desire-laced voice that was both teasing and confident.

He knew she was still not completely comfortable with this, and he understood how all of this was new to her. He would not push her, but he knew that when a deed needs doing, it is best to do it quickly. So, without furthering her discomfort, he took her mouth with a kiss.

He wanted her and he made no effort to hide it. He knew she had feelings for him—feelings that grew stronger each time they were together, with each kiss they shared. He knew she was both puzzled and curious by it all, considering her limited knowledge in matters of the heart.

He still couldn't understand that. What was wrong with the Scots males? So, she lived on an island. To get to a woman like Kenna, he would have crossed a dozen lakes, swimming until he reached her island, if that were the only way he could be near her.

He did not understand his own seeming obsession for her. It wasn't something that he had experienced before. He liked women, and for a time imagined himself in love with one or another of them, but his interest soon waned, and his love for the sea called out to him.

With Kenna, it was different. He was in no hurry to go anywhere, unless she was there. His desire for her became a driving need to mate with her, even though he was thinking somewhere in his mind that Kenna was a woman who deserved more.

His hands were on her beautiful breasts, so soft and full, and the weight of them felt glorious in his hands. There wasn't a part of her he did not desire, or anything he would not do for her. He wondered if they were going to end up making love right here, because she was melting against him and responding like she never had before. She was ready. He was ready. Hell and damnation! He had been ready since he first saw her.

"Colin, we cannot…not here…please stop."

He eased his hold and sat there, not saying anything. He was feeling plenty, however… Like someone had sliced a vein, and he was watching his life flow out of his body. They were so close. He knew that. He also knew better. A man can never predict what a woman will do, or say, or how she will react. Isn't that what his own mother had told him when he was in the first years of his yearning?

He leaned his head back, took a deep breath and smiled.

"I expected you to be angry, yet you smile. Why?"

"I was recalling something my mother once told me."

"Which was?"

"'Colin, there are three things you must remember about a woman. Never take her for granted. Never think you know what she is thinking. And never think you know what she will do in a given situation. A woman is like smoke. She will curl seductively around you one moment, burn your eyes the next, tickle your throat until you cough, and then poof! She is gone. She is a mirage. She is a thunderstorm. She is a sailboat on a sunny mirrored lake. She will run when you reach for her, and come to you when you wish her away. You can solve a problem. You can analyze logic. You can explain how vapor turns into water. But you cannot understand the mind of a woman. And do you know why? Because she does not understand herself.'"

"Then what do you do?"

"You love her and deal with her in all honesty. You earn her trust. And then you trust the Almighty, who made women the way they are, believing that He knew what he was doing."

"What if that doesn't help?"

"Blame Him."

# *Twenty*

The trenchant blade, Toledo trusty,
For want of fighting was grown rusty,
And eat into it self, for lack
Of some body to hew and hack.
—Samuel Butler (1612-1680),
English satirist. *Hudibras* (1663).

The clash of swords; the ring of steel…

From the sound of it, pandemonium had broken out in the great hall of Durness Castle. In time, the staff and any visitors who happened by would become accustomed to the daily chaos, and they would know the clattering din was not due to a wild uproar, or otherworldly chaos.

But today, they did not know that, and for this reason, throughout the castle, the household help dropped what they were doing and rushed to the great hall, expecting to meet the scourge of the human race, a raid of Viking warriors, the return of the Spanish Armada, or even the resurrection of William the Conqueror.

What they found were two women making sport with the silvered blade as they engaged each other in practice.

For a moment, no one said anything, so stunned they were to see Lady Kenna Lennox and Josette Revel parry and thrust their way across the vast hall and back.

It wasn't an uncivilized horde, after all. Nor was it a Viking raid.

"It is only Attila the Hen," said Ewen McNab when he arrived and found the gathered throng. "Now, back to work with you."

The crowd dispersed, leaving behind only two men, Colin and Alejandro, who came to observe, and ended up squashed, mashed and shoved against the wall.

Sometimes, Colin would close his eyes and listen to the rhythm of the foils, the hollow ring of steel against steel, the accompanying sound of feet moving swiftly, and once in a while, her triumphant laugh when she scored a hit.

Kenna…day by day his feeling for her was growing stronger, while at the same time his concern over her determination to have a final confrontation between herself and Lord Walter. It was not something he could talk to her about, for he had tried that once, thinking he could persuade her to put down the foil and let someone else fight her battle…namely him. It took her very few words to let him know that Lord Walter was no one else's concern but hers. "If I would not allow my family to intervene, what makes you think I would even consider allowing your acting on my behalf?"

He knew he had done all he could do, and nothing had changed. She would continue to practice daily with Josette, and wait for the appearance of Lord Walter. There was no place for him in this. She made that abundantly clear. His ship was ready to sail, and today he would sail out of her life, but she would never be out of his heart.

"If you care for her so much, why are you giving up so easily?" Alejandro asked.

His glance told Alejandro what he thought of his comment. "That is what she needs, isn't it? Me hanging around here, a daily distraction, who causes her to lose her concentration and her focus, while I fill her head with romantic ideas, and then I can stand aside and watch her face her nemesis unprepared."

The two of them fell silent, and continued to observe quietly, until they ended the practice and placed their foils in the rack.

Kenna approached Colin, her face rosy from exertion. She had picked up a towel after she put away the foil, and now she blotted the perspiration from her forehead. Her breathing was labored. He was distracted by the way her breasts moved beneath the soft cotton shirt she wore with her fencing skirt. Her mouth was pink and shiny, and so perfect for kissing, he wanted to send Josette and Alejandro off on a fool's errand, so he could carry her away and make love to her for the rest of the day.

"It grows warm," she said. "I wish I had time for a swim in the loch."

"Take time."

"You know I cannot."

It was a phrase she said a great deal, for she was always busy. "Are you going to the distillery, then?"

"Yes, for a while, once I change out of these clothes. I plan to be back here later, for another match with Josette."

"You are undertaking a great deal."

"I prefer to stay busy, with my hands never idle. I hired a man this morning. Owen Fletcher is his name. He is going to help with getting the distillery operating again."

"I hope you will be pleased with the results. Finding good help is difficult, and doubly so when you live in an isolated place like this."

"Oh, I am already pleased. He started taking inventory of the boilers, pipes and furnaces this morning. He will let me know which are operable and those we must replace. He knows whom to contact to get estimates for the wood and carpentry work, the water wheel, and the malt barn. There is a growing list of supplies we need to order…things I am not familiar with, like a saccharometer and a hydrometer. Do you know what they are?"

His expression was one of amusement. "They are not part of my vocabulary, if that is what you mean."

Her eyes were lovely and bright with humor. "Take a guess."

"I am falling back on my Latin for this," he said. "*Saccharon* is sugar, and mēnsūra is measure, thus a device to measure sugar content. As for hydrometer…a measure of water density."

"Oh, you are very good at this," she said. "A saccharometer measures the strength of sugar solutions by measuring its density. A hydrometer determines the specific gravity, or density, of a liquid."

"I can hardly wait to pass on that bit of information," he said. "I am sure others will find me a charming conversationalist because of it."

They both laughed, and then their eyes met and held. He took her hand in his, and kissed it in a way that was softly intimate. "You were fortunate to find someone with Owen's knowledge."

She took her hand back. "Yes, it is true enough. I know I would not be able to do this without someone like him to teach me, although there is a growing list of other people I must hire—a malt man, bollman, someone for the tun and cooler, and each of these needs an assistant. That is only the beginning of the list. The most important position will be difficult to fill, according to him, and that is a distillery manager. These are all terms I was unfamiliar with a few days ago."

"I am glad to see you happy. Your body, your voice and your eyes express it beautifully."

"I am happy. I never dreamt I would be in these high spirits when I made the decision to live here. It is ironic that what started as a result of misfortune ended with a blessing."

"It is good to see you this way." His eyes searched her face. "Be happy, but remember it isn't over yet. You still have Lord Walter lurking in your future. Be cautious, Kenna. He will come when you least expect it.

Don't let your other endeavors distract you to the point that you are unprepared."

What she was unprepared for was his next statement, when he told her *Dancing Water* would be sailing as soon as he was on board.

At first, her expression was blank, as if his words had not penetrated her consciousness. Then came surprise. "You did not tell me you were leaving," she said, a hint of anger in her voice.

"I told you we would be leaving as soon as the ship was mended, which it is."

Her brows knitted together in a frown, and he knew that look well enough by now to know she was weighing and balancing things in her mind, while she tried to decide if she should try to detain him for a while longer, or take the more flippant attitude and tell him she would miss him.

He was not a man to grovel, no matter how much he cared. He would make it easy for her. "I came to tell you goodbye."

"Without having lunch?"

His smile, he knew, did not hide the bittersweet mood he was in. "We have a galley on the ship, remember?"

"Then this is goodbye?"

He stroked her cheek. "Only because it is a part of leave-taking."

"You will be back, won't you?"

He smiled at her and said in his customary teasing way, "Is that an invitation?"

"Of course," she said, and then, as if she did not

want to commit herself, she added, "You know you are always welcome here."

He nodded. "Your warm words will be comforting, I am sure, on a long, lonely journey." He put his hands on her arms and held her fast, so he could look into her eyes, where he saw nothing to give him encouragement, so he gently kissed her on the forehead. "Stay safe," he said, and he turned and walked from the hall.

Kenna continued to stare after him, long after he was gone, with only the rhythm of his boots on the stone floors telling her that he had been here at all.

"Damn!" she said, and shoved a chair out of her way as she strode from the hall.

She planned to have lunch, but she ended up on the battlements instead, where she had a good view of the bay and *Dancing Water* as she awaited the arrival of her captain.

It was not long until she saw Colin and Ewen ride down the beach to rendezvous with Alejandro, who stood with Josette by his side, which reminded her that was where she should have been—down there as well, to see Colin off.

There were not many times in Kenna's life when she felt very, very small, but today was one of them.

She decided she would stay until they were in the boat and rowed out to the ship. But when they disappeared on the decks of *Dancing Water,* she decided she would remain until the ship sailed.

She saw Ewen was holding the reins of the horses, and realized there were only three of them, which meant Josette rode down there on the same horse with

Alejandro. It was only so she could ride the horse back, she told herself, choosing to ignore the fact that Ewen had come to take Colin's horse and could have easily taken Alejandro's as well.

In the end, she stayed until Colin and his ship sailed out of the bay and disappeared in the vastness, where the heavens met the sea.

Kenna wasn't hungry after all, she realized once she was back inside the castle, so she went to the distillery where she would work, until time to meet Josette in the great hall.

Owen was a godsend, and Kenna was more than pleased with the work he was doing, but she desperately needed someone knowledgeable about the distilling process, and to hire the workers needed to run it. She had talked with a man named Dougal Allan, who managed a distillery at one time. She hoped he would agree to take over the management of her distillery, which meant she had to wait until he let her know what his decision was, and Kenna was awfully impatient when it came to waiting patiently.

She knew there was a lot to learn, and for the past week, she had been studying the books in the distillery, and she understood the process, but that was a long way from actually transforming those words into a bottle of whisky.

The stills were cleaned and set up, but no one knew positively that they were set up correctly, or if they were too outdated to use, which Owen suspected. The two of them discussed this and other distillery matters for quite some time before she had to leave to meet Josette.

\* \* \*

Prior to sailing from Durness Castle, Colin decided to take the gold seized from the French, who had seized it from the Spanish, to his grandfather, who would know who could be trusted to get the money into the hands of the Highlanders who needed it most.

Colin knew many Scots had emigrated to America, for he had transported a great many of them in his ship. Large numbers had also fled to France and Australia, and there would be innumerable waves of them in the future—those who could no longer support themselves due to the changes that were sure to come, and the Jacobites who were now in hiding, desperate to escape Scotland before the British found them. The desperate highlanders saw their situation grow more hopeless with each day that passed, for they needed money for transportation out of Scotland, and additional cash to help them settle in a new country. For those who chose to remain in Scotland, things could only get worse.

Colin and his grandfather, Hugh Montgomery, the twelfth Baron of Fairlie, did not get along well because of the long-standing resentment his grandfather had for Colin's father, Alexander. The baron had never forgiven his son for moving to America and leaving Baron Fairlie with no one to take over the family castle after his death. It was a crushing blow to him to think that after thirteen generations, the title would become extinct. It did not help that Alexander was so frank in his rejection, when he wrote:

*The castle falling into ruin matters not one iota to me. I owe naught to Scotland, and my only indebtedness to you is due to your having sired me.*

Having failed to persuade Alexander, the baron began to work on Colin, with hopes of convincing him to become the thirteenth Baron of Fairlie, by telling him the title could be legally passed to his grandson, which made Colin feel like his father, in that he did not care one iota to become the thirteenth of anything.

Colin felt sorry for the old man, for there had been much sorrow in his life—a wife who died along with her unborn child, and the subsequent deaths of three of his four sons and both daughters—and for a while Colin attempted to form some sort of relationship with him, but the baron was bitter and his resolve was as hard as the Cairngorms' granite.

The thing that kept Colin going back and subjecting himself to his grandfather's harsh ways was simply the fact that, unlike his father, Colin felt an inexplicable need to honor the blood connection to his grandfather.

"That is not something you inherited from me," Colin's father said, when Colin explained how he felt. "Go ahead and befriend him if you like, but in time he will wear you down to a nub. He is obstinate, flinty-hearted and as dour as a Puritan. Scotland will sap the humanity out of you, and give you nothing in return."

Because the baron's home, Barroleigh Castle, looked out upon Dunnet Bay, on the Pentland Firth, it was only a day's sail from Durness Castle. Colin decided to stop at Barroleigh, where they would unload the two chests of gold. Alejandro would then take the ship on to Edinburgh for repairs. Colin would stay with his grandfather a day or two, to make certain the gold was in a safe place, then he would go back to Durness. Part of the reason was he did not like the way things were left between himself and Kenna, but there was another, more important reason, and that was Colin had a persistent feeling that he should go back. He did not know why, only that something kept urging him to return.

He decided it was best to go back, even on a wild-goose chase, than stay away and learn later that something happened he could have prevented.

*Dancing Water* was anchored in Dunnet Bay, with Alejandro in command of the gold and the ship, while Colin called on his grandfather.

Colin waited for the baron in the library, where he refreshed his memory of the maps hung on the dark stone walls, the old, leather-bound books crowded into bookshelves, and the compartments overhead crammed with manuscripts, journals, loose papers and a few unidentifiables. He was about to peruse the items on the library table when the baron entered the room.

From his earliest recollections of his grandfather, Colin always thought the baron's entry into a room should be accompanied by music, so commanding a presence had he.

"Each time you leave, I know it will be the last time I see you, and each time you come back, I am forced to admit I am wrong."

"I know how you hate to be wrong," Colin said, "so perhaps you should learn from your mistakes and stop predicting my comings and goings. You are looking well, Grandfather."

"I don't know why I should be, when there isn't a part of me that isn't wearing out. I couldn't live long enough to list all my aches and pains."

Colin smiled in spite of himself. "I see you are as cantankerous as ever, so you must be in better health than you think."

"What brings you here this time? I know this isn't a social call. The American branch of the family seems to have lost all memory when it comes to social graces."

"I still remember how to curtsy."

"Don't be flippant. That is a woman's foolishness."

"If I had said I remember my social graces enough to visit you each time I come to Scotland, you would have labeled me deceptive. Either way I lose."

Enveloped in silence now, the two of them stared at each other from opposite sides of the room. Colin could see his grandfather had aged a great deal since he was here last, and there was something else…not age, but more a battle weariness that had settled over him like a mantle.

"Well, I suppose there is a reason you are here… God knows you did not come to forge a bond with me."

"You are right about the first and could not be more wrong about the second. But, if you mean by bond, my willingness to become the thirteenth Baron of Fairlie, you are right. Thirteen is an unlucky number, and I have enough bad luck on my own, without inheriting thirteen centuries of it."

"You have the devil's confidence…superstitious, are you?"

"Only when I'm in Scotland."

Colin thought his grandfather came quite close to smiling. "I am going to need a cart or some strong horses."

"Did your ship run aground near here?"

"No, the news is better than that. You might say I ran into some good fortune, and I have two chests of gold on my ship that I want to leave with you."

The baron's face turned a deep red, and his voice was rock hard and laced with anger. "I'll not hide your ill-gotten loot for you."

"I don't want you to hide it. I am giving it to you. I want it distributed in the Highlands. I know you will know the best way to get the gold into the hands of those who need it the most."

"How did you come about it?"

Colin grinned and walked to stand in front of the baron. "If you will pour the both of us a glass of whisky, I will tell you everything."

They had two glasses of whisky while they waited for the baron's men to fetch the chests and lock them in the dungeon. They had a third glass after dinner, as they continued to discuss the distribution of the gold. His grandfather might be old, but he was as sharp-minded and as shrewd as he had ever been.

Colin saw the weathered face and the shock of white hair, but those light blue eyes were as young as they had ever been. He saw something different in the baron, something that seemed to have energized him, but whether it was his enjoyment of having something exciting to do for a change, or the result of too much whisky, Colin might never know.

"So, you will be staying here until tomorrow, then?"

"Yes, at least until I can get passage to Durness Castle."

"Why are you going to Durness?"

The question threw him off, and the baron was quick to pick up on the fact, for his eyes twinkled with a sort of glee as he said, "So it is a woman who draws you there?"

The answer was written all over Colin's face.

It did not evoke a laugh from the baron, but he did manage a chuckle, and Colin could never remember his grandfather doing that before.

"Is she a MacKay?"

"Her mother was the daughter of the earl."

"Aah, she married the youngest son of the Duke of Sutherland?"

"Yes."

His grandfather seemed to go off somewhere and did not come back for a little while. "Tell me, does your lass have red hair?"

"Oh, does she!"

The baron slapped his leg. "Tell me about her."

Colin ended up having a fourth glass of whisky with the baron while he told him about Kenna.

By the time Colin finished his story, neither of them could have managed to stand if they had had a fifth glass of whisky, so they stumbled off to bed.

The next morning, Colin set off for Durness Castle with some of the baron's men.

# Twenty-One

At length the morn and
cold indifference came.
—Nicholas Rowe (1674-1718),
English playwright.
*The Fair Penitent* (1703).

She knew it was not going to be an ordinary day when she went to bed that night and heard the clock strike thirteen.

When she crawled into bed, she was distractedly conscious of Colin's absence and haunted by the cold indifference of her goodbye. She could not do anything to change what had happened any more than she could call back the day, so she might start anew and live it all over again.

After much thought, it seemed to her way of thinking, that if she could not change it, she should not keep thinking about it. But she did.

Consequently, she did not fall asleep straightaway,

kept awake, as she was, by guilty thoughts about Colin's departure, and later, by the dark menace of foreboding that persisted in lingering, even when she bid it to go. When sleep did take her, she was overcome with an emotional restlessness.

She did not know if she actually slept, of if she only imagined she did; whichever it was, she gave a start and sat straight up in the bed, gripped in a clammy, cold sweat. She thought she heard a sound, a tapping, like someone walking, or drumming their fingers on a table.

Her eyes were wide open now, and another noise crept into her consciousness, coming, she was certain, from outside, perhaps on the parapets beyond her window.

She groped across the small table by her bed, with hopes she would be fortunate enough to put her hand on the tinderbox, or bump into the candle. She located the tinderbox, and eventually, the candle, too, and tried again and again, but the candle would not light. She recalled prior to closing her eyes in what she thought was sleep, the sound of the candle guttering, before it went out.

It was darker than the blackest black in the room, and the velvet draperies were drawn so not even the moonlight could enter. Outside, she heard a gale blowing wildly and her spirits sank like cold dread, while everything inside seemed eerily quiet. She wriggled backward to brace her back against the headboard and sat quietly listening, afraid to breathe until the moment it was critical. She heard nothing but the wind, yet everything seemed out of harmony.

With a sigh, she decided it must have been a bad dream, and she worked her way back to a sleeping position. But her heart was pounding loudly in her ears and her mouth felt chalky and dry. She closed her eyes and heard the clock strike thirteen again. Eyes open. Did someone turn the handle on her door? Something creaked; a slice of yellow light appeared on the threshold and quickly disappeared. The hand was on her door again.

"Josette?" she whispered, and received no reply. Fear knotted in her stomach; cold fingers fluttered up and down her spine.

Something howled; something that did not sound like a dog. She recognized the sound of wind rushing up the chimney, as it did when a door was opened and the wind rushed in, drawn up the chimney in an updraft. Somewhere in the castle, someone must have left a door partially shut and the wind had blown it open. That must be the explanation.

She reminded herself the dogs were belowstairs and if anyone entered, they would bark. Unless the dogs went out when the door was opened. She relaxed; she was not alone; there was the castle's staff.

Her frantic heartbeat slowed. She sucked in a long breath and willed herself to relax. Her eyes were heavy now; heavier still, they closed.

The house settled about her; easing the nervous tension. It was too quiet...unnaturally quiet...quiet like death. She relaxed with a sigh, eager now to fall asleep and leave the menace behind. But it was not to be a deep sleep; it was fraught with dreams, strange and creepy, until she could not decipher what was a dream and what was real.

A muffled sound, like something small being moved; a book pushed aside; the palm of a hand skimming along a stone wall. Her eyes opened again, straining now to see in the dark interior of her room where the creeping chill was unnatural and uncommon, yet it continued until she could feel the ice of it seeping into her bones.

There was something or someone in the castle who had no business being there; someone with evil in their heart. She sensed someone was in her room now, breathing and taking away her air; she gasped and felt a presence beside the bed. She was too paralyzed to move.

She remembered the *comte*'s sword was lying on top of the chest at the foot of her bed. She began to turn and move slowly toward it. Time stretched as thin as her nerves, and she was a hair's breadth away from shouting, "I know you are in here!" But she said nothing.

The sound of a door opening and then closing came from far away, as if it were in a tunnel. Another sound near her window, the one that looked over the parapets. Perhaps someone in the castle had suddenly taken ill. What if Josette was trying to waken her because she needed help?

I might as well go and check, she thought, for I will get precious little sleep this night. She felt around for her dressing gown and her hand bumped against the handle of the *comte*'s sword. Relief washed over her, even though the hand that held the sword trembled. She eased her feet to the floor and stood. She walked with slow, measured steps to the door and opened it cautiously. She could not see a thing, for it was as dark on the other side of the door as it was within.

A strange odor reached her nose. Her eyes began to tear. She returned to her room to fetch the tinderbox and groped her way back toward the desk, relieved to find a candle she had left there. It flared to life on the third strike of steel against flint.

She turned around to leave the room, and in a state of numb and bewildered curiosity, she remained transfixed as she watched a peculiar, swirling mist slowly encroach upon the privacy of her room. She wondered, what was this intruder that slithered uninvited into her bedchamber in the middle of the night? The gripping sense of fear within her screamed ghosts, but the logic of her mind searched for other clues, ones that were more explicable as well as reasonable.

She inched her way toward the door, breathing in the odd smell that was now choking her with a pungent bitterness. Scent and fog mingled in her consciousness as she searched to put a name to it. Hypnotic to watch, the eerie gray vapor tinged with brown crossed the threshold like searching fingers, so fascinating that she was completely absorbed in a drowsy consciousness as if from a sleep-inducing drug. Her sluggish mind had difficulty understanding this was not beautiful, but dangerous. This was no swirling mist that came slowly creeping into her room. This was smoke. The same smoke that filled the room, choked her throat and burned her eyes; smoke that did not belong here.

Smoke, whose mate was fire.

She saw rays of light pushing into the room from the windows behind her drapes. She put the candle on a table and hurried to throw back the heavy velvet, hoping it was the sun and not a worse alternative. The light of early morning washed into the room to snap her from her trancelike state. Infused with a burst of energy that suddenly kicked in, she ran into the hallway and threw open the door to Josette's room. A hot blast of smoke rushed over her; she could see flames now, flames that licked at the draperies over the windows.

The room was stifling hot; she dropped her sword by the door, put her hand over her mouth and moved into the room until she bumped against the bed. She groped for her friend and began to shake Josette. "Get up! Your room is on fire! Wake up, Josette! Please wake up!"

She shook her harder; the only response was a moan. She began to scream now, then she screamed louder, still shaking Josette, while she called for help. She had no idea how long it would take the flames to reach the bed. Panic beat in her lungs like a trapped bird. The fumes were starting to affect her. She ran to the stand that held a basin and a pitcher of water. She grabbed the pitcher, rushed back to the bed and threw the water in Josette's face.

Josette sputtered and coughed and coughed again. Kenna dropped the pitcher on the bed and wiped burning tears from her own face and screamed for help again.

The draperies nearest her burst into flames. A second later they leaped like a devouring monster to the bed.

"Someone, please help!"

She smelled singed hair and reached for Josette again, just as she heard the sound of footsteps running on the floor below. Something crashed and a voice called out, but she could not hear as she tried to drag Josette from the bed. The flames were consuming everything in sight.

Someone was rushing up the stairs; the door to Josette's room flew back and banged against the wall.

Strong hands grabbed her shoulders and pushed her out of the way; her head flew up as Colin scooped Josette from the bed and slung her over his shoulder. His other arm snaked around Kenna and drew her close.

"Hurry," he said. "This way, quickly! Before it spreads and we can't reach the stairs."

Smoke was thick in the corridor outside the door, but it began to grow thinner as they approached the stairs. They were halfway down when they were met by a group of MacKays rushing up the stairs with buckets of water.

Colin managed to get both of them outside. Josette was coughing violently, but at least she was breathing.

"Wait here," he said, "and don't go back in for any reason. Understand?"

She nodded and he caressed her cheek, then disappeared back inside the house.

It seemed he was gone for an unbearably long time...so long that she began to worry he might have been trapped in one of the rooms above. She came to her feet and started to go back into the house, and remembered what he said.

"*Mon Dieu!* What happened?" Josette choked out.

Kenna turned around. "There has been a fire. I think it started in your room. When I arrived to awaken you, your draperies were alight."

Josette coughed again. "Thank God you thought to come and help me."

Kenna put her arm around her. "I would never leave you to that kind of fate, Josette. Never."

She sat down next to her friend, holding her trembling hand, and started to cry when Josette squeezed it and put her head on Kenna's shoulder.

They were friends now, truly, resolutely, and forever friends, and she knew that somewhere the *comte* was smiling.

More time passed and eventually the MacKays began to straggle through the door.

"Is the fire out?" she asked.

"Yes, it was only in the one bedchamber on the second floor," a MacKay responded.

Kenna was starting to worry about Colin all over again when he stepped through the doorway and came toward them. He had a wet cloth in his hand and he handed it to Josette. "Put this over your nose and breathe through it. The moisture will ease the burning in your lungs."

Josette covered her face and began to breathe deeply, in and out.

Colin stood near Kenna, while his gaze searched her face.

"Even with the charcoaled face of an urchin, you are still beautiful." His voice was laced with sadness, and she was reminded of the mood between them when he saw her last. His hand stroked the top of her hair and she felt the singed ends break off at his touch. "Your lovely hair is burned, but not badly."

A voice came from inside the cloth as it lifted. "I'm almost dead, and the two of you are making love?" The cloth fell back into place.

Colin gave a start and then laughed out loud.

"She is definitely feeling better," Kenna said, and smiled with relief.

Josette removed the cloth and looked as cross as two sticks. "You would not feel so jolly if it were your breathing machine that was scorched," she said in her grumpiest tone. "How bad is it?"

"Did the fire spread to my room?" Kenna asked.

"No, just the smoke, which will leave some damage," Colin answered.

Josette frowned. "And my room?"

"The drapes and the bed are gone, I'm afraid. The rest can probably be salvaged."

Kenna looked from Josette to Colin. "The fire was only in one room?"

Colin nodded. "Yes, we checked all the other rooms on that floor and found only lingering smoke, so we opened the windows."

"That is strange," Kenna said. "I don't understand how it could have happened."

"It could have been a candle," he said.

Josette was quick to knock that suggestion down. "I

did not burn a candle last night. I had a headache and went to bed after dinner...before dark."

Kenna was amassing the facts and put them together to form a mental picture. Slow awareness dawned. "I think it was started intentionally," she said.

"But why...who...?" Suddenly, Josette paused and her gaze locked with Kenna's. "Your friend," she said. "The monster that killed the *comte*."

"He was never my friend, but yes, I think it was Lord Walter. I think there is a calculated method to his madness. It isn't only me he is after. He intends to kill everyone around me first, all those I care about, one by one, then he will kill me."

Josette turned her head to one side with a questioning look. "How would that satisfy his sick hunger?"

"It will give him pleasure, satisfaction if you will. Do I think he is insane? Of course, but sometimes genius hides in the lunatic mind, which is even more dangerous. Each time he kills someone I know, he will see it as making me suffer twice, giving me as much pain as possible before he kills me is what it's all about. A weird sort of satisfaction for a demented mind."

Worry and concern produced a frown on Colin's brow. "Don't talk about that now. You've been through a great ordeal this morning. What you don't need is more agitation. Let's go inside. The mist coming in from the water is cool and damp. You don't need to catch a chill."

Kenna was the first to move, but Colin reached for her arm and detained her with a light touch. She glanced at his hand and back at him. "I want to ask you something."

"You need to hold my arm to ask me something?"

He released her. "Do you have a knife...a dirk?"

"Of course I do."

"Wear it."

"Wear it? What are you talking about?"

"I am talking about safety. You've got a murderer running loose around here trying to kill people. You don't know where he will strike next. I would feel better if you had your knife with you all the time." She made a move to roll her eyes and thought better of it.

"Is it such a big thing to ask? Only a fool would go out unarmed when her life was in danger."

He did not know why she was so obstinate. Was she this way with everyone, or just him?

"All right. I'll wear it."

"All the time."

A sigh. "All the time...except when I bathe and when I sleep."

"Keep it by your bed at night."

"Agreed. *Now* may I go in?"

He bowed and she swept past.

They ended up in the small dining room because it was cozier than the great hall. They settled themselves and sat around, quietly talking until dear Ewen came in with a tea tray that also contained milk, honey and scones.

Kenna always gave him a smile to reinforce her words. "You always anticipate, and it is always appreciated. Would you mind bringing another wet cloth?"

With a nod, he scurried from the room in that endearing half walk, half hobble particular to him.

Kenna was relaxed on the sofa. Colin sat next to her, but he was careful not to get close enough that they touched.

"Do you realize we have on our nightgowns?" Kenna said.

"I do not care" was Josette's emphatic reply. "Naked would have been fine, too, if that's what it took to save my life. Kenna, if you had not awakened when you did, if you had thought to save only yourself... Why did you wake up? The fire wasn't in your room."

Kenna started with the clock striking thirteen times, twice, and gave them the entire story of what transpired: the noises she heard, the presence she sensed in the house; the certainty that someone entered her room; how afraid she had been lying in her bed; the smoke she mistook in the beginning for a swirling mist, and the terror that gripped her when she could not awaken Josette. She even mentioned strapping on her dirk, and thinking she heard a dog howl at some point.

Josette had an odd expression. "Where *are* the dogs?"

Ewen returned with a wet cloth for all three of them, and two small blankets he gave to Kenna and Josette. When he started from the room, Kenna called out to him. "Ewen, have you seen the dogs this morning?"

Ewen shook his head and hurried from the room.

"That was odd," Kenna said, "and quite unlike him. Do you think he knows something and doesn't want to tell? He was very attached to them. He would have noticed their absence immediately."

"I will speak to him when the confusion has died down. Right now, he is going in five directions."

Josette wiped her face and Kenna saw how exhausted she was. "If you want to rest, you can go in any of the empty bedchambers. Ewen can have the maids move what's left of your things to whichever one you choose."

Kenna wrapped the blanket around her shoulders, to cover her gown as much as she could. She noticed Josette left hers folded across her lap, as if someone seeing her in her nightgown was not on her present list of worries.

Kenna saw the grave expression of Colin's face and it occurred to her that he was saying very little. "When did you arrive? I was surprised you repaired *Dancing Water* so fast."

"And where is Alejandro?" Josette added.

"I got here shortly before I heard you scream for help. *Dancing Water* is in Edinburgh undergoing repairs with Alejandro and the crew."

"Edinburgh?" Kenna asked. "You couldn't have gone to Edinburgh and back so fast."

"I did not go to Edinburgh. We sailed to Dunnet Bay where my grandfather lives, stopped long enough to drop me off, then they sailed on to Edinburgh. My grandfather had his men bring me back here."

"Why did you come back here so soon?" Kenna asked.

"It was a strong feeling I had...instinctive, if you will. You would call it intuition. Whatever the term, I could not disassociate myself from it. I planned to go to Edinburgh. I needed to go to Edinburgh. I did not want to disrespect your wishes, but I am a man and, instinctively, I want to protect. You are an independent woman—you want to take care of yourself. I understand the tension you live with, the constant worry about Lord Walter, but we disagree on how to deal with it. In the end, I decided it was better to return and be sent away, than to learn later that I should have come."

"It was a good thing you listened to your inner voice and returned," Josette said, "at least it is from my perspective."

Kenna was conscious of the way Josette was looking at her. It lay somewhere between accusatory and sympathetic, and Kenna did not want to deal with that right now, so she brushed it aside.

"Why did you stop to see your grandfather, if you needed to be in Edinburgh?"

Colin spent the next few minutes detailing his visit, the securing of the gold in his grandfather's dungeon, and the arrangement he had worked out for his grandfather to manage getting the gold into the hands of needy Highlanders. "I also realized the two of you did not get a share of the gold, and I made provisions for that as well."

"Did you take a share?" Kenna asked.

"Are you wearing your dirk?"

She came close to smiling. "As a matter of fact, I am."

"Good."

"Did you take a share?" she asked again.

"No."

"Did Alejandro?" Josette asked.

"No. Like me, he feels the Highlanders need it more than we do."

"You must have wealthy families," Kenna said.

"While there is truth to that, we like to seek our own fortunes."

"The life of a privateer must be a lucrative one," Josette said.

"I don't make my living privateering, because I give away most of what I plunder, as you saw with the Spanish gold."

"Then how do you seek your fortune?" Kenna asked.

"Shipping."

"Shipping?" she repeated. "Isn't your ship a bit small for that?"

"*Dancing Water* is not the only ship I own, love."

"Really? How many do you have, then?" she asked, knowing she was being incredibly nosy, but allowing her curiosity to dictate.

A half smile played around his lips. "I haven't been asked this many questions since I was in school. I have five ships, Lady Lennox, including *Dancing Water*. Is there anything else you would like to know?"

"Not at the present, but I may think of something later on."

"Then you better hurry."

"Why do you say that?"

"As I said, I came back because I felt I should, and that bit of instinct turned out to be on target. Now that the danger is past, I know you will want me to go and not interfere, even if it is against my best judgment."

Josette stood and put her teacup down. "This sounds like a battle being waged between forces of opposing angels. Either both sides win, or neither one does. I know the sun is up and I have had breakfast, but I'm going to see if I can go back to sleep. I know that does not sound normal, but absolutely nothing has been normal about this day from the start." She put the blanket around her shoulders and departed.

Kenna was thinking about offering Colin an apology when he stood and said, "I think I will go have that talk with Ewen now."

She watched him go, and the emptiness of the room closed in around her.

Kenna went upstairs to survey the damage to her own room, which turned out to be only a faint smoky smell, thanks to the MacKays, who had opened the windows earlier in order to freshen the air. The room was a bit drafty, so she went to close all the windows but one. It was on the third window that she glanced toward the courtyard and saw two MacKays in a horse cart about to go through the gate. She caught a glimpse of Colin as he stepped into her view and walked toward the cart. She heard him call out, and the cart stopped. They spoke for a moment and one of the men climbed down. Colin walked with him to the back of the cart, and as the man pulled back a piece of burlap, Kenna gasped.

Inside, she saw the two deerhounds. Later, when Colin returned, he told her, "Their throats were cut."

Everyone had their boiling point and Kenna had reached hers. It was the turning point; the final and un-

bearable misfortune; the last horrible deed at the end
of too many tragedies; the camel's back that was broken by one little straw; the one occurrence that made
the entire situation unbearable. And that is what
prompted her to vow she would search for a way to
force his hand—a way so compelling that Lord Walter would come out into the open and make his move.

# Twenty-Two

The bright day is done,
And we are for the dark.
—William Shakespeare (1564-1616),
    English poet and playwright.
*Antony and Cleopatra* (1606-1607),
    Act V, Scene 2.

The candles had never shone brighter in Durness Castle than they did that night when the three of them sat down to dinner. The food was good, but dinner was a dreadful affair, and Kenna barely touched anything on her plate. It gave her an odd feeling to sit with two people she cared so much for, and to listen to their lighthearted banter, knowing that she was not a part of it.

Oh, she partook of the conversation, certainly, but her heart was not in it. She felt like a watch with some of its springs removed. It looked fine, but anyone who checked inside could see that it was broken.

As soon as the meal ended, she said, "It has been a long, exhausting day. If you will excuse me."

But she did not retire to her room as she had planned, but found herself instead navigating the quiet passages of vaulted stone past the chapel, robed in the scarlet and gold of the past. How many heartfelt prayers had been sent heavenward like birds on the wing, now set free?

The fragrance of candle wax scented the corridors, and made her wonder if anyone had ever found their way, blinded, and guided by its scent alone.

She pushed open the heavy door of the tower and climbed the steps of timeworn stone, narrow and steep, until she reached the top and stepped out onto the parapet, to look out on the beauty of Sutherland, where the veins of rivers flowed through fallow fields and into lochs, cold and deep.

The sunlight was almost gone, the last thin slice of it perching like a bird on a craggy pinnacle, barely visible in the distance. Overhead a few small clouds floated by: a backdrop for an occasional swallow or kittiwake.

She found the stone ledge that ran around the parapet—and pegged it the perfect seat.

As she sat down, night embraced her, the warm russet and gold of the day now turned to a deeper, darker shade, the usurper stealing the last light, and replacing it with her colors of mulberry, indigo, violet and red; colors that bled into the purpled dye of a cardinal's robe.

A quiet hush settled over the moors. The toothed rim

of crags disappeared beneath the cloak of night, moving across the horizon and dipping her hand into her silvered bag to glitter the sky with stars.

The peace of the evening penetrated, softening even her bones, and Kenna leaned her head back against the cold stones, and willed the cobwebs in her mind to be swept away. She felt stretched to a dozen points, unable to align herself on her axis. And as always, thoughts of Colin crept forward to curl at her feet, silent and mysterious as a cat.

The intimacy they previously enjoyed had been superseded by a discomforting constraint that stayed between them like a pane of clear glass. They could see each other and talk to each other, but the glass prevented them from actually stepping into each other's world.

She missed the warm familiarity, but did not know how to go about getting it back…or if she should even try.

She did not realize she was so tired until she began to relax. She closed her eyes and listened to the tinkle of a sheep's bell, the bark of a dog driving the herd home.

The door she had come through earlier clanked, then scraped across stones and was thrown back. "You little fool! Don't you know everyone in the castle has been looking for you?"

She opened her eyes to the golden glow of a candle in a lantern, almost touching her face. She drew her head back, and watched Colin wave it over the parapet as he called out, "I have found her up here. She is safe."

He put the lamp down. Light and shadow transformed the handsome planes of his face into that of a gargoyle, reminding her of the one that had fallen and hit her shoulder; was Colin her bad omen? Still groggy from having dozed off, she closed her eyes and wished he would disappear, but when she opened them again, he was still there, too handsome by far to be looking at her so angrily.

"There was no need to sound the alarm. I was not planning to jump from the parapet. I don't know why you are so upset. Perhaps it makes you feel important."

"I am important, at least to some people. But, that isn't the issue here."

"What is the issue?"

"How about your total disregard of others. Where is your empathy? Are you so wrapped up in your own world that you can effectively cut everyone else out? What do you mean, you don't see why we are upset? Someone tried to kill your friend and burn the place down last night. How can you be flippant and act as if it never happened? You tell us you know it was Lord Walter, and we believe you because he has already killed your father, three brothers and now the *comte*. Then you disappear tonight while we frantically search for you. Would it have stressed you too much to tell us where you were going? I guess it was too much to ask someone devoid of empathy, which is, in case you are unfamiliar with the word, the ability to understand another person's feelings, to put yourself in their place and see it from their point of view."

"I did not think…"

"Well, lady, you better damn well start thinking before you end up getting what you want and find yourself completely alone. What in the hell were you doing up here all this time? Without bothering to tell anyone that you never intended going to bed?"

"I didn't know I was coming up here until I was almost to the staircase. I do not see why you are so furious because I sought a little peace and quiet in a place where I could think."

A breeze ruffled his hair, and his face looked as dark as a pirate's. She decided this was not a good time to discuss anything with him. "Is this some contest, then, to see which of us can stare moodily at the other for the longest amount of time? If there is a prize, you take it, because I am going to bed."

"You aren't going anywhere."

"This is my home and you are neither my father nor my husband. I can go where I please, when I please and do as I please. I am not your responsibility or your concern. I can support myself and take care of myself. In other words, I don't need you…."

She intended to say she did not need him shouting at her all the time, that she was new at this and would naturally make mistakes. She was a human being, for God's sake, and therefore created imperfect, but she did not get to say those things because he cut her off.

"You're right, you don't need me or anyone. I saw how well you were taking care of yourself and those around you this morning when I came into Josette's room and pulled her out of a burning bed. What were you going to do? Stand there wringing your hands, calling for help and offering her moral support as she burned to death, all in the name of doing everything your way?"

"That was an exception."

"Your entire life is an exception."

"I was going to say it was an exception in that we normally don't have fires intentionally started in our bedchambers when we are sleeping in there."

"*Mea culpa!* You are right. I guess by now 'normal' in your life is to have a father and two brothers ambushed, another brother poisoned, your sister almost starved to death, a friend brutally stabbed and another almost burned alive. Have you become so desensitized by your suffering that you have lost all contact with what is factual, what is real?"

She glanced toward the door.

He crossed his arms and regarded her impassively. "Go ahead," he said. "Try it, and see how far you get."

She had come too far to back down now, and she swore she would not even try to mollify him. She stood and faced him, but he did not give her time to throw any words at him.

"I ought to turn you over my knee. If your father had done so when you were younger, you would not be so obstinate and uncaring."

"I care, but not for you!" The minute the words were out, she wanted to snatch them back, but she could tell by the dark, angry look on his face that it was too late for that. His face was both stubborn and stern. I'll not give in and ask his forgiveness, she thought with a hint of desperation; I give in and melt each time he touches me.

The faint notes of a mandolin floated upward. Someone was playing in the courtyard below. The unfamiliar melody was lovely. She took a deep breath. The music had intervened at the right time; music to soothe a savage beast.

She heard voices carried on the wind and turned away from him to lean against the parapet. Below them, one of the MacKays was building a fire. She watched the orange flames leap hungrily upward, wild they looked, seeking something to devour. She had a sudden impulse to shove Colin toward the ravenous flames and say, "Here, take him."

The thought of it pleased her, even if the reality of it did not. Someone plucked a few strings of the mandolin and began to play again.

She stood on her toes in order to see what was happening. "What are they doing down there?" She did not turn around.

"Ewen said some of the men were going to build a fire and play a few songs. They asked Josette to bring you when we found you."

She might have known he would get the conversation back to that. She was trying, really trying not to have another argument like they had in the distillery, so she clamped her mouth shut in order to remain quiet, for tonight everything she said seemed to raise his ire. She did not know how long they stood there, neither of them speaking, but at some point, he must have grown tired, for he stepped up to the parapet and stood beside her.

They leaned into the stones and watched the activity below, standing side by side, their bodies touching lightly. Yet, neither of them spoke as they looked upon the shadowed courtyard, beneath the light of a gibbous moon.

She was about to speak when the mellow tones of violins floated over them, and the golden glow of the fire danced across the faces below. Those standing near the flames began to move back, and Kenna saw Josette, and knew she was going for the first time to see her dance.

Josette danced the same way she lived her life, with a passion, her eyes wide, head alert and her body ready to confront whatever challenge she was handed. Kenna did not need to be down there to know her exotic, dark eyes would be hypnotic to anyone who dared gaze into them.

Her well-controlled body twirled to each pulsing note, as if aware only of the passionate rhythm pounding in her ears. She was telling a story of her people, a tale that was seductive, oppressive and sad. It was so poignant and graceful, it was easy to confuse it with reality.

She had never seen anyone dance the way Josette danced. It was as if it were a part of her, an ancient rhythm placed inside her long before she was born. There was such emphasis on the graceful movements of her arms, hips and shoulders, and the expressive twists and turns of her hands, all from the wrists. And all the while, she held her black skirt, emphasizing each move with the skirt, played like an instrument with her hands.

It was provocative, worldly, seductive, carnal. Kenna could feel the coiling spiral of desire surrounding her and slowly drawing her forward, pulling her into its powerful embrace. Her throat was dry. Yearning made her aware of her body in a way she had never known. She wanted Colin, wanted him now; to kiss her, to touch her in all the right places. She felt warm and thick, as if a rush of feeling jammed in her throat, blocking her ability to communicate.

She hardened her resolve and felt her body stiffen in resistance—of him, of her desire for him, of any thought of there ever being something between them.

"Why must you be so hard-hearted and stubborn? Can't we find a halfway mark in all of this? Couldn't you at least try?"

"I cannot. You know I must keep my focus upon Lord Walter until I have settled the matter. And please do not say I should let you or anyone handle it. It is something I must do alone. I can't face Lord Walter with my mind distracted."

"Who said anything about breaking your heart?"

"I'm not asking to settle it for you…only to be here in case you need me."

"I cannot risk another life lost because of me—especially yours. I know you don't understand, but I can't explain it any other way. I have always seen this as my fight, because it is. I have already lost someone dear to me by letting my guard down and thinking I could live a normal life, and I lost sight of the fact that I will always fail in that regard simply because Lord Walter is not normal. I've told you this dozens of times, but you still do not understand, and now I think I know why—you don't want to understand because you want everything your way."

She studied his face, waiting for him to say something, to respond to her, to keep their communication open so they remained in the same army, instead of withdrawing into separate forces that would eventually evolve and start to grow apart, until they reached the point where they became enemies. But his face was hard; his expression inscrutable; his mouth unsmiling.

Sometimes, silence can be an answer.

She wished with all her heart he could understand, and his not doing so left her unsettled and disappointed. She had opened herself to him, and then she had pressed him, wanting—no, needing to hear some expression to tell her that he understood, that he loved her enough to stand by her, even when he did not disagree with her.

There was nothing—only the feel of his eyes boring into her. She was a fool for being too naive to understand that a man can want a woman but not *want* her; that he can want her body, but not the commitment; that he can draw out her spirit and her soul, and give nothing back.

And then she is nothing but an empty shell. She would not settle for that. It left her angry with herself for fishing for some assurance from him.

"It is getting late. I'm going back inside."

He was left standing on the parapet, listening to the sound of her feet that hurried down the narrow steps. When he turned to follow her with his gaze, he saw her use both hands to pull back the heavy door before she disappeared behind it.

She was greeted by the same scent of candles as before, and saw that someone had come along to light the torches that cast a dim light down the passageway. She hurried on and was almost to the chapel when she heard the scrape of the parapet door; the sound of it closing loudly behind her.

The rapid staccato of footfalls echoed down the passageway, telling her he was coming after her. She quickened her step and felt, a moment later, the tight grip of his hand close around her arm. He whirled her around to face him.

"What is wrong with you?"

"Please do not touch me like this. Someone may come by."

He looked around. "In here," he said, and pulled her into the dim chapel.

She made a scoffing sound. "The chapel, a perfect choice. Are we here to create new sins, confess our old ones, or just to pray for the forgiveness of them?"

He crossed his arms and leaned against a column. "How do you see it?"

"All those ways," she said.

"Damned if I understand you."

"I have not noticed you trying."

"I have invested more effort into understanding you than you know."

"Ha!"

"Do you know what I think the problem is?" he asked. "You wear your feelings on your sleeve, and your heart is too easily bruised because everything by-passes your intellect."

She shrugged and kept her gaze focused on the floor. This was going nowhere. She could not bare her heart to him because he gave her no reason to. She was glad, at least, that he could not see her feelings for him in her eyes, her face. She sighed deeply.

She would not be the first lass to lose her heart to a man who cared naught. It was a painful realization, but it would not be forever, she knew. The pain she felt now would eventually heal, and in the gaping hole where love had dwelled there would be wisdom.

"You must have someone special. A fiancée? A certain woman waiting for you in America?"

"No, there is no one special in my life."

His words stung. Well, what did she expect? Did she truly think he would say that she was his someone special? Foolish woman. Couldn't she understand how easy she would be for him to forget?

She was nothing more than someone to amuse him while he was in Scotland. She would not boost his ego any further by allowing him to think it bothered her. It was best this way, she told herself. There was no time for her to deal with matters of the heart.

"I think it is time for you to go," she said. She turned and, without a word, fled from the chapel.

# *Twenty-Three*

The only way to be absolutely safe
is never to try anything for the first time.
—Attributed to J. A. D. Ingres (1780-1867),
French artist.

Kenna was waiting for Josette in the great hall the next morning, when she walked in. "I did not mean to be so late," she said.

"It is all right, but unlike you. I have grown accustomed to your punctuality. Did you oversleep?"

"No, I had breakfast and Colin was there. He was getting ready to leave, and I offered to ride down to the bay with him so I could bring the horse back."

"He left? How did he go? His ship is not yet ready."

"Perhaps you should have thought about that before you told him it was time for him to leave."

Kenna stared at Josette in amazement. "Are you taking his side in this?"

"I am not taking sides at all, but I think you were wrong to say that to him."

"He was wrong to tell you."

"I asked why he was leaving when he had only just arrived. He said it was time for him to go. Of course I disagreed, but he said I should talk to you about it, because those were your words, not his."

"How did he leave without a boat?"

"He heard there was a large ship in the bay that just happened to be heading to Edinburgh. You did not know he was leaving, did you?"

"No, but it does not surprise me. We have not had the smooth road of love running between us for some time."

"I'm sorry."

"Yes, so am I, but at least now I can focus all my energy on besting you each time we have a match."

"Then by all means, come and we will let you beat me…if you can."

"That is the problem. Each time I get better, you do as well."

Josette smiled. "That sounds remarkably like something I told the *comte* when he first began to teach me."

Kenna placed her foil on the table and folded her arms across her middle. "How *did* you and the *comte* end up together?"

A wan smile settled upon Josette's mouth and her face took on a faraway look, as if she had traveled back to another place, a special event in her life that she held a particular fondness for. "He found me in Aix.

There was a dispute at a fair. Everyone blamed it on the Gypsys. The *gendarmes* began to round us up. My parents and a great many others were arrested and taken to the *gendarmerie*—the police station. The *gendarmes* did not want to bother with me, so I was left behind with the ragged remnant that escaped arrest. When the fair was over, the rest of the Gypsies broke camp and left. No one bothered to look for me."

"Where were you?"

"Asleep under a tree near one of the wagons. I like to think they simply climbed up and did not notice me, because Gypsies are very close and most of them are good parents."

"And the *comte* found you there?"

"No, when I became hungry I wandered into Aix. The children there ran after me, taunting me and pulling my hair, while they called me assorted names, none of them kind. I tried to run away, but I fell near a…the English word escapes me. That happens sometimes when I get emotional. I lose my English. In French, it is a *fontaine,* a *petit réservoir.*"

"A cistern."

She smiled. "Yes, I fell and cracked my head against a cistern. The children all ran away. No one came to help me. My head, it was very painful and it bled all over my new dress. I did not know where to go, so I sat down by the cistern. I stayed there all day. It was hot and the flies kept buzzing around my head. Sometimes one of the children would come by and laugh. It was almost dark and I started to cry…for the first time, mind you.

"I heard a coach approach and it sped by the cistern,

throwing dust over me, and stopped at a nearby inn. It was a beautiful coach with a crest on the door and six matched gray horses. There was a footman, and four liveried postilions. I thought it was the king of France. And then a man stepped out. He was tall, slender and so graceful; and his clothes looked as if they were spun from silver. He started toward the inn. I was still crying. He must have heard me, for he turned around. For a moment, he simply stood there looking at me. I remember I stopped crying and stared at him, because I decided he was not the king of France or an angel. In my eyes, he looked more like God. And then he did the most remarkable thing. He came across to me and I was suddenly afraid and scrambled to my feet. In that split second, between the time I was on my feet and the moment the command to run reached my brain, he smiled at me, and said, *'ma petite.'*"

Tears began to spill down Josette's face, but she did not pause. "He stopped in front of me in a squat, and he said, *'Ne pleurez pas. Je prendrai soin de vous, ma petite.'*"

Kenna was not even aware she whispered the translation: "Don't cry. I will take care of you, my little one."

"His voice was like music. I had never heard anyone speak such educated French, you understand. I was frozen, captivated by this beautiful man, whom, by this time, I had demoted, for he was no longer God, but back to being an angel in my mind, because I knew angels were beautiful, and I had never seen a picture of God. He picked me up and took me inside the inn. He ordered a bath and sent someone to find me new clothes. It was late, but they found the clothes and they were so beautiful I did not at first want to put them on. I was afraid I would be arrested, but he assured me I would not. And then, when I was in my new dress and shoes, and my hair had been dressed by the innkeeper's wife, he picked me up and he carried me down to dinner, and on the way there he said, *'Personne ne vous blesseront jamais encore. Vous avez ma promesse.'"*

Kenna translated again, only this time Josette was crying and she spoke loud enough that Josette heard: "No one will ever hurt you again. I promise."

"And no one ever did, until the night he was murdered."

They had to cancel their match that morning.

Instead of fencing, Kenna took Josette on a tour of the distillery. In the afternoon, they met again in the great hall for their afternoon match.

Afterward, Josette went upstairs to see if everything had been moved into her new room. Kenna was on her way to change out of her fencing clothes when she decided to go back to the distillery to see if Dougal and Owen were still there, or if they had locked up and gone home.

She had become quite attached to these two men in the short period of time they had been working to get the distillery operational. At first, Dougal Allan hadn't been certain he wanted to run a distillery again, but after Culloden things had not been so good, so he decided to take the position Kenna had offered him. He'd started to work only a few days ago. It was good that he already knew Owen Fletcher. The two of them had previously worked together, and they promised they would soon have the malt barns full and the peat stores enough to last several months, and would fill the new storage barns with oak barrels to age the premier whisky.

The kilns were next on the list of repairs, and before long, they would be drying malted barley around the clock.

When she reached the distillery, she was about to put her key in the lock, when she noticed it had been forced.

She pushed the door open slowly and quietly stepped inside.

The cabinet door was ajar.

A lone candle burned on the long, wooden table. Her heart pounded and then stilled.

Dear God…he was here.

Lord Walter, the devil incarnate, was on the opposite side of the table, his back toward her. She could see that he was rummaging through papers he had removed from the cabinet.

She took a step back, intending to turn and slip back through the door, but before she could do so, he turned around slowly.

He had not changed all that much. He was thinner, but he had always been the thin sort, and his hair was peppered with more gray than when she had seen him last. But the evil eyes that burned like Satan's furnace were the same.

"What are you doing here?"

"I was in the neighborhood and thought I would stop by for a visit. I was here once before, but I missed you. I did leave a message. Did you find it?"

He came closer, until he was standing dangerously near, not more than a foot away.

He backhanded her. Her head snapped back and whipped around. The force of the blow sent her slamming against the table, her hip receiving the brunt of it, sending an excruciating pain shooting down her leg.

"Bitch, how do you feel about that midnight ride to Edinburgh now? Do you think it has been worth it? No? Well, don't worry. There are a lot more surprises to come, so many creative things I have in store for you. Do you know, I bet that by the time I am through, you will be begging me to kill you."

"I don't beg weak, cowardly bastards for anything."

He hit her again and she could feel her lip bleeding. Spots flashed in her eyes and she wobbled dizzily on her feet. She turned her head away. He grabbed her by the hair and jerked her around to face him. "Do not call me a bastard again, or I might decide to kill you sooner than I planned, and that would rob me of so much pleasure."

She wiped the blood from her mouth. "Take your hand off me or I will scream, and whether you kill me or not, you won't leave this place alive."

She stared into vacant pits of hell, for his eyes were void of any spark of life—nothing more than two orbs, of a flat black color. No windows on the soul there.

He released her. "I like a woman who fights back." He grabbed her and shoved her against the wall, and kissed her, rudely, while he pressed himself into her. When he broke the kiss, he kept his forearm against her throat and began raising her skirts, until he could touch her.

Her left hand was behind her back, caught against the wall, but she could move it slightly because it was trapped in the cove of the small of her back. She had to endure his groping as she inched her fingers slowly along her waist until she felt them close around the handle of her dirk.

With one coordinated move, she slammed her knee into him, while at the same time bringing the tip of her dirk to rest against his throat. She pressed the point until a trickle of blood seeped out. "Back off, you bastard. Do it now! Step back… Move, I said! Ten paces back, right now!"

He leered down at her. She pressed the point and the trickle became a thin but solid flow. "Move, you bastard, or I will sever your windpipe and enjoy every minute of it."

He began to back away.

She was breathing heavily, both from exertion and fear, but the fear had already begun to leach away in the face of self-confidence.

"I will be back, you bitch."

"I am hoping you will be, and when you come, you better bring your rapier, otherwise I will take pleasure in carving your stinking carcass into so many wee pieces I'll prove you don't have a spine."

As soon as she said the words, she knew there would be no turning back now. She was committed. The Rubicon was not only behind her; it was off her map. If she was ever going to get the chance to bait him, it would have to be now. Her mind was searching for the opening, and it surprised her when he was the one who provided it.

"This is not the end of this," he said. "I will return and you will be sorry."

"You don't have the courage to come back and face me again. Your liver is too yellow for that. You aren't very smart, but you are smart enough to know it will be the end of you the next time we meet, because from this moment on, I will have my sword strapped to my side even when I sleep. I've known for a long time that you lack the nerve to face another man in a test of skill with a sword, but now I know you're even less of a man than I thought, because you are too cowardly to even fight a woman, which is a good thing for you, because I would soon have your heart dangling from the tip of my foil."

She paused and stared him in the eye, never looking off, not even once. "Now, get out before I change my mind and carve you up."

"I will be back to finish you."

"I long for the moment."

She watched him slither toward the door, and like all of hell's creatures, he vanished completely. She would not have been surprised to catch a whiff of sulphur.

After it was all over, Kenna collapsed weakly against the wall, her limbs jellied. She kept thanking

God, repeating over and over, how thankful she was that Colin had made her wear her dirk.

From now on, she would not be without her sword, and she prayed she would have the guts to use it. She wiped the blood from her mouth and waited a moment to let her breathing return to normal. A wave of nausea hit her, and for a moment, she thought she would be sick. Her hip throbbed, and she wondered if that would impede her fencing skill.

She was still leaning against the wall, weak and in pain, when Josette walked in. "There you are— *Mon Dieu!* What happened to you?"

Kenna started to explain what happened when several of the MacKays rushed into the room. "I am glad to see you and your men, Gavin MacKay."

Gavin came toward her. "We saw a man run out of here. I don't think I need to ask if it was the Englishman. Are you all right?"

"I have felt better."

"I will have one of my men take you back. Do you think you can walk?"

"I can walk, and Josette will help me. If you would not mind locking everything before you go, I will be in your debt."

"First I will have the distillery searched to make certain no one else is here, then we will lock it. I have already posted extra guards around the castle."

"Thank you, and now I think I'd like to go lie down."

She leaned on Josette's arm and the two of them walked slowly out.

Once Kenna was back inside the castle, she decided

to rest awhile downstairs before she tried to tackle the long climb up the stairs. Her hip still throbbed, her lip was swollen and she felt defiled where he had put his hand on her. Already the maids were heating water for her bath so she could wash his taint and scum from her body.

Ewen brought them tea in the solar, and warned her he had taken the liberty of adding a dram of whisky to hers to ease her suffering a bit. After he left, she and Josette talked about Kenna's challenge to Lord Walter, and whether or not they thought he was smart enough to figure out she had baited him, or whether his warped pride and confidence would make him face her with a sword.

Kenna was about to make a point, when Ewen came into the room looking grave, his skin ashen. A sense of dread gripped her, for she knew something had happened, something far worse than the fate of the two sweet deerhounds.

"What is it, Ewen? What has happened?"

Outside, she could hear shouts and the sound of booted feet running.

"They found Dougal and Owen with their throats cut, and someone has set fire to the distillery. It could spread to the castle."

The faces of Dougal and Owen floated through her mind, as she recalled the bond of friendship she had formed with them during the hours they worked together in the distillery. Even now, she could hear the sound of their laughter, which was so frequent, and played an important role in making her feel at home.

She said a prayer for them, and whispered, "I shall miss you terribly, dear friends. I'm so sorry...so very sorry."

Their deaths made her more determined than ever to stop Lord Walter, and she vowed to do so before another life was lost.

Kenna and Josette went out to see where Gavin was, but she did not see him. It was not utter chaos, but men and horses were scrambling, buckets were brought out and bucket lines formed near the well. Already they could smell the smoke and saw the black smoke billowing upward to form fat gray clouds.

It was a terrible blow to her, and Kenna wondered if this nightmare would ever end.

Josette sensed her despair and tried to offer her encouragement.

"I am losing heart, Josette. I grow weary. Everything I try is hurled back in my face. Defeat is behind each door that I open. I am so weary of death and watching those I care about disappear out of my life. I'm sick of trying. I feel I have lost the best years of my life, and for what? For each dragon that I slay, two more spring up. I have had enough. I turn in my sword. I am ready to leave Scotland altogether." She went back inside and slumped into a chair.

Josette followed her inside. "You cannot give up now. Every hero has his dark moment, and only those who are strong grow stronger. It is when you are cast into the deepest pit and experience your darkest moments of despair that you must call forth all your reserves in order to stand firm. You said you issued a challenge to him today. You cannot crumple now. What if he accepts the challenge? What will happen if you are unprepared, if you are not ready?"

"Why is this happening?"

"We all have trials and demons we must face from time to time, and only the weak are defeated. You have worked too hard and paid too great a price to get this far. You cannot quit now. I won't let you."

"I don't know how you can stop me."

"If you don't fight back, if you don't face your enemy, then I will do it for you."

"Don't be silly, Josette. You said yourself that you have no stomach for drawing blood."

"One of us has to try. It will be either me or you."

"You are foolish to consider it. The *comte* would tell you that if he were here right now, and you know it. You are not strong enough with the sword to withstand Lord Walter."

"Perhaps not, but I am strong enough to face him."

Josette left the room and Kenna dropped her head into her hands. She could not cry. There were no tears left. They had all been expended long ago.

It was close to midnight when Gavin MacKay came into the solar, where Kenna and Josette waited for the occasional reports on the fire's progress, wondering whether or not they would have to abandon Durness altogether.

They looked up with expectant faces. His clothes were burned, his face blackened, his hair singed, but his spirits seemed high. "We have fought back and beaten down the last of the flames."

Kenna expelled the breath she had been holding. "Oh, thank God."

Suddenly, the faces of Dougal and Owen came back to haunt her, and she knew it would be a long time before she would be able to think of them without a stabbing pain of loss. Dear God, she prayed, let there be no more deaths. With her heart pounding, she asked the question she dreaded, yet knew she had to ask. "And the men? How do they fare? Any injuries?"

"They fare much better now, milady, than they did earlier. Good news always makes a man's fighting arm stronger. Their spirits are high, since they know the worst is over. There are no serious injuries, just a few burns and a lot of dirty faces."

"There is no danger to the castle?"

"No, milady. All is well for the castle, but the distillery could not be saved. I'm sorry. We did the best we could."

Kenna shook her head and thought, so much work wiped out in a few hours. She spoke to Gavin. "I am certain the fire was set and we both know the villain who set it. But, tell me, Gavin, how was he able to get close enough to do such a dastardly deed, when you had posted extra guards and all the men were about?"

"It is my opinion that he never left after he attacked you. I think he found a place to hide, and then went back later and set the fire."

"That makes sense," Josette said.

"Then that is the first thing about all of this that has made sense," Josette said.

After Gavin left, Kenna and Josette fell silent, each

seeking their own counsel. Nothing was said for quite some time, until Kenna spoke. "You were right, Josette, and I thank you for trying to talk some sense into my hard head. I am not ready to give up. I simply allowed myself to become overwhelmed for a while."

"It is easy to do, and we have all done it at one time or the other. The important thing to focus on now is being certain that you are prepared. I agree with your idea to draw him out and to make a stand. Otherwise, God only knows how many more innocent people he might kill. What I don't understand is how will you do it. I know you have challenged him, and you feel he will react positively. But *where* will he react? Where will he suddenly appear? What will you be doing when you look up and see him standing there with a sword in his hand? You need a plan, Kenna."

"First, I plan to have my sword belted around my waist at all times. I shall even sleep with it."

"All right. You have a plan to have your weapon available. What about the place? Where do you think he will strike? Is there anything you can do to draw him to a place of your choosing?"

"I have thought about that and I need to choose a place I know or feel might be advantageous to me. Then I must decide how I can make him come to me. One idea would be to form a pattern of behavior, to do the same thing around the same time every day."

"You mean something like riding your horse down to the bay every morning?"

"Yes, that way he could plan to hide somewhere and jump out to surprise me."

"What strategy do you have to put things in your favor?"

Her question was inspiring. "Lord Walter is puffed up with pride, arrogance, vanity and an overabundance of self-confidence. He is in possession of a minor English title—enough to fill him with a nobleman's idea of defending his personal honor if it were impugned. He is also a man who is easy to incite to anger. If I can make him angry, it is to my good, because we both know that such a man cannot fight with a sword as skillfully as one in control."

"And you will make him angry, how?"

"I have been thinking if I can find the right insults to taunt him with during our match. If I can wear him down mentally, then he will defeat himself."

"Good," Josette said. "Very good. You fence like your fencing master, now you are starting to sound like him."

# Twenty-Four

You are not worth the dust which the rude wind
Blows in your face.
—William Shakespeare (1564-1616),
English poet and playwright.
*King Lear* (1605-1606), Act IV, Scene 2.

"I have an idea," Josette said as she walked into Kenna's room.

Kenna looked up from the book she was reading. "An idea about what?"

"How we manipulate Lord Walter into attacking you."

She put the book down. "Go on."

"I mentioned it the other day as an example, but it has been sticking with me these many days. I believe I said you needed to have some habit that he can identify, like riding down to the bay every morning. I think it's actually a great idea."

"Hmm, I don't know."

"Kenna, hear me out. You and I will start riding down to the bay about ten o'clock every day. The weather is still warm, so we can take a blanket and find the right spot to relax. We can read, or play cards, but the point is, we can position ourselves so we have the sea to our back."

"I am not comfortable involving you in this."

"I will be only a prop. I won't fight…unless it is to save your life, of course. Are you thinking he might not come if I am with you?"

"It is always possible, I suppose. However, we could try it for a while and if he never shows, then we think of something else."

The plan laid, they began their daily excursions down to the bay the next day.

By the Monday morning of the third week, they were starting to consider other ideas. "We will finish out this week and start afresh with a new idea next week," Kenna said.

Already dressed in her fencing attire, Kenna fastened her sword around her waist and followed Josette out of the room.

The horses, a chestnut mare and a sorrel gelding, were saddled and waiting. The groom gave them each a boost into the saddle and held the reins until they had adjusted their skirts. Once they were settled, he handed them the reins and they turned the horses and rode through the gates of Durness, and followed the track that wound down to the bay.

They made their way among gorse bushes, scrub and heather scattered along the rocky hillside, as they

headed for the bay descent. Overhead, the cry of kitti-
wakes and razorbills soaring overhead was almost
drowned out by the pounding of the surf. When they
reached the sandy beach, waves were breaking against
the rocks, where a few seals sunned themselves. Two
of the seals slipped into the water as the horses approached.

They rode to their customary spot, dismounted and
tied the horses to a large piece of driftwood, as big as
a tree trunk, which is what it had been at one time.

Josette spread the blanket and tossed a deck of cards
on top, while Kenna removed her sword belt, withdrew
the sword, and placed it on the blanket next to her. Josette did the same.

Josette shuffled, Kenna dealt, and they were soon
into the game, talking low together, and occasionally
finding something amusing enough to produce a
smile or even a laugh. They did not talk about Lord
Walter; they had exhausted that topic weeks ago and
Kenna did not believe in giving too much attention to
the Devil. "I will not glorify that parasite by talking
about him."

As the weeks had passed and Kenna's nemesis
failed to appear, they had given up speculation about
it. "He will come when he comes," Josette said.

During their game, they did, from time to time, scan
the horizon, the track or even the beach for a sign of
him, and as usual, saw nothing.

That did not mean he was not there.

It was the horses snorting that first alerted them, a
stomping of feet, a whinny or two, but their restless be-

havior did not elicit much notice beyond Josette's query to Kenna: "Do you see anything?"

Kenna placed a ten of spades on the blanket and let her gaze scan the hillside they had ridden down. "No, not yet."

Josette played a jack of hearts. "Still nothing?"

Kenna was rearranging her cards. "No, still nothing."

Josette was about to lay down a king of hearts when she gave a start and looked up at the same time Kenna did. Lord Walter was striding down the beach toward them.

*He came by water,* she realized when she glanced behind him and saw a boat beached on the sand. How could they have been so stupid? He had outfoxed them. The first round went to him.

Cards abandoned, they were on their feet, Kenna with her blade drawn, her dirk at her waist.

His empty eyes darted to the sword in Kenna's hand. "I see you came prepared."

"We always come prepared," she said. "We never know when vermin might appear. Take you, for instance."

A muscle clenched in his jaw. "Did you think I would find two swords more intimidating?"

Kenna laughed in his face. "Actually, I don't think of you at all. Why should I?" She looked him over with a sneer. "Just look at you, a maggoty worm, low in status, low in rank, low in importance—you are insignificant."

Lord Walter's face paled. A cruel smile appeared.

"You'll not think me so insignificant when I make short work of you and leave you to rot in the sun, picked at by scavengers."

He is taking the bait, Kenna thought, and it was a calming balm. Her insults had cut the surface of his vanity and he was attempting to reclaim his prowess. The only sign Kenna gave that she had heard him at all was the raising of a languid brow, then she added new insult with a trifling glance that made her appear almost bored.

"I would believe now," sneered Lord Walter, "that you have not only studied the sword, but also at a school of acting. You are very good."

"Feign or feint? I see you brought your sword. Does that mean you know how to use it?"

"I will let you be the judge. Name the place."

"Over there, where the track ends on the smooth layer of rock."

Josette appeared distraught. "Kenna, think! If you do this, you will be a murderer."

"And a boil on the face of humanity will be lanced. Worth it at any price, I would say." Kenna started toward the layer of rock she had indicated, her stride one that indicated haste to arrive.

He approached slowly, and she waited with marked impatience. "I have one question to ask you before we start."

"And what is that?"

"What is your preference?"

"My preference for what?" he asked, already showing agitation.

"Your preference for what happens to your body after I kill you," she said with casual disinterest.

A startled face was followed by an uncertain laugh. "You surely jest."

"I am *dead* certain. Unfortunately, you will not be alive to check the truth of my words. Would you like them carved upon your gravestone?"

"We shall soon see who the victor is," he said, taking a peacock stance, which was wasted on this audience.

"Then why waste my time with your talking. The victor awaits you. Draw your sword, monsieur." She used the French word to honor the *comte*.

Once they faced each other, Kenna unfastened her skirt and let it drop to reveal the fitted black trews beneath, where her shirt was tucked. The surprise worked, for Lord Walter looked disconcerted. She knew by his expression that he was well aware he had lost one big advantage: the lack of mobility a long skirt would have given her.

They took their positions.

"Your youth and inexperience does stack the dice against you. Don't you want to say a prayer of confession?" he asked, with a surge of shaky confidence.

"I will say it afterward, when I have a murder to confess."

"On guard!" he cried, and attacked vigorously. He began the match with the obvious intent of catching her off guard and ending the fight with due haste. An intent that began to look less obvious almost immediately. He was accustomed to facing those who yielded ground easily and took it if they could, who advanced and retreated, and took the advantage whenever possible. But now he began to see that she fought in a different style, for she barely moved at all, giving no ground, nor taking any. He had a mental image of how it must look, with him doing his fencing maneuvers while she practically stood in place and deflected each thrust with an effortless parry.

He tried a few of his tricks, and even a secret thrust, and found his point easily parried each time. He retreated to draw her away, and she held her ground. He advanced with an attack and she moved not.

She was all defense and no attack. He doubted this was in any fencing manual. His mental stress was distracting, and he was beginning to tire, while she had not even broken a sweat.

"Are you sufficiently warmed up now, *monsieur?*" she asked. "For I am ready to begin this match."

His anger flared. "You call that fencing?"

She smiled. "I understand your confusion, *monsieur,* for it is apparent your maneuvers have all been self-taught."

Lord Walter responded with a forward feint and a lunge. Kenna encircled the blade, knocked it clear and touched her tip to his throat. Enraged that she had foiled him so easily, he attacked again, ready for her to hold her ground and not move, when she surprised him by retreating swiftly. He followed her, with force, but it was smoothly met. He was seriously winded now, and fell back to pause. He was paying a dear price for his rash confidence that he would finish her off quickly, and the hot and fast pace he had maintained because of it. He realized too late that had been her intent all along. Furious now, he was enraged to know his pomposity had cost him dearly.

"*Mon Dieu!* I thought you wished to fight. Have you changed your mind, then?"

"I shall lift your head from your shoulders as easily as I did your brother's."

She expected such references beforehand and had prepared her mind to accept the painful reminders with cold calm. "You are beginning to feel, I think, some of the same awareness of approaching death that you gave to my family. How does it feel, *monsieur,* to know your life is all but over?"

Driven by his anger, he attacked when he should have conserved his strength, and Kenna, knowing he was winded, refused to allow him to rest. She exposed her low lines to invite his expected lunge, and whirled away when he followed through, which caused him to waste the move on empty air, which put her inside his guard, right where she needed to be, and she drove her blade to pierce him from one side to the other, and render him motionless.

It was done with such precision and speed that Kenna recovered before Josette realized the monster had been hit, for Lord Walter was still standing, his eyes wide with astonishment, his expression a mixture of terror, amazement and awe.

A tremble coursed through his body at the same time a faint moan escaped his lips, and he slowly sank, as one in quicksand, and fell forward at an angle that broke her sword in two.

Trembling and weak enough to faint, Kenna stood over him, and spoke the epitaph she had long held inside:

"When you are gone, you will vanish into nothing. Your name will be blotted out, no one will grieve, no grave will record your existence, even Hell will reject you. You are nothing, an empty space, a void. You will not be revered, you will not be missed, you will not be remembered, because you do not exist."

She heard the hiss of his last breath leaving him like a demonic vapor, and she recited the Lord's Prayer, because she had killed a man, and to protect her from any evil he might have left behind.

She swayed and felt the rise of nausea, and hated him anew for driving her to the point where she had no choice but to end his life so others might be spared. It would forever change her, and the memory of what she had done here this day would linger for the rest of her life.

She felt Josette's arm go around her, and she wished it was Colin who stood at her side.

# *Twenty-Five*

Beauty itself doth of itself persuade
The eyes of men without an orator.
    —William Shakespeare (1564-1616),
        English poet and playwright.

Revered and ancient, the brooding black crags of Castle Rock came into view. An extinct volcano, its ridges carved by glaciers, it seemed proud of its past—Bronze Age fort, thriving Roman settlement, royal residence, military garrison, prison and place of refuge.

Like Rome, Edinburgh was built on seven hills; like Rome, it had been attacked and rebuilt numerous times. And like Kenna Lennox, it had a turbulent past, and seemed destined to repeat it—at least that had been true in the past.

These were the memories that occupied her mind as she made her way along the quay, as she began to search the harbor for a ship flying an American pennant among a throng of foreign flags.

And then she saw it.

*Dancing Water...*

Her heart began to pound. Her mind filled with questions and self-doubt. Was she doing the right thing? Would he even be on the ship? Would he agree to see her?

She saw a man loading a few supplies into a small boat. She headed his way and stopped next to him. He took no notice of her until she cleared her throat and spoke. "Would you be available for hire? I need someone to row me to the ship *Dancing Water.*"

This time, she did not haggle over the price but paid it gladly, for this trip was worth a king's ransom to her. She stepped into the small boat, and kept company with her thoughts as the boatman rowed her closer to the moment when she would know if this trip had been a wise move or fool's chase.

As she was helped on board *Dancing Water,* she said, "I would like to speak to Captain Montgomery."

The man who turned to face her was a hot-blooded Latin, and her eyes lit up at the sight of him. She smiled at the sight of his dear face. "Are you Alejandro Feliciano Enrique de Calderón?"

His face was alive with humor. "*Señorita,* I am anyone you wish me to be, and I am entirely at your service," he said with a bow.

Tears rolled down her face as she said, "It is so good to see you again, dearest Alejandro."

He smiled and opened his arms, and she stepped into the circle and left a few tears on his shoulder.

"It is good that you have come," he said. "I have not

had anyone to tease for these many weeks. What took you so long to get here?"

She stepped back to look at him, with his long black hair, queued back, smoldering eyes and a smile whose sole purpose was to persuade women, and she remembered one woman in particular whom he had persuaded.

"There is someone I think you would like to see. She is waiting at the Edinburgh Inn."

A smile appeared. "And do you think I would like this woman?"

"Oh, very much, for she is the perfect complement for a man such as you."

"I shall go see for myself," he said, "as soon as I take care of you. Come this way, *señorita,* and I will take you to our captain."

What he needed was a woman.

Not just any woman, but one with fire in her heart and her hair, and eyes as golden as doubloons…and an excellent sword arm, he added as an afterthought.

This was not the best time for someone to puncture his dreams with a loud knock at the door.

He stared moodily at the door; the urge to choke whoever was on the other side growing with each breath he drew.

Another knock, this one louder. Alejandro's voice called out, "You have a visitor, Captain. A *female* visitor."

"Of course I do. Now, go away."

Alejandro swore he was not joking. "Truly, Captain,

there is a woman here to see you…a woman you will want to see."

"Of course there is. I can see her now, this woman who simply appeared on my ship, asking for me. Shall I tell you how she looks?"

"No, Captain, let me tell *you* how she looks. She has hair as red as a sunset, and eyes the color of Incan gold. She is obviously of noble class, for her clothes are finely made, and she wears a sword of a most unusual design."

The door opened and Colin's head snapped back and his jaw dropped at the sight of her flaming curls peeking from the hood of her green cape, with her lovely face turned toward him.

The impact of it hit him like a fist in the gut, and he knew for the second time in his life that he had made a mistake in letting her go…a terrible mistake.

"I hope you are not angry that I have come," she said.

"That all depends on why you are here."

She looked him over—so alluring in his well-fitting tan pants and a white ruffled shirt, and it set her heart racing. "My circumstances have changed," she said.

"What circumstances might that be?"

"I am no longer encumbered by the past and devoted to the sport or the cause that took up my time."

He stood and came around the desk, and stopped not more than a foot away.

"What makes you think that would interest me?" he asked.

"I have heard you are a man of much wisdom and good judgment, who never passes on a sure thing."

"Does it involve a woman?"

"Yes."

"I have sworn off women."

"A very wise man once told me there are three things you must remember about a woman."

"Which are?"

"Never take her for granted. Never think you know what she is thinking. And never think you know what she will do in a given situation."

"I find women difficult to understand."

"That is true. A woman is like smoke. She will curl seductively around you one moment, burn your eyes the next, tickle your throat until you cough, and then poof! She is gone. She is a mirage. She is a thunderstorm. She is a sailboat on a mirrored lake. She will run when you reach for her, and come to you when you wish her away. You can solve a problem. You can analyze logic. You can explain how vapor turns into water. But you cannot understand the mind of a woman. And do you know why? Because she does not understand herself."

"Then what does one do?"

"You love her and deal with her in all honesty. You earn her trust. And then you put your faith in the Almighty, who made women the way they are, believing that He knew what He was doing."

"And you believe this story?"

"With all my heart."

He took her in his arms, and he was so achingly familiar to that impossible-to-blot-out image she carried of him in her mind every moment that they were apart. And she was here now, impossible though it was, in Edinburgh and in his arms.

"I love you, Colin, and I am so sorry for…"

He kissed her to silence, and then asked, "Lord Walter? What of him?"

"Lord Walter is dead."

He held her more tightly. "I should have been there. The thought of it scares the hell out of me even now. I could have lost you."

"As you can see, you have not, and I am here for good, if you will have me."

A wicked gleam came into his eyes. "Lady Lennox, are you proposing to me?"

"I am."

"And if I refuse?"

"I have brought my persuasion with me, to change your mind." She put her hand on the sword at her side.

"I don't have to spend the rest of my life sleeping with that between us, do I?"

"Never, for as long as you are at my side, what need do I have for it?"

"Do you have any idea what you have put me through and how long I have waited for this?" The moment he said that, he could see she was finished with this game she played.

She put her hands on her hips. "Is that a no or a yes, Colin?"

"Do you need to ask?"

"No," she said, and stepped into his arms, where she belonged. "Take me home, Colin, to Loch Lomond and Lennox Castle, for I long to see my family and to have them meet you."

"I have a better idea. Why don't we invite them to a wedding in Edinburgh?"

"On your ship?"

"If it pleases you."

She had her fairy-tale wedding, on the deck of his ship, and she would never forget the way he looked. His black cape swirled around his feet, the wind tugging it back just enough to expose the merest whisper of a tucked white shirt, in a manner wickedly pleasing. It intrigued her and made her wonder just what else lay hidden beneath that cloak.

Later that night, she found out.

From *New York Times* bestselling author

# SUSAN WIGGS

Before an estranged couple is killed in an unthinkable tragedy,
they designate two guardians for their children—Lily Robinson
and Sean McGuire. Brought together by tragedy, the two
strangers are joined in grief and their mutual love for these
orphaned children. Sean and Lily are about to embark on the
journey of ups and downs, love and hope that makes a family....

## Table *for* Five

"Wiggs has done an excellent job of depicting
what lies beneath the surface of relationships."—*Booklist*

*Available the first week of April 2006, wherever paperbacks are sold!*

If you enjoyed what you just read,
then we've got an offer you can't resist!

# Take 2 novels FREE!
# Plus get a FREE surprise gift!

## Clip this page and mail it to The Reader Service

**IN U.S.A.**
3010 Walden Ave.
P.O. Box 1867
Buffalo, N.Y. 14240-1867

**IN CANADA**
P.O. Box 609
Fort Erie, Ontario
L2A 5X3

**YES!** Please send me 2 free novels from the Romance/Suspense Collection and my free surprise gift. After receiving them, if I don't wish to receive any more, I can return the shipping statement marked "cancel". If I don't cancel, I will receive 4 brand-new novels every month, before they're available in stores! In the U.S.A., bill me at the bargain price of $5.24 plus 25¢ shipping and handling per book and applicable sales tax, if any*. In Canada, bill me at the bargain price of $5.74 plus 25¢ shipping and handling per book and applicable taxes**. That's the complete price and a savings of over 10% off the cover prices—what a great deal! I understand that accepting the 2 free books and gift places me under no obligation ever to buy any books. I can always return a shipment and cancel at any time. Even if I never buy another book, the 2 free books and gift are mine to keep forever.

185 MDN EFVD
385 MDN EFVP

| Name | (PLEASE PRINT) | |
|---|---|---|
| Address | Apt.# | |
| City | State/Prov. | Zip/Postal Code |

**Not valid to current subscribers of the Romance Collection,
the Suspense Collection or the Romance/Suspense Collection.**

**Want to try two free books from another series?
Call 1-800-873-8635 or visit www.morefreebooks.com.**

\* Terms and prices subject to change without notice. Sales tax applicable in N.Y.
\*\* Canadian residents will be charged applicable provincial taxes and GST.

All orders subject to approval. Offer limited to one per household. Credit or debit balances in a customer's account(s) may be offset by any other outstanding balance owed by or to the customer. Please allow 4 to 6 weeks for delivery.
® and ™ are trademarks owned and used by the trademark owner and/or its licensee.

BOB06R

© 2004 Harlequin Enterprises Limited

# ELAINE COFFMAN

| | | |
|---|---|---|
| 32092 LET ME BE YOUR HERO | ___ $6.99 U.S. | ___ $8.50 CAN. |
| 66738 HIGHLANDER | ___ $6.99 U.S. | ___ $8.50 CAN. |
| 66842 THE FIFTH DAUGHTER | ___ $6.99 U.S. | ___ $8.50 CAN. |
| 66946 THE ITALIAN | ___ $6.99 U.S. | ___ $8.50 CAN. |

*(limited quantities available)*

| | |
|---|---|
| TOTAL AMOUNT | $ _____ |
| POSTAGE & HANDLING | $ _____ |
| ($1.00 FOR 1 BOOK, 50¢ for each additional) | |
| APPLICABLE TAXES* | $ _____ |
| TOTAL PAYABLE | $ _____ |

*(check or money order—please do not send cash)*

**MIRA®**

**www.MIRABooks.com**

MEC0406BL